A LIAR'S GRAVE

Emily Slate Mystery Thriller
Book 8

ALEX SIGMORE

Dark Woods Press

A LIAR'S GRAVE: EMILY SLATE MYSTERY THRILLER BOOK 8

1st Edition

ebook ISBN 978-1-957536-28-6

Print ISBN 978-1-957536-29-3

Prologue

As Duncan Schmidt sat at the small table, he couldn't tamp down the butterflies in his stomach. This was the first "date" he'd been on in over six months, and he didn't want to screw things up like he always did. It didn't use to be like this—he never used to have trouble finding a date for Saturday night. But ever since his little "slip-up", the well had run dry. Which meant matching on those dating sites was a complete bust. Everyone had the entire internet at their fingers, and it only took them a second to look him up. Trying to pick up women at bars wasn't much better, unless he wanted to use a false name. That was fine for a one-night stand, but he couldn't build a meaningful relationship off of something like that. And despite what his therapist said, no one had been willing to give him a second chance.

Not until tonight.

With a shaky hand, he grabbed the glass of water sitting closest to him and drank half of it down in one go. What he really needed was a solid drink, but as the therapist had reminded him, that was how he got in trouble to begin with. No, if this was going to have any chance of working out, he needed to be completely sober.

Duncan inadvertently picked at the wooden table as he anxiously looked around the restaurant, sure that he was being stood up. This whole thing was probably just a prank, someone having a bit of fun at his expense. It wouldn't be the first time, and he doubted it would be the last. He checked his watch, noting that she was already ten minutes late. He'd wait another five, then he was out of here.

All around him, raucous couples and groups of friends conversed over their meals, all of them oblivious to his misery. And why should they care? He was just a middle-aged man who was losing his hair and developing the same paunch that had plagued his father. Ten years ago he was a specimen, but as he turned the corner to forty, things had just started to fall apart. Now his back ached every morning and occasionally his knee would flare up, probably a consequence of all that running he did in high school. Getting old was hell, and combined with his "other" history, it was no wonder he couldn't get a date.

Just as Duncan stood up, prepared to throw a five on the table for wasting the waitress's time, he spotted her.

Her auburn hair perfectly framed her face, and her green eyes were piercing, complemented by the dramatic red dress she was wearing. Duncan realized that more than a few people had taken notice of her when she walked in, and how could they not? She was dressed to the nines, her dress barely reaching the middle of her thighs and six-inch heels showing off her sculpted calves and long legs.

She looked around a minute, then spotted him, a smirk appearing on her face.

Suddenly, those butterflies in his stomach started flapping a lot harder.

God, she was hot. That dress of hers accentuated every curve of her body, and Duncan found he couldn't pull his gaze away from her as she made her way through the restaurant.

"Duncan?" she asked as she approached. Her voice was

light and velvety, and was it his imagination, or was there an undercurrent of mischievousness there as well?

"Y-yes. Julie?" he replied, sticking out his hand. She took it for a moment, her skin baby soft.

"That's me." She removed the purse from her exposed shoulder, setting it in the booth. "I'm sorry I'm late. I got held up."

"That's okay." He anxiously took the seat across from her, doing everything he could not to drool all over this woman. Images of them in bed assaulted his mind, and what it would feel like with her on top of him. He couldn't believe his luck. After six months of nothing, he'd finally hit the jackpot. It was time to get this train rolling, and for Duncan to get his game back. "Aren't you cold?" he asked, noting her lack of coat or jacket.

"Nah, not really," she replied, a little giggle escaping her lips. "You're sweet to ask though. You haven't ordered anything yet, have you?"

"No...just," he looked down at his half-empty water glass. "No, I haven't."

She leaned forward, just enough so that he could get a good look at her cleavage, which was clearly on display. Was she wanting him to look? It had been so long since he'd been on one of these, he'd forgotten how they went. "I don't usually do this, you know," she said in a conspiratorial voice. "But I just got out of a messy divorce. So it's my first time back out in the dating world."

Duncan's heart fell. Prior marriages meant baggage. Namely in the form of kids, which he wasn't ready for. Kids were out of the question.

"Oh," he said. "I didn't know you were married before. It didn't say anything about that on your profile."

She giggled again. "I know, I'm sorry for not telling you before, but I was afraid you might not come meet me if you knew I just went through a divorce."

He looked her up and down again. Maybe she wasn't the long-term relationship he was looking for, but with a body like that he could at least have a fun night ahead of him. "Do you have any kids?"

She shook her head. "No. Thank goodness. I can't stand my ex. Trying to raise a child with him would have been a nightmare."

His spirits lifted again. "Tell me about it. How long were you together?"

"About five years," she replied. "But let's not talk about him. I want to get to know you." She turned, looking for the waitress. "How about some wine?"

Duncan glanced over at his sad little water glass. Wine would loosen him up, but at the same time, all he could hear were his therapist's words in his head. Still, an opportunity like this didn't come along every day. He needed to take advantage of it. Who knew when he'd get another date like this? The last thing he wanted to do was disappoint this girl before he got her back to his place. The fact that she didn't have children put her right back into the "eligible" category. And with a body like that, how could she say no?

"Sure, wine sounds great." He motioned until he caught the waitress's attention. "A bottle of Pinot Noir, on the double."

The waitress gave him a quick sneer, but what did he care? He wasn't on a date with her. He was here with the prettiest girl in the entire restaurant. "You don't look thirty-five," he said once the waitress had left.

"I hope I don't look older!" Julie replied, though it was clear she was joking.

"No, not at all. High twenties, at best."

"Whew," she said. "That's a relief. You scared me for a second." She batted her eyelashes. Man, she was *really* into him. He hadn't lost his touch after all. "Tell me about you. What brings you to the wonderful world of dating?"

She was kind of funny; he liked that. But it wasn't like he could tell her the entire truth, not right now anyway. Maybe later, after they'd gotten to know each other better. But he knew from prior experience if he told her everything now, she'd be out that door like a shot. Still, she was already so familiar to him. That had to be a good sign, right?

Before he could open his mouth, the waitress returned with two wine glasses and a bottle of what he knew was very expensive wine. "Here you are, sir," she said, setting down the glasses. "*Tignanello*, one of our finest."

Duncan reached out and took the waitress by the arm before she could pour. The girl was so startled she froze. "I didn't say bring me the most expensive bottle in the building."

The girl looked down at her arm and Duncan realized he was squeezing. If he wasn't careful, he'd screw this whole thing up.

"I…" the girl stammered before Duncan released his grip.

"It's fine," he finally said. "But I want to speak to your manager. Right now."

The girl headed off, looking like she was about to burst into tears. These kids today, they just couldn't handle the simplest of tasks. And when they were faced with even the smallest bit of confrontation, they crumpled.

Duncan looked over at Julie, whose eyes were wide. "I'm sorry you had to see that. But I'm not about to let them take advantage of me here."

Julie blinked and for a brief second, Duncan thought he might have miscalculated; that she was one of those bleeding heart types. But she just gave him a grin and waved it off. "Sometimes it's so hard to find good help. The girl who does my hair is the exact same way. Can't handle even the smallest amount of criticism."

"Right?" he said, relieved. "It's so refreshing to hear you say that. So many people today are so concerned with tiptoeing around other people's feelings and all it's doing is contributing to the erosion of our entire society. Back when I was a kid, you had to deal with it. There weren't all these excuses and touchy-feely reasons not to do your job."

"Sir, is there a problem here?" a heavyset man said, coming over with the waitress in tow.

"Yes," Duncan said, sticking out his chest, hoping to continue to impress Julie. "I asked for a bottle of red wine and your waitress brought *this* over." He indicated the opened bottle on the table. "I feel like your establishment is intentionally trying to gouge me."

"I can assure you, that is not the case," the man said. He turned to the waitress. "Ashley, did this man order this bottle?"

"Well…no," she stammered. "But…"

"I know you know this is a two-hundred dollar bottle of wine," he shot back. "Are you trying to rip off our customers?"

"Mr. Malden, you should have heard how he spoke to me, like I was his slave or something," Ashley replied, tears in her eyes. "I just…"

"That's it," the manager replied. "You're fired. And I'm taking the cost of this bottle out of your last paycheck. Get your things."

"Mr. Malden, you can't do that, I need this job!" the waitress protested.

The man turned back to Duncan. "I'm very sorry about all of this. Please enjoy this bottle on us. I'll send Monica over to serve you for the rest of the evening." He took Ashley by the arm, just as Duncan had and let her away, even as she continued to blubber.

Duncan, satisfied with the whole encounter, sat back, a smug look on his lips. "Would you like me to pour you a glass?"

Julie was looking after them as they left, but when she turned back to Duncan, that smile was still there. "Sure, I'd love one."

Duncan took the bottle and poured them both a generous serving. He needed something to calm his nerves, especially if he was planning on closing the deal with Julie tonight. "Does that happen to you often?" she asked.

"Sometimes people just have to be put in their place, you know?" he said, tipping his glass forward. Julie did the same and clinked the glasses together in a toast.

"You couldn't be more right."

TWO HOURS AND AN ENTIRE BOTTLE OF EXPENSIVE WINE LATER, Duncan was too drunk to drive back home. And if his date was any indication, she wouldn't be able to get them there either, not without wrecking his car. Which meant they'd have to take a ride-share.

As they stood out on the curb, waiting for the car to arrive, Julie stumbled a little, leaning into him. She was a lot drunker than he was, that much he knew. She could barely keep her eyes open, and the cold was probably the only thing keeping her awake.

What a lightweight, Duncan thought. He needed to get her back to his place so she could warm up.

As soon as the car arrived, Duncan helped her in and Julie slumped over to the side, half-asleep. They rode in silence for a while before Duncan decided to try his luck. It had been more than six months after all. And after everything he'd been through, didn't he deserve a little something? All because of a little misunderstanding. Things had been blown out of proportion; he'd never meant any harm.

Duncan nudged Julie but she barely stirred. He couldn't help but stare at her long legs, barely covered up by that dress. He reached out and placed his hand on her knee. When she didn't stir, he moved his hand down a little further, feeling the warmth of her thigh…

"Here you are."

Duncan snapped his head up, realizing they'd arrived back at his place. He glanced at the driver in the rearview who was giving him a stern look. "Is she okay?" he asked.

"She'll be fine," Duncan said, opening the door and nudging Julie a few times. She finally stirred and seemed to be in almost a trance as she got out of the car, unstable on her feet.

"Miss? Are you sure you're all right?" the driver asked.

"She's fine, just had a bit too much to drink," Duncan said and slammed the door, eager to get away from the nosy driver. He practically had to hold Julie up as they walked up to his apartment door. She was mumbling something, but he couldn't make it out. He just needed to get her inside as fast as possible, before any of his neighbors saw them.

Finally, he got the door open and escorted her in, helping her down on the couch. She looked up at him and smiled before her eyes closed again and she slumped over to the side, just as she had done in the car.

Duncan locked his door and went to the kitchen for a glass of water, which he greedily drank down. He couldn't believe this was happening. Right here in his apartment, she was less than ten feet from him, and she decides to go to sleep *now*? What luck. He happened to snag the hottest woman he'd ever met and she falls asleep before anything could happen.

Then again, she had come back to his place with him. And dressed like that, she had to be planning on doing something, right? Who else would have worn such a short dress on a night like this? She definitely wasn't a prude, not based on the height of those heels. No, she wanted this to happen as much as he did. She just happened to fall asleep before the main event.

Duncan came back into the living room and took a seat beside her. "Julie," he said, feeling her cheek. Only her small, soft breaths came in response; she was completely out.

Duncan looked down at the hem of her dress again, his eyes going wide when he saw it had hitched up and a small piece of her underwear was exposed.

He couldn't help himself; he placed his hand on her inner thigh again, running it along the inside edge as he began breathing harder, feeling himself grow in his pants. This was right, this was what she had wanted. He leaned into her delicate neck and began kissing, not believing this was actually going to happen. "You're so beautiful," he said.

As his hand reached up under her dress, he felt her stiffen at his touch.

Finally, a response, he thought.

Suddenly he felt a sharp pain in his neck. When he pulled away, his eyes went wide with terror. In that moment, he knew he had screwed up.

It was the last thought that went through his mind.

Chapter One

"HAPPY BIRTHDAY!"

I jump back, startled so much I back into Liam, whose hands hold my shoulders as the lights in the apartment flick on and five people look at me expectantly with large grins on their faces.

The person at the very front of the group, Zara Foley, my best friend and some would say partner-in-crime, runs into me, smashing me between herself and Liam Coll, my boyfriend.

"We got you good," she exclaims, the joy in her voice palpable. "You should have seen your face!"

"Z, you're crushing me," I say. Zara is what most people would call petite, but she's got some strength behind her. It must be all those training classes at work. She said she'd been putting in extra hours, now I believe it.

She pulls back, her grin as big as her face. "Were you surprised? You had no idea, did you?"

I finally extricate myself so I'm back on my own two feet and turn back to Liam, who sports a grin similar to Zara's. "No, *someone*, it seems, is quite the actor."

He shrugs. "What can I say? I had to make it convincing."

"We knew you'd be suspecting something on your actual birthday, so what better way to surprise you than to hit you with it five days before?" Zara asks, winking at me.

I have to admit, I am surprised. I thought Liam and I were just coming over for a regular game night with Zara and her newish boyfriend Raoul. They've only been seeing each other about a month, ever since the FBI nearly imploded in on itself.

"You're not mad, are you?" Liam asks in my ear as we enter the apartment to all the other smiling faces.

I turn to him. "I know I've never told you this, but I love surprise parties." Though usually I like for them to be a little more low-key. Zara has outdone herself with all the decorations. Streamers run across all the ceilings, and balloons hang from every surface. I can already tell by the smells that she's brought in a ton of food, though I won't complain about that part. I'm famished from having not eaten all day.

"Here, come with me, you need to meet everyone," Zara says, taking my hand and pulling me away from Liam.

"Only you would invite people I don't know to my birthday party," I tell her, allowing myself to be dragged along.

"Four people does not a party make," she replies with a stiff upper lip. "This is Richard, Raoul's roommate," she says, landing me in front of a short man who is probably in his early thirties. He's got a dark crop of hair down his back and sports a KISS t-shirt.

"Nice to meet you," I say. "Sorry you got dragged into this."

He offers me a quick smile. "No problem. Raoul told me his girlfriend would kill me if I didn't show. Also free food, so…"

"Thanks anyway," I tell him as Zara pulls me to the next person.

"This is Grace Wang, who lives four doors down," Zara

says, planting me in front of a woman with sharp features and jet-black hair. She offers me a wan smile.

"Thanks for coming," I say.

"It was no trouble. I've always liked Zara," Grace says. "Plus, birthday parties are always fun."

I'd like a second to speak with her more, but Zara grins and hauls me away from her before I can say anything else. "You really went to too much trouble. I didn't need all of this," I tell her, looking around to see where Liam went before she makes me meet more people.

"Nonsense! It's your twenty-ninth birthday. After this you don't get any more. You get to be twenty-nine forever, so we have to do it up big."

I smile despite myself before seeing who she's about to introduce me to next. Immediately I stiffen upon seeing their faces. "Zara, what are they doing here?"

The two people she's bringing me to are deep in conversation before they see us coming and immediately stop what they're doing, turning to us.

"Emily, you know Agents Nadia Kane and Elliott Sandel," Zara says.

"Of course," I say, holding out my hand and giving each of theirs a shake. "I don't think we've formally met in the office yet—"

"Things have been chaotic," Agent Sandel says. He's brusque, and sports a pronounced chin and deep-set brown eyes. Though he's probably our age, he looks about ten years older, like the job has really taken its toll on him.

"Though we appreciated the invite," Agent Kane says. She's about half a head shorter than me, and her long, dark hair is tied back, though I know from seeing her around the office it goes halfway down her back. Agent Kane reminds me of a movie star with her flawless skin and hair without a strand out of place, but she's always so quiet and reserved at work. Both Agents Kane and Sandel came in after the whole debacle with Cochran, an effort by Congress to get the FBI back on track after such a huge breach of security. They're only two of the dozens of agents who have now been assigned to the different departments that were under Cochran in an effort to reinforce the public's trust in the institution after it was revealed that one of the deputy directors was actually a mole.

A mole that Liam, Zara, and I were able to expose for the world to see. But it left my workplace in tatters. And we've all spent the better part of the last month trying to figure out just how much damage Cochran did and how to begin repairing it all.

As a result of his actions, the FBI has been reorganized, and as soon as the new president is sworn in, will be completely rebuilt from the ground up. Despite all my efforts to keep my position here in D.C., I still may find myself in a field office somewhere else. It was determined the D.C. office, our headquarters, was compromised, so we have all had to undergo serious evaluation to prove we're loyal agents and not part of some other, shadow organization.

I remember Zara and I thought things were bad after DuBois was exposed. This has been ten times worse.

As a result, agents like Kane and Sandel have come in to clean up our mess, and thus haven't been exactly friendly toward any of the people who operated under Cochran's watch. Even those of us who managed to expose him. Their directive is to get the FBI's house back in order, no matter what it takes. I've noticed we've lost quite a few people in our office since they joined. To me, they're acting like some sort of cleanup crew. And while I know Zara, Liam, and I are loyal, I imagine it doesn't take much of an excuse to get on their bad side. Why the *hell* did Zara invite them?

"You really didn't have to come," I tell both of them. "But thank you for making the effort." I quietly excuse myself and pull Zara to the side, out of earshot. "What are you thinking, bringing them here?"

She looks at me like I've gone crazy. "What do you mean? We need to be working with them, right? We don't want to get swept up in all the changes, so I figured what better way than to bring them into the group? I mean c'mon. Out of all the people they assigned to our office, who else would you want here? You want me to invite that guy Wooler? Who looks like he takes the second amendment a little *too* seriously? Or what about Venegas, who'd probably tell us to turn down the music and put on something *a little nicer?*"

I sigh. Sometimes there is just no reasoning with her. "I guess if you had to invite anyone...but still, don't you feel like you're being watched with them here? I mean, the entire reason they've been assigned to the office was because Congress wants to make sure there's no one else like Cochran or DuBois there."

She gives me a playful shove. "Just wait until they've had a few tequila shots. Trust me, that will loosen them right up. Here." Somehow we've made it back over to the kitchen and she's already got a drink for me in hand.

"What's this?"

"Straight whiskey, just how you like it," she says, plunking a round piece of ice in the glass, causing some of it to splash over the sides. She then clinks my glass with her own, which is much more colorful and probably contains ten times the amount of sugar as my drink. "Happy Birthday, Em."

I take a sip and smile, grateful to have someone willing to do this for me. "Thanks," I say.

"Now it's time to get it started. And I've got just the thing for you." The mischievous grin on her face tells me I'm in for it now.

"No. Not that."

"Karaoke!" she yells and a few other people cheer. Zara immediately turns up the volume on the speaker connected to her phone and runs to the other side of the apartment to grab a microphone. While she's keeping everyone distracted, I search out Liam, who has managed to hide himself in one of her spare rooms, talking to Zara's boyfriend, Raoul, who I haven't seen yet tonight.

"Gentlemen," I say, walking in. "Having your own get-together?"

"Emily, happy birthday," Raoul says, giving me a quick side hug. He's sort of lanky, with dark-rimmed glasses and a trim beard. He's got that sort of European vibe to him, though I'm not sure he's actually from Europe. Annoyingly, Zara has been light on the details. But he's also an architect, and she can be a sucker for smart guys so I can't say I'm completely surprised. Even though they've only been together a month, they seem to be hitting it off well.

"Thanks," I say, before giving Liam a gentle smack on the chest. "Nice subterfuge there. We'll get you into undercover work before you know it."

"Couldn't be helped," he replies, a sheepish smile on his face. "I was under strict orders not to reveal the plans."

"Uh-huh. I guess this just means I'll need to be more careful around you in the future." I shoot him a wink. "So what are you boys conspiring about in here?"

"I just knew it was going to get loud out there," Raoul replies. Already I can hear Zara belting out the lyrics to *What is Love* by Haddaway.

I turn back to Liam. "Did you know Kane and Sandel would be here?"

He shakes his head. "I was given as little information as possible. I don't think she trusted me to keep the secret. Why, is there a problem?"

I turn back to the open door, expecting to see one of them standing there, staring at me. "No, no problem. Just…I dunno. Maybe I'm being stupid."

"Well, if there's one day where you're allowed to be

stupid," Raoul says, then raises his beer to me and takes a swig. "I'll leave you two lovebirds alone for a minute. Room's yours if you want it." He chuckles and dodges my half-hearted swing as he leaves us by ourselves.

"You're not seriously worried about them, are you?" Liam asks, once we're by ourselves. "It's been a month already. I think we've more than proven to be loyal agents. Especially you, you're the one who helped bring Cochran down."

"Yeah, I know," I reply. "I just can't get this nagging feeling out of my stomach. Like I'm being spied on."

"Bad memories," he says. "Camille is gone, the Organization is all but disbanded and powerless. You shouldn't have to worry about that on your birthday."

He's right. Though I'm not so sure about the Organization being disbanded. Cochran was just the tip of the iceberg. The FBI is working closely with Interpol to determine if any other potential members might have fled the country or be operating overseas, but without a complete picture, it's difficult to be sure.

"Em…this isn't about the letter, is it?" Liam asks. I can tell by the way he phrases the question he's trying to be gentle, but even the very mention of that letter sets my teeth on edge.

I drain my drink in one gulp. "No, of course not. We agreed not to talk about that, remember?"

"We did, but I'm starting to think that might not be the healthiest way to deal with this. I mean, it was a letter from your dead mother. You need to talk to someone about it."

The more he says the more I feel the urge to get out of the room. I can't explain it, but the very thought of that letter sends a chill down my back, and I can't deal with that right now. Not with all these people here expecting me to be present for the party and the other two agents that I *know* are watching my every move. I still can't get *why* Zara thought inviting them was a good idea. Sometimes she can be a little bubble-headed, but never this bad.

"I need a refill," I say and leave him alone in the room, heading back out into the raucous. Zara has been replaced by Richard, who is doing a passable job on a KISS song.

Zara spots me, pulling me close so I can hear her over Richard's off-key singing. "So what do you think?" she asks, beads of sweat pouring down her face from her performance. Raoul is in the kitchen behind her, doing a poor imitation of a dance to the music.

"It's great," I say, more enthusiastic than I feel. "But you didn't have to go to all this trouble."

"It's no trouble for you," she beams. "I couldn't just let you sit around playing board games all night for your birthday! And I know how much you hate clubs. So this is the best of both worlds." She grabs the bottle of whiskey and refills my drink. I notice her glance over my shoulder and take a look myself, seeing Liam come out of the room, his attention focused on Richard singing his heart out.

"Everything okay?" she asks.

I smile. "Sure." Though I feel a pit in my stomach as I say it. I haven't told Zara about the letter yet. In fact, I haven't even looked at it again since the day it came. I wanted to tear it up, throw it away, but Liam wouldn't let me. Because I know it's nothing more than a prank; someone's idea of a sick joke.

Still, I get a nauseous feeling in my stomach every time I think about it, so I shake it out of my thoughts and try to focus on the party.

"Em, is there something—" Zara begins before Raoul comes up behind her, wrapping his arms around her tiny waist and practically lifting her into the air.

"Time to dance, Tinkerbell," he says.

"I told you not to call me that," Zara chides, but she's laughing as she says it. He whisks her away to the middle of the living room where all the furniture has been moved away. Combined with the music and Zara's particular choice of lighting, it really does feel like something of a club in here.

I take the opportunity—mentally thanking Raoul for getting me out of a tough spot—to peruse the food selections, as I am famished. I find a couple of small roll sandwiches with what looks like ham and peppercorn spread on them before popping one in my mouth. The flavors are delicious, and I lose myself in it for a minute before I feel a presence behind me. I turn, thinking it's Liam, only to find Agent Sandal standing there, a full drink still in his hand.

So much for getting them trashed.

"Agent Slate," he says. His body posture is stiff, like he doesn't know what to do with himself.

"Sandwich?" I offer, pointing to the tray.

"Thanks." He takes one, then enjoys a bite. "I'm not really sure what I'm doing here. But your friend insisted we come." I look around him at Agent Kane, who seems as uncomfortable as he is.

"Zara is something of a closeted extrovert," I say. I don't want to let my guard down around him, but Zara's right, neither he nor Agent Kane have done anything to make me suspect something. It's just hard not to after everything I went through with Camille, Agent DuBois and Cochran.

"I think we should probably go, we don't want to ruin your party," he says, setting his drink down on the counter.

"No, you don't have—"

He motions for Kane to join him, who looks far too eager to leave. "Tell Agent Foley thank you for the invitation, and again, happy birthday."

Kane comes up beside him and sets her glass down as well. "Happy Birthday, Agent Slate," she says, ducking out without even looking at me. They're both gone before I can even process what happened. Was there something about my body language that made them uncomfortable? Or was it the fact that Zara invited them to a stranger's birthday party?

"Hey," Liam says, coming up beside me.

"Hey."

"Sorry about…before. This isn't the time or place."

"That's okay," I reply. I notice that Grace has taken over for Richard and is attempting a Sublime song, which I have to admit is entertaining coming from someone at least ten years older than me.

"What happened to those two?" Liam asks as he nods at the closed door.

"No idea. I think they were as confused as to why they were here as I was."

"Well, they don't know what they're missing," he says, pulling me in close and kissing the top of my head. "You are definitely something to celebrate."

I don't feel like something to celebrate. I'm not good being the center of attention in any situation, but even more so when it's my birthday. I just feel like I have to…perform for people, otherwise they'll be disappointed. And the last thing I feel like doing tonight is performing.

As the evening wears on, I find myself a few more drinks in than I'd anticipated. But it at least dulls the nagging sense that something is wrong. Either with the agents at the party, or the fact that now that Liam has mentioned it, I can't get that damn letter out of my mind. But another drink or two and I won't have to worry about it at all.

"Okay, here we go," Zara says, stumbling her way over to me. She grabs me by the hand and hoists it high into the air, like I've won a medal or something. "Here's to Emily! Many happy returns!"

Everyone else in the room similarly raises their hands, all holding glasses in a toast and they all shout some variation of *Happy Birthday*.

Suddenly I feel myself overcome with emotion, not joy or belonging or anything that a person should feel at a time like this, but instead of absolute dread, like a dark shadow is waiting for me. I manage to flash everyone a smile, doing everything I can to pretend like it's all okay until Zara releases my hand and pulls me into a hug. Before I know it, tears are falling down my cheeks as she embraces me, wishing me a happy birthday for what seems like the thirtieth time tonight. I hope to pull away from her without her seeing my face, but she catches a glimpse of it anyway and I bolt for the bathroom, excusing myself from everyone for a moment.

Once I'm inside it's like I'm enveloped by a feeling I can't even describe. It feels like I don't even belong in my own body, that *Emily* is just an imposter and she's not even real. That everything I've ever done has all been a farce in some way. I can feel myself spiraling and I have no way to stop myself.

It's all-encompassing. And it feels like I'll never find my way out.

Chapter Two

"OKAY, Emily, let's talk about last night."

I look up, realizing I'm holding myself a little too tight and I relax. Dr. Kurt Frost sits across from me, one leg crossed over the other with a pen and small notepad in his hand. He's in his late fifties, his full, gray beard bushy but not unwieldy, which matches the color of the rest of his hair. A pair of round-rimmed spectacles sit perched on his nose. I've noticed he likes to look over the edge of those glasses any time he thinks he's made a good point or whenever he thinks I need to pay closer attention.

Today marks session number nine with Dr. Frost, part of my FBI mandated therapy sessions following everything that happened with Camille, the Organization, and Cochran. Given everything I've been through, I can't really blame them. A D.C. cop was murdered right in front of me, I was held captive, and was almost killed via lethal injection. Not to mention my boss's boss, the deputy director of the FBI, was actually my husband's presumed-dead father, and he had ordered it all. James Hunter, or Cochran as I first knew him, had been running subterfuge in the FBI, using his position to advance the goals of his Organization, and making sure certain agents like DuBois, were in place in the event they needed to be activated. When DuBois failed to kill me, Cochran took it upon himself to devise an elaborate trap that would make it look like I'd died in the line of duty. But his hubris—or maybe it was his sentimentality—had determined he owed me an explanation, which was the only way I made it out alive. But not before finding out *he* was the one responsible for Matt's death, and the hit on Camille. It was only by sheer luck that I didn't die that night.

And in their infinite wisdom, the FBI mandated me and some of the other agents to twice-weekly therapy while everything else was sorted out.

So here I am, yet again.

I realize that Dr. Frost is still staring at me, waiting for me to respond. He does that a lot; I guess all therapists do. He waits for me to begin talking and doesn't try to push me along or rush me. Apparently, that's what the process is all about.

"What was last night?" I ask, thinking back to my panic attack in the bathroom. I don't know what came over me in there. It was gone as suddenly as it came on, like it had never even happened. I'm not sure how to explain it. But I didn't tell anyone about it, so I don't know how he could know. Have I been subconsciously sending signals that something happened? Therapists can be so difficult to read sometimes. They're so…stoic.

"Your birthday party?" he prompts.

"Oh," I say, relaxing even further. "You know about that."

"Agent Foley let it slip when she was making the arrangements. So how was it?"

I shrug. "It was a party, I guess."

"Did you have fun?"

"Sure."

He lowers his gaze and looks at me over the rim of those glasses. "Really?"

I let out a long breath. "I mean, yeah, it was fun. I just…I don't do great being the center of attention."

"Why is that do you think?"

I take a deep breath in through my nose. "I mean, I enjoy the thought. It's comforting to know that someone thinks enough of me to do something like that."

"Let's go with that a moment," he says. "You said it's comforting. Can you tell me a little more about that?"

He does this sometimes; he gets stuck on a word I use. Though, more often than not, it leads to me exploring deeper parts of myself that I wouldn't normally. "It's…I don't know…comforting. I don't know a better word to use."

"When you feel that sort of comfort, what other feelings do you associate with it?" He wags his pen back and forth over his pad. Part of me isn't sure this is doing me any good, but Wallace was adamant I take these sessions if I wanted to continue field work. And somehow he got Janice to agree with him.

"Like I belong, I guess," I say.

"That's been tough for you, hasn't it?" he asks. "After everything with your family."

I nod. "It seems like no matter what I do, I'm destined to lose people."

He scribbles something on his pad. "You've said that before. Let's explore it a bit more."

I glance up at the clock, hoping that time is almost up, but we're only halfway done. "What's there to say? So far, I've lost everyone that was important to me."

"Not *everyone*," he replies.

"Not yet," I counter. "But my parents, my husband, my brother, and sister-in-law. I barely have anyone left."

"Which makes you feel alone," he says.

"Wouldn't you?" I ask, trying to keep my voice light, but it almost cracks.

"You still have your friends. Your boyfriend."

"Yeah." But the truth is I can see a day when they're gone too. Either taken from me in the line of duty or I'll do something stupid to push them away. I was aware of it before, but since coming to these sessions with Dr. Frost, I've fully realized just how alone I am.

"Let's go back to the party," Frost says. "You said you felt comforted. Did you feel loved? Cherished?"

I can't say that I didn't. Zara pulled out all the stops to make it a birthday to remember. And Liam really went the extra mile to make sure I was surprised. They wouldn't have done that if they didn't love me on some fundamental level. I can't let any pity I feel for myself overshadow that fact. Not to mention Raoul surely helped Zara with everything. Even though I've only known him a month, he seems like a genuine guy.

"I guess I did," I say.

"Why did you hesitate just now?" he asks.

Can I tell him about the other two agents that were there, seemingly randomly? They do work in this office, after all, and I have no idea if he's counseling either of them. Though I don't know why he would be, seeing as they're transfers and haven't suffered through any of what the rest of us have.

I glance down, rubbing my hands together. "There were a few people there that I didn't know very well. Zara invited them because she wanted to have a big blowout, and she couldn't invite any of my other friends because I don't have any. So she was forced to invite neighbors and...coworkers."

He nods, taking his time with his notes. "And how did that make you feel?"

"Like I was under surveillance. I know she didn't mean any harm, but...I'm not the best around new people."

"Considering what you've gone through the past few months, I'm not sure anyone could blame you."

I think back to not only what happened, but the aftermath, a big part of which was Rodriguez's funeral. I'd opted to go alone, telling Liam and Zara I owed it to Detective Rodriguez's family to be there. But the entire time all I got from them were dirty looks and sneers. They blamed me for what happened to her. I realize now I probably shouldn't have gone.

"Where are you just now?" he asks, pulling me out of the memory.

"At Detective Rodriguez's funeral," I say.

"The officer who was killed on the farm where you were captured," he says.

"I was covered in her blood," I say, thinking back. "They had to use a pressure washer to get me clean."

He drops his leg and crosses the other. "Why did you go back to that memory?"

"You said something about everything I had been through the past few months. It just came to mind."

"Because you feel guilty."

I bite back a retort. Every time I've tried to argue this point with him, I inevitably lose. "Maybe."

"Emily, we've talked about your guilt. And how if you're not careful, it can come to define you." I nod, not looking at him. He uncrossed his leg again and leans forward. "You know what strikes me? That when I mention the last few months the first memory that comes to mind isn't that of your husband."

I play with my fingers, keeping my gaze down. "Why would it?"

"Well, seeing as your discovery that his death was not a suicide was the primary driving factor for you for months, it seems reasonable that—"

"I don't want to talk about Matt," I say. As far as I'm concerned, that book is closed. I found out that he was planning on exposing the Organization before his father had him killed. And while his last act might have been noble, the fact that he was part of that Organization for so long and did nothing doesn't sit right with me.

"We're going to have to talk about him eventually," Dr. Frost says. I know he's right, but it's just not something I'm ready for today, not after everything last night. I don't even want to get into why I almost lost it in the bathroom.

He sits back and I notice him glance at the clock behind me. "Tell you what, let's pick this back up during your next session. I think we've covered enough for today."

I'm out of my seat before he changes his mind. "Sounds good, see you then," I say and I'm out the door before he can say another word. As soon as I'm out in the hall my entire body shivers, like I'm shaking off all the feelings I'd just absorbed. I'm about to go back into work and I can't be anything other than on the top of my game in there.

I head back to the elevators and take them up to my floor. I use the reflective surface of the doors to make sure I look presentable. The last thing I need is Wallace thinking that I'm not able to handle the stresses of the job after all this therapy.

When I enter through the double doors, I spot Zara immediately, her eyes half closed and a steaming cup of coffee beside her on her desk. I make my way over and slam my fist on her desk, startling her so much she almost flies out of her chair.

"What was that for?" she demands once she's managed to compose herself.

I chuckle. "No reason. You just seem to get the drop on me often enough, I figured it was time for some payback."

"How do you not have a headache?" she asks, taking a sip from her coffee cup.

"Because some of us didn't go hog wild last night," I tell her.

"It's your birthday, you're *supposed* to go hog wild."

I take a seat at my desk directly across from her. "Thanks again for the party, you didn't have to do that."

"I kinda did, you needed it." She takes another sip before turning up her nose and setting the cup back down. "I need like four more shots of sugar in this thing." She looks up. "Is everything okay? Last night you seemed…"

I wait for her to finish, but she just leaves the words hanging. "Yeah, of course," I reply. "I'm good, you know me."

My phone trills before she can say anything else. "Slate," I say.

"Good, you're back at your desk. I need to see you a minute." It's Wallace. I don't know why it's so hard for him to just walk to his door and call me in like a normal boss, I barely sit fifteen feet from his office.

"Be right there," I say and hang up.

"I'm telling you; you should have taken the week off," Zara says, wagging her finger at me. "It's not like you don't have the time accrued."

I shake my head. "That would just give me too much time to sit around and think. I'd much rather keep my mind busy."

She gives me a sad sort of smile as I get up and head for Wallace's office, wondering what fresh hell I'm about to face now.

Chapter Three

I POKE my head into SAC Fletcher Wallace's office to find him sitting behind his desk, per usual. He notices and motions me in. "Close the door," he says as I enter.

Great. It's going to be one of *those* meetings.

I barely keep myself from rolling my eyes and manage to take my seat across from him. He's got his signature horn rim glasses on, and his dark gray suit is immaculate, as always. When Wallace was first brought in to replace Janice, he had wanted to have me transferred to another field office, seeing as our styles of working didn't exactly mesh. That may or may not have been partially my fault, seeing as I'd been relegated to desk duty under his watch. But after everything that came out about Hunter and given that Janice is *his* boss now, I no longer have any doubts about my job security and I'm back in the field. He's still my boss, but I like to think we've developed a tolerable working relationship for the time being.

"I've been reviewing your reports from Dr. Frost," he says, without looking up. "How do you feel like those sessions are going?"

"Fine," I reply. I don't know what he's after, but I'm definitely not talking to him about my private life.

"Good. Well, based on his recommendations, I don't see any reason not to keep you on active duty," Wallace says.

I sit up straighter. "Wait a second, is that what these sessions have been about? I thought you just wanted me to have someone to talk to after everything that happened."

"I did," he replies. "But I also needed to assess your operational fitness. You're no good to us if you're traumatized by recent events." He says it completely without emotion. Like it's no big deal that I almost died twice.

"Does Janice know about this?" I ask.

"Listen," he says, catching my gaze for the first time. "I know you two are friends and that you had a good working relationship for a long time. But you are under my direction now, and it's my job to assess your ability to handle the job. If Dr. Frost had found any reason that you weren't fit for duty, even a friendship with the president wouldn't have made any difference."

I can feel my cheeks burning, but I manage to keep quiet.

"Slate, this isn't personal," he adds. "I'm having several agents evaluated. If it makes you feel any better, I never had any doubts you'd be cleared for duty."

"Then why—"

"Because when you're in my position, there has to be a reason and a paper trail behind every decision you make. I can't just *declare* people fit for duty without something to back it up. I know you think I'm picking on you because of our history, but I can promise you I'm not."

I sit back, unsure how to respond. I can't really blame him, seeing as his argument makes sense. But at the same time, I wish I'd known the stakes. He's already tried to have me sent to another office; I wouldn't put him above firing me if he thought there was good cause.

"Still, I want you to continue seeing Dr. Frost for the foreseeable future. I know from experience things like this don't work themselves out in a month or two."

I had really hoped my time with Dr. Frost would be limited. But I don't guess I'd mind continuing to see him, as long as it doesn't interfere with my work. "Is this what you called me in here about?"

He shakes his head, pulling a file out of one of his drawers and handing it to me. "Something came across my desk this morning and I want you on it. It's one of those cases that should be right up your alley."

I carefully take the file. The last time he spoke like this I ended up tracking down a case that wasn't a case at all, and instead was an elaborate trap. "Oh-kay," I say, cautious.

"We've been contacted by Jim Rice, a D.A. up in New Hampshire." I open the file to reveal four different dossiers. "Every Saturday for the past month, someone has been murdered in a different town up there, all in the same general area and all under his jurisdiction. This past Saturday it was the brother of a police officer in a town called Collins."

I begin flipping through the dossiers, looking over the preliminary information. "Are we looking at a serial here?"

He nods. "Definitely. Local news hasn't made the connection yet because they've all been so far apart, but it won't be long. Take a look at the autopsy reports."

I pause a moment to peruse the documents. When I begin reading the details, my stomach turns and I have to bite the inside of my lip to keep from groaning. "Wow…that's—"

"—extreme, I know," Wallace says. "But the local cops up there aren't making any headway and given this most recent killing is a relative of a police officer, D.A. Rice thinks it's better that they bring us in, seeing as we'll be an impartial party."

"Do they have any leads?" I ask, incredulous.

He shakes his head. "Four bodies and nothing so far. If it is the same killer—and I don't see how it can't be—they aren't leaving any traces behind. At least, none that they've managed to detect yet." He looks at his watch. "I want you up there by tomorrow. If the pattern holds, there will be another death on Saturday. I know it's asking a lot, but we need to try and stop it if possible."

It's already Wednesday. "That doesn't give me a lot of time to get up to speed."

"I know. But I'm having all the files and everything they've gathered so far sent over to your profile. You can review it on your way up there."

"Great, when does my flight leave?" I ask.

He glares at me under hooded eyes. "Remember what I said about you never getting on a plane again on the government's dime? I meant it. You'll drive."

I sputter. "But…that's—it's like a twelve-hour drive."

"Ten if you keep the stops to a minimum." He looks at his watch again. "If I were you, I'd get home and start packing. You'll want to get on the road as soon as possible."

Wow. One would think if he wanted me up there as soon as possible he'd put me on the next flight out of Dulles. But it seems like SAC Wallace isn't playing games, and my indiscretion last month where I *accidentally* booked a private plane hasn't been so easily forgotten.

"I'm going to need help," I say.

"I figured you would," he replies. "Agent Foley will accompany you. Once you've assessed the situation, I want you back in contact with me to let me know what other resources you think you may need. I don't want to cause a national panic up there. You know as soon as the media gets a hold of this it'll be on every seven-o'clock news across the country."

I nod. "Find a killer, stop them, and do it all before someone else dies or the media gets wind of it," I say. "Seems simple enough."

He takes a deep breath, blowing it out through his nose. "Slate, being a smartass doesn't do you nearly as much good as you think it does."

"Do I at least get a company car, so I don't end up putting a couple thousand miles on mine?" I ask.

"See Grafton down in the garage. He'll get you squared away."

I nod, standing with the file in my hand. A new case is intriguing, and it will help keep my mind off everything I talked about with Frost this morning. "Anything else?"

"Just keep me updated," he says. "And no unnecessary expenditures, got it?"

I give him my widest, most placating smile. "Yes, sir." He glares at me a moment before turning back to his work and I head back out into the bullpen. I happen to catch a look from Agent Kane from across the room. As soon as she sees me, she turns away, like she wasn't looking at all.

A shiver runs down my back. I don't know what it is, but I don't like the idea of her or Agent Sandel keeping an eye on me, sanctioned or not. At least with this case I'll have the opportunity to get out of town for a few days.

"Hey."

I nearly jump out of my skin, and even though it's just Liam, he still managed to startle me. I didn't even see him coming toward me. "Whoa, you okay?"

"Yeah," I say. "Sorry, I just…I didn't see you there."

"Is everything okay?" he asks.

"Yep."

"Everything go okay with Frost this morning?"

I look down and realize he's holding two cups of coffee. I tuck the file under my arm and take the one he's offering me. "Yeah, fine, why?"

He lowers his voice. "Emily, are you okay? Something seems…wrong."

"I'm fine," I tell him. "Wallace just assigned me a new case." I motion to the file under my arm. "Looks like it's going to be a gruesome one. I'll have to be in New Hampshire for a few days. Do you mind watching Timber for me?"

"Of course not, you don't even have to ask," he says, almost hurt. I don't know why, but things seem a little strained between us lately. It's like we're on different wavelengths, different than a month or so ago, anyway. Then again, we haven't had the most normal relationship. Liam is technically my rebound, though I don't think of him like that. But he is the first guy I've dated since Matt. And there are still a lot of... feelings there.

"Hey, can we talk tonight after work? Before you leave? I think there's some things we should discuss."

"Umm, yeah," I say. "Sure, just...I have to be out early in the morning, so I'll need to get to bed early."

"Right, of course," he says, straightening back up. "I'll see you back at your place then."

"Sounds good," I tell him, though I'm relieved when he heads back to his station. Liam has only been in the Bureau a few months, and thus he's still relegated to the grunt work they make all the newbies do. All the same stuff I had to do when I first joined. It may not be glamorous, but he'll get his feet wet soon enough. He's certainly been through enough.

I return to my desk and slap the file folder down, causing a half-asleep Zara to snap awake again. "Wha—?"

"Sleepy time is over. Check your email. We've got a new case."

Chapter Four

I MANAGE to get home over an hour earlier than I normally do, and before I'm through the door I'm almost run down my Timber, my pittie who has been the one constant in my life ever since Matt died. We rescued him from a dogfighting ring the FBI managed to break up and he's been the perfect dog ever since. Sometimes I don't know what I would do without him. For a long time I think I was using him as a security blanket, or a last connection to Matt, since we rescued him together. But in the days and months that followed Matt's death, Timber and I created our own bond, different than the one we had when Matt was still alive. He seems to know my moods, especially when things get hard. And he's been my gentle companion ever since.

But every time I look at him, I think about how I almost betrayed him. Back before I knew who or what my brother and sister-in-law actually were, they almost managed to convince me to leave Timber with them. They said my lifestyle was too dangerous for him, that I was gone too much. Little did I know both of them were actively plotting my death and so for a while, I listened to them. Some days I have a hard time forgiving myself for that until I remember what Dr. Frost said about my guilt.

You're not responsible for everyone else's actions, Emily.

I take a deep breath, give Timber a good face squish and get in the house so I can start packing. I have no idea how long I'll be in New Hampshire, but I know they already have snow on the ground, so I'll need to pack for cold weather. After Timber takes his afternoon potty break and I get him a pre-dinner snack, I get to packing. It can get cold in D.C. in the winter, but nothing like up in New England. That's ski lodge country, and the mountains draw the cold in and protect it all winter long. Even though we're a good month away from the official start of winter I'm sure all the ski resorts are already in full swing.

As I'm pulling out long underwear and anything I can find that's warm, I accidentally graze the corner of the letter I received last month at the bottom of my drawer. I haven't looked at it since the day it arrived. In fact, had Liam not stopped me, it would be nothing but ashes right now. So I stuffed it in the bottom of one of my drawers, determined never to look at it again.

But as I stand there, frozen over the letter, I can't help but feel that same dread I felt last night at the party. I don't know what it is, or why I feel that way when I look at it, but I manage to cover it up with a bunch of socks and slam the drawer shut.

Timber looks up at me, whining.

"It's okay," I tell him. "Nothing to worry about."

Thirty minutes and one packed suitcase later there's a knock on my door. I already know who it is, but I double-check the peephole anyway. Six months of being hunted by an international assassin will make anyone a little paranoid.

I open the door, a smirk on my face. "You have a key for a reason."

"I know," Liam says. "Still, I feel like it's the polite thing to do." He leans in and gives me a passionate kiss that I'm not expecting and almost knocks me off balance.

"What was that for?" I ask as he pulls away.

"Just letting you know how much I'll miss you."

"Is that your way of saying you'd rather being going instead of Zara?" I give him a quick wink.

"I wouldn't mind," he says. "But Wallace seems determined to keep me out of the field until he believes I'm ready. Until then I get to answer tip lines, write reports, and occasionally get someone a coffee."

"I dunno," I say, wrapping my arms around him. "I think you make a good coffee boy."

He leans in again but before he gets very far, I feel a warm, thick mass wriggling itself between my legs and his. We both look down at the same time at Timber who has inserted himself between us.

"Someone is attention-starved," Liam says.

I laugh and let go while he rubs Timber down. "Want anything to drink? I've just finished packing."

"I'm good, thanks. Do you at least get a last meal?"

I check the time on my phone. It's almost six. Zara and I agreed to leave before sunrise tomorrow seeing as my GPS has the trip as taking close to eleven hours without stops. "We'll need to make it quick. I want to get at least six hours sleep seeing as I have half a day's worth of driving ahead of me."

"Do you think Wallace would have ponied up for a plane if you hadn't pulled that stunt last month?" Liam asks as I get Timber's bowl and fill it with his kibble. That should cover him until we get back.

"I doubt it. He's such a hard ass anyway. He reminds me of an accountant sometimes, the way he's looking at every single dollar coming in and going out. I don't remember Janice being that strict with it."

"Maybe he just likes to be thorough," Liam suggests as I close the door and lock it behind me.

"And maybe he's just an asshat with nothing better to do. You do remember he's the one who wanted to send me off to Flagstaff or wherever, right?"

As we descend the stairs toward my car I can feel the air heavy with something unspoken. I'm sure he's about to broach whatever subject he wanted to discuss earlier today, and I know from his stiff posture I'm not going to like it.

"Before we head out," he says as we reach my car. "I wanted to check in with you, make sure everything was okay."

"You keep asking me that," I say. "And I keep telling you I'm fine."

"You weren't fine last night," he says.

I stop short and meet his gaze. "What?"

"When you left the party to go to the bathroom."

"I wasn't feeling well. I'd had a lot to drink."

"You'd had a total of two drinks. And I've seen you put away a lot more than that before you make a run like the one you made last night."

I square my shoulders as I face him. "What are you saying? Are you accusing me of something?"

"No, nothing like that. Em, I just want to help. You seem like something is…I don't know. Off, somehow. I don't know how to describe it."

"I'm not sure I like what you're implying. Do you think I'm not fit for duty? Because I just met with Dr. Frost today and he says—"

"No, Em, it's nothing like that," he says, clearly exasperated. He looks up at the night sky and takes a deep breath before facing me again. "Ever since you got that letter in the mail you haven't seemed like yourself. I don't understand why you won't at least try to find out who sent it or send it off to Quantico so they can analyze the hand—"

"Stop," I tell him, my gaze boring into his. "That's enough." Wisely, he stops trying to argue. "I shouldn't have to explain myself to you. I've already told you I don't want anything to do with that letter. My mother is dead, it's obviously a prankster or someone who is trying to get something from me. And I'm not playing that game. After everything I had to go through with Matt, I don't have the bandwidth to deal with that. I just want to get back to work, do my job, enjoy my life with my boyfriend and live my life. Is that so wrong?"

He screws up his features. "Of course not. But you can't just shut that away forever and bury it. You're going to have to face it someday. And I'm afraid it's taking more of a toll on you than you think."

"Is that your professional opinion, *doctor*?" I chide without a hint of playfulness in my voice.

"Have you even told Dr. Frost about it?" he asks.

I set my lips in a line. "You know what? I'm not really hungry anymore." I turn back to the apartment. "I really need to get some sleep."

"Em, c'mon," Liam says, smartly not coming after me.

I shake my head as I climb the steps to my door. "It's fine. Just make sure you come by tomorrow morning to get Timber. I'll feed him breakfast and take him out before we leave."

"Emily," he says. I hate the longing in how he says my name. I don't get what's so hard to understand about this. It's a stupid prank, and I don't need to pay it any attention.

I turn back to him when I reach my door. "You'll be here in the morning?"

He waits a beat then nods. "I will." He holds up his key. "He'll be in good hands while you're gone."

"Thank you," I say. "I'll see you when we get back."

He looks like he's about to say something else but thinks better of it and heads back to his car. I want him to come after me, to realize that I'm not being irrational about this, but Liam just doesn't get it. I hate this is how we're going to leave things, but the fact that he can't see my point of view is infuriating.

I don't wait to watch him drive away, instead I walk back into my apartment and slam my door behind me. Timber, who is still perched over his bowl, stops eating for a minute and looks at me, confused as to why I'm back here so soon.

"It's okay, you can keep eating," I tell him, and he doesn't waste any time going back to his bowl.

I stomp through the house, making a beeline for my bedroom and snatch the letter out of the bottom of the drawer. My name and address are still scrawled across the front in that same, familiar font I'd recognize anywhere. I make my way back into the kitchen and stand over the trash can, the letter in both hands. I'm about to rip it in half, but something stops me. I've been doing good to keep this letter out of my mind for the past month but I'm tired of it plaguing me. Why can't I just tear it up and be done with it already?

Maybe it's because some deep part of me realizes that Liam might be right. What if it's *not* a prank? What if it really is from my mother...somehow?

I shake my head. That's impossible. Mom died seventeen years ago; I know, I was there. Her illness developed slowly at first, so little that I—being a preteen—had no clue what was going on. Then one day she was suddenly in the hospital. I remember thinking it was just something small, and she'd be home soon. And she was, but her visits to the hospital became more and more frequent, until one day she finally went and never came back home.

Dad and I would spend countless nights there with her, waiting, me reading or sleeping while mom lay in that bed, dying. I didn't really get it at the time. I thought they'd find a way to make her better. I couldn't imagine a world without my mom because I'd never lived in one before. And when that day finally came when they woke me up and told me she was gone, I didn't know how to respond. I still thought maybe there was a chance for a miracle—a way to bring her back.

But as the hours and eventually days wore on, I realized that this was my new reality.

I remember being so angry at her back then for leaving me. I tucked myself away in my room, refusing to come out for anything. Eventually Dad managed to coax me out for the funeral and that's where I think it really hit me. It was a closed casket, thankfully, but still, there was a picture of her beside the casket, from the year before, looking as alive and well as anyone else in the world. It didn't make sense that she was dead.

I withdrew from everything for a long time after that. I think that's probably why I don't let very many people in. My mom was my best friend; she was the woman I looked up to more than anyone and the person I relied on for everything. And even though Dad was still there, I considered myself alone after she died. Growing up without brothers or sisters, and not having a particularly close family meant I relied on them for everything. Until I left for college it was just me and Dad most of the time. I'm sure that's why I'm as self-sufficient as I am and why being alone doesn't bother me very much.

Looking down at the envelope again, a tiny rip streaks across the top from where I almost tore it in half. I remove the letter itself from the envelope, open it and flatten it out on the kitchen table. For the first time in a month, I read the words written in her handwriting:

Dearest Emily,
You look so pretty on TV. I can't wait to see you again soon.
—Mom

I thought maybe I might have read something wrong the first time, but it's exactly the same. What I don't understand is what anyone would gain by sending this to me. Anyone who knows me at all knows that my mother is dead. So why pretend like she's alive? What's even more disturbing, is they have somehow managed to replicate her handwriting.

Liam's wrong. I don't need to send this thing down to Quantico for them to do a handwriting analysis. I know it's her script. Or a very close approximation. But if this is someone's attempt at convincing me that my mother is in fact alive after all these years, they have failed massively. A wave of unease washes over me again and I fold the letter back up, stuffing it back in the envelope. By now Timber has finished eating and is looking up at me as I take the letter and throw it in the trash. I'm not going to be anyone's pawn in some sick game—I've already been down that road and I'd rather not repeat the experience. Though deep down I need to know who could have possibly sent that letter, something tells me it's better if I let it go. Whatever I've been feeling ever since it arrived is tearing me up, and I have a job that needs my full attention.

Satisfied I've made the right decision, I go to the fridge and pull out a microwave meal and an opened bottle of wine that'll end up being my dinner.

Ten minutes later I'm sitting on the couch, with a mug of wine sitting on the table as Timber whines for a bite of mostly-warmed-up lasagna, doing my best not to think about what's in the can behind me.

Chapter Five

"Em, hey, Em, wake up."

I try to stretch out, a cramp in my neck causing me to wince before I can fully open my eyes. I groan, then attempt to roll over before I realize I've been restrained by a seatbelt. There's a flash of half a second where my half-awake mind thinks I'm back in the car with Rossovich, headed to my death before my eyes snap open and I realize I'm still in the passenger seat of the company's Black Escalade, Zara sitting right beside me. She's tuned the radio to a nineties station and it's blaring *Tony! Toni! Tone!* How did I sleep through that? "What?" I say, rubbing my eyes.

"Look at this."

I reach over and push the button on the side of my seat raising it back up so I'm in an upright position to see one of the most gorgeous sunsets over snowcapped mountains I've ever seen. "Oh, wow."

"Right?" Zara says. "I couldn't let you sleep through that."

"Thanks," I say, admiring the sunset for a moment. The entire sky is a deep pink, transitioning to purple, the blue of the mountains in the distance a cold contrast to the rays peeking over them. "What time is it?"

"Almost six-thirty, we're nearly there."

"I see why people love it up here." The road in front of us is deserted, Zara having turned off the interstate some time back. These are the country roads that head into the mountains, and there doesn't look to be another car around. A blanket of snow covers the ground, though it doesn't look very deep. "Are we sure we're in the right place?"

"You saw the report, the D.A. is stationed in Collins, so I figure that's probably the best place to start. Though it's going to be a little late to get started tonight."

"Ugh," I say, checking my phone. "We've already lost the entire day to this stupid drive. I can't believe Wallace couldn't just make an exception, especially if we know our killer is probably going to go after another victim in two days."

Zara shakes her head. "I think you're right about him. He's too bogged down in the balance sheets and it's going to end up getting someone killed."

"Maybe we can do some light recon tonight, get the lay of the land," I suggest as the sun finally disappears behind the tallest mountain ahead of us. Even though the sky is still light, it feels like someone has shut off the lights, as everything seems immediately darker. The mountains surround us and seem much larger than the upper Appalachians should be.

"Do these look sort of like the Rockies to you?" I lean forward so I can get a better look out the windshield.

"I don't know, I've never seen the Rockies," she replies. "Why?"

"No reason, they just seem...ominous."

We drive for another twenty minutes before coming over a pass and down into a small valley. Before we even get into the town proper, we pass lone homes out on the roads, most lit up with Christmas lights, and a few that even have blow-up decorations in their massive yards. By the time we reach the town of Collins proper, the streetlights are decorated with large light-up candy canes and there's a festive atmosphere about the place. All of the snow in the town has been pushed to the side off the main roads and has accumulated in drifts. "I hope you brought snow boots," I tell Zara.

"Are you kidding? If we get extra time I'm going snowboarding," she replies with a grin.

"You don't even know how to snowboard." I laugh.

"Yeah, but what better time to learn? Plus, what Wallace doesn't know won't hurt him. I still need to make up for not being on that private jet."

I place my head in my hands. "I am never going to live that down."

She pats my back a few times. "No ma'am, you are not."

As we're driving through town we pass the local police station: an old brick building that looks like it's been there for at least a hundred years. "Guess we'll be headed in there first thing in the morning."

"They're going to love us," Zara says. "Coming in to take over where they couldn't cut it."

I sigh. "Maybe it won't be so bad this time. There have been a few that actually accept our help."

She gives me *the look* and I have to relent. "Yeah, probably not. Where are we staying anyway?"

"We're only about five minutes away," she says, and we both check the GPS. The address listed is right on the edge of the far side of the town.

When we finally pull up, I furrow my brow then look back at the accommodation arrangements that were made by central. "This can't be right."

"Hey," Zara says. "Don't look a gift horse in the mouth." In front of us sits an old Victorian home, complete with a turret on one side and a sharp pitched roof. The entire building is decorated in lighted garland and there is a wreath around the pole out front which sports a sign: *Mantokee Bed and Breakfast*.

"You didn't," I say. "Wallace is going to kill us."

"What was I supposed to do?" she asks. "The only hotels in this town are up on the mountain for the tourists and ski people. It was either this or face a twenty-minute drive up and down a treacherous mountain road in the snow every day."

"Zara," I chide.

"Okay, okay, so maybe that's a little exaggeration. But I'm serious. There's one old motel about ten minutes out of town, but from the online pictures it looked like it had been condemned a decade or so ago."

"Fine," I say, gathering my bags. "You get to explain to Wallace why we're in a swanky B&B. Maybe that will get him off my case for a while."

"I figured we might as well enjoy ourselves while we're here," she says, turning off the car and getting out.

I open the passenger door and am immediately hit with a blast of chilly air. "God! That's cold." I go to the trunk to pull my suitcase out, hoping I've packed enough for this weather. "Do we just leave the car here or…"

She shrugs. "This place doesn't look like it has a traffic problem. I'm sure they can tell us inside."

I can't help but laugh as we make our way up the walkway to the stairs leading to the front door. "You're incorrigible, you know that?"

"It's one of my best qualities," she replies.

Before we can reach the front door, it opens to reveal a woman in her early sixties, her white hair pulled back into a bun. She's sporting a Christmas sweater covered in bells and reindeer and has a wide smile on her face. "You must be the FBI agents!" she nearly shouts.

"Yes, ma'am, I'm Special Agent Emily Slate and this is Special Agent Zara Foley," I say as we finish climbing the stairs and reach the door.

"I'm Andrea Bale, proprietor of Mantokee with my husband, Matt." The name catches me off guard for a second, but I recover quickly. "We're so excited to have you joining us. You're here for the week, is that right?"

"Maybe longer," Zara says. "When I made the reservation online it said I could keep it open-ended."

"Yes, of course," Andrea says. "Come in, come in, it's already so chilly out."

"Is this typical for this time of year?" I ask as we step inside, and she shuts the cold out. I get my first good look inside the old house and realize that Andrea—or someone here—takes Christmas seriously. There's a large tree in the foyer, lit with more lights than I can count and covered in tasteful ornaments, almost like the whole tree is a piece of art. The banister leading to the second floor is wrapped in lit garland, and even more ornaments hang from each spindle. In fact, everywhere I look the place has been decorated in some fashion or another.

"We're just going through a cold snap," Andrea says. "It'll warm up again in a day or two. Let's get you two settled." She leads us over to an adjacent room which acts as sort of an office for the home. Now that I'm getting a good look at it, it's a lot larger than it seemed from the street.

"We've got you in the mountain suite. Two queen beds, is that right?"

Zara nods. "With an en suite."

Andrea gives her a wide smile. "We renovated this house before we opened and made sure each of our rooms had a separate bathroom. You wouldn't believe how much that has helped occupancy rates."

I exchange a quick glance with Zara.

"Do you have a vehicle?" she asks.

"We left it out at—"

"Here," Andrea says, holding out a little yellow hang tag. "Clip this on your car when you're not driving it. We have a small parking area around the back, but you can leave it on the street for tonight. But without this tag, the parking authority will think it's been abandoned and tow you." She pauses for a moment, then lets out what I can only describe as a cackle. "Wouldn't that be a hoot? Them, towing an FBI car? I'd pay money to see Wendel's face if that happened." She pulls the tag back out of Zara's reach. "You wouldn't want to try it, would you?"

I reach out and take the tag out of her hand. "We'll place it on the car. We don't have time to deal with being towed."

For a second she seems disappointed, then shrugs. "Ah, too bad. Would've been a great trick. Okay, the mountain suite is up the stairs, second door on the right. It's got the little mountain with the cute goats on the door. You can't miss it. Breakfast begins at five a.m., and we serve until about nine." She leans a little closer. "But if you really need something, the kitchen's always open. Just come on down and make yourself a snack."

"That's very generous, thank you," I say.

"We also watch Jeopardy each night in the main gathering room over there." She points past us, across the entryway to a large sitting room with three couches around a large TV Inexplicably, there's *another* decorated tree in the bay window, about half as large as the one in the hallway. "And we have plenty of games or books if you get bored."

"Thanks," Zara says. "But we'll probably just be here for sleeping."

Andrea beams at us. "You're here because of those men that keep dying, aren't you?"

I exchange another look with Zara. I guess in a town this small, word is bound to get around. "What do you know about them?" I ask.

She gives me a noncommittal shrug. "Nothing much. Just heard that boy got killed last Saturday, though they haven't released his name yet. But we all know it was Duncan. He hasn't been back to the hardware store since that day and he's always over there, giving old Henry a hard time about some

tool or another. And I've got a cousin, Darlene, over in Highburg who told me that another boy got killed over there three
weeks ago, but she didn't know much else. Just said it was
brutal. She owns the salon over there and overheard the
woman who lived next to him talking about how the police
had to bring in some kind of special crew to clean up the
mess? Can't imagine what might have happened." She pauses
and bats her eyes at us. "Don't suppose you could give me any
hints, could you?"

"Sorry," I say. "We can't comment on ongoing investi-
gations."

She leans back in her chair. "Well, if you're feeling like
sharing, just let me know. I'm always happy to lend an ear."

I take the key from the counter. "Thank you. We'll see you
bright and early for breakfast."

"You two sleep good now, y'hear?" she calls after us. We
give her a final wave before climbing the stairs with all of our
luggage.

"I am going to kill you," I whisper to Zara as we reach the
top and make a left turn, looking for our room.

"What? She's nice," Zara says, playfully.

"Yeah, and she's going to be all in our business the entire
time we're here." Sure enough, there's a door with a mountain
painted on it, complete with small goats. Though I don't think
there are any mountain goats in New Hampshire. I turn the
key and the door opens to reveal the room.

It's larger than I expected, both beds set next to each other
with a small nightstand between them. We're in the room that
is the upper floor of the turret, which means the windows
offer us a wide view of the small town beyond, all of it decorated in festive lights. There's a dresser and a few other small
pieces of furniture, including a small chair, and a plush rug on
what look like hundred-year-old hardwoods. Just inside the
door is another door which leads to the small bathroom. It
only has one vanity and a shower/tub combo, but it's enough

for our needs. Better than sharing a bathroom with a bunch of other guests.

"Well?" Zara says, setting her stuff down on one of the beds. "Did I come through or didn't I?"

"Yeah," I say, looking around again. "I guess I can't complain."

Chapter Six

ON THE WAY up Zara and I took turns driving every couple of hours so neither of us would be exhausted. This meant that when one of us wasn't driving, we were reviewing the case notes Wallace had given us, or, occasionally sleeping. But going over case notes while driving and actively sitting down and putting our heads together are two separate things.

After we finished dropping off our stuff at the Mantokee B&B, Zara and I headed out to find a place to eat and to see if we could get a good read on the town. Sometimes you can learn a lot about a place by just watching the people that live there. We've already learned from Andrea that word has gotten around about the most recent victim: Duncan Schmidt. It doesn't help things that he was the brother of one of the local cops, but we'll deal with that snake pit tomorrow. Right now all I want to do is get something good to eat and figure out how we want to approach this.

Since Zara took the last leg of driving, I offer to find us a place serving dinner. The town itself is sparse and spread out, which is a lot different to the small towns I'm used to seeing. In fact, it's like a town that's out of time, like it was built in the 1700s and never updated. A large, white church sits at what

I'd call the center of town, surrounded by a smattering of smaller buildings. But what's interesting about Collins is how much green space is around. The buildings are set far off from the main street running through town, and all of them are freestanding buildings. None of the rows of brick storefronts like I'm used to in the southern parts of the country.

"Looks like a nice place to raise some livestock," Zara says as we pass a pasture on the left. In the distance dark shapes stand out against the inky night. I can only assume they are cows.

"It's very…traditional," I say.

"Look! A bookie's office," she laughs, pointing at a bright neon sign. It's the only flashing sign in the entire town.

"We're definitely out of my element here," I say. "Do people eat out around here or does everyone just cook something on their pot-bellied stove?"

"That looks like something," Zara says, pointing to the other side of the street. There's a sign that says *Birchwood Eats*. I slow the car and pull in a gravel driveway which turns into a makeshift parking lot. The building doesn't look like a restaurant, in fact it resembles a colonial-style home, complete with a full-length porch and columns supporting it. There are four other vehicles in the parking lot, three of them pickup trucks.

"Seems like as good a place as any," I say and kill the engine. When we get it out I'm hit by that cold again and I shiver, despite wearing my warmest coat. "It's going to take me some time to get used to this cold."

"I love it," Zara says. "It's brisk. Not like those puny winters we get back home."

We make our way to the door, which requires me putting my shoulder into before it will budge. When I finally get it open, we enter as all eyes in the place turn to look at us. There's no hostess stand anywhere, but the guy at the bar clears his throat. "Ya'll just take a seat anywhere. We'll be with you in a minute."

We nod our thanks and make our way into the place. Right inside the door is a bar that runs halfway down the restaurant, complete with half a dozen stools, three of them already occupied. Otherwise, there are a couple of highboy tables up against the wall. In the room beyond the bar there are larger tables, all situated in front of an ancient-looking fireplace. Even with all the alterations, it's easy to tell someone converted an old house into this restaurant.

Zara and I make our way past the bar into the great room, and take a seat at a table close to one of the windows along the side of the house.

"Do you feel like you just walked into the O-K Saloon?" she asks.

"Yeah, they're definitely putting out that vibe. And based on what our proprietor told us, I'm betting this is a very close-knit community."

A few minutes later a woman comes along with two waters, both without ice and leaves again without saying a word. We're far enough away from anyone else that I don't expect anyone will be able to hear us, but at the same time, I'm not about to do anything else to draw attention to us. So we just sit in silence, waiting for the waitress to return, which she does, a few minutes later, carrying two menus.

"We got Bud Light and Red Rocks on tap," she says. "And we have a couple of local brews if ya'll want to try somethin' fresh."

"Water's fine for me," I say.

"Do you guys have any ciders?" Zara asks.

"Apple Orchard and Bosch. That'll be it," the waitress replies, then pop's the gum she's chewing in her cheek.

"That's okay," Zara says. "Thanks anyway."

"Ya'll here for the skiing?" she asks.

"Is it that obvious?" I ask.

She shrugs. "Most tourists stay up on the mountain. But a couple make it down here every now and again." She hesitates a moment, and I can't figure out what she's looking at. "Ya'll lesbians?"

My eyes go wide as Zara turns to hide her face. I know she's doing everything she can to keep from laughing her ass off.

"No, nothing like that. We're just friends," I manage to say.

"Uh-huh," she replies. "Well just so you know, we respect Jesus here." She points to a large cross that's high up on the old fireplace. "Ya'll keep that in mind. I'll be back in a minute to get your order." She turns and heads off.

Zara finally peeks out, her entire face has gone beet red, and I know it's taking all her willpower not to lose it completely. "Did'ya hear that, Em? Can't be doing any of that lesbian stuff while you're here."

"Shut up," I tell her, doing my best not to crack a smile as I read the menu. "Where have you brought us?"

"Aw c'mon, it's kinda cute, if not a little sexist," she says, peeking over her own menu.

"I'm reserving judgment on that one."

AFTER THE WAITRESS RETURNS AND TAKES OUR ORDER, WE finally get down to brass tacks. I pull up the file information on my phone so we can go over what we know before we face the firing squad in the morning. "Okay, four victims so far, each of them from a different town around here."

"Right," Zara says, looking at her phone. "The most recent being from Collins. Duncan Schmidt."

"All we have connecting all four of them is that they were all killed on a Saturday night, and they all exhibit the same method of death. The throats of each victim are punctured by an unknown weapon before their genitals were removed."

"Someone is trying to make a point," Zara says.

"And not a subtle one. Obviously, someone has a real problem with these guys. Did you have any time to pull background information on any of them?"

She shakes her head. "Not beyond what was in the file; I haven't had the time. Why, what are you thinking?"

"I'm just wondering about the families. We know Schmidt has a brother on the force. But I'm wondering if there's anything else that connects them. Could they have known each other? Maybe even gone to school together at some point? Something has to tie them together, something that makes them targets." I scroll through the information again, though there's not a lot in the files. Why can't local LEOs ever fill these things out fully? I swear it's like pulling teeth to get full reports sometimes.

"What do you think the motivation is behind the genitals?" Zara asks just as the waitress appears with our food. Zara immediately goes still, not taking her wide eyes off mine as the waitress sets our food in front of us. She clears her throat then looks up at that cross again before she returns to the kitchen.

Zara bursts out laughing. "Okay, I *swear* I didn't do that on purpose."

"You're gonna get us kicked out of here before I even get to taste it," I tell her. Looking down at my plate the food looks delicious. I ordered a seafood platter while Zara got a club sandwich with chips. About half the items on my plate are fried, but at the moment I don't really care. We didn't stop much on the trip and I'm starving. Not to mention for some reason sitting in a car all day wears me out. "But to answer your question, it could be a number of things. Scorned lover, jealous competitor, the usual. And then there's always the possibility that someone is doing it to throw us off."

"That's a lot of trouble just to throw us off. Plus, it's not like we don't know *how* they're being killed." She takes a bite of her sandwich and her eyes go wide again. "This is really good."

"So if we discount the possibility it's some sort of smoke-screen, then whoever is doing this has some sexual motivation for doing so. We just don't know what, yet." I take a few fried shrimp and pop them in my mouth. She's right, it *is* good.

"I dunno, Em. Why start now? What kicked this whole thing off a month ago? And why is it only every Saturday?"

I shake my head. "No clue. Hopefully we'll get some more information tomorrow when we talk to Collins Police. Maybe since they knew Duncan Schmidt they'll be able to give us some more insight into who he was. The only way we're going to find out who's doing this is by figuring out what they want."

"Apparently they want to cut off a bunch of dicks," Zara says under her breath and I almost spit out a popcorn shrimp.

After I recover, I scroll through a couple more pages. "I just wish we had more time. We need to talk to each of the family members and that's a lot of ground to cover."

"We could split up," she suggests. "I'm sure Collins Police would give us an extra vehicle."

"I wouldn't bet on that. We'd have better luck with a car rental place in town but we don't have time for that. Best case scenario we'll be able to talk to a couple of the families. Maybe that will give us enough to go on to find our killer."

"You don't really believe that, do you?" she asks, her sandwich forgotten on her plate.

I want to. But the truth is we're not miracle workers. I'm not sure what Wallace expects, but there is no way we can find and stop this person in less than forty-eight hours. "I want to. We'll just have to do the best we can with what we have."

"And if there's another body on Sunday?" Zara asks.

I take a deep breath, disturbed by the reality of what we're facing. "Then at least we'll get to look at a fresh crime scene."

Chapter Seven

I never sleep well when I know a big case is on the horizon. But I can't deny the bed at Mantokee was a lot more comfortable than I'd expected. Though at some point during the night I thought I heard someone coming up and down the stairs. It was probably just one of the other guests, heading down to the kitchen for a midnight snack. Still, it kept me awake enough that I'm a little bleary-eyed when we get up.

After a hearty breakfast at the courtesy of Andrea, Zara and I head to the Collins Police Department, determined to get there as early as possible. When we walk inside, a desk sergeant sits behind a partition that reminds me of the kinds they have in the principal's office at school.

"Good morning," I tell the officer, holding up my badge. "Special Agents Slate and Foley with the FBI. We're looking for Chief Eastly."

"He won't be in until nine," the desk sergeant says, his face completely impassive.

"Okay," I say, nodding. "What about Sergeant Schmidt? Could we speak with him?"

"He's out on leave. His brother was killed last weekend, in

case you didn't know." I shoot Zara a glance. The grimace on her face tells me she was expecting a slightly warmer welcome.

"Then who would you suggest we speak with?" Zara asks. "We've been assigned to take the Schmidt case."

The desk sergeant just shrugs. "Chief's handling that one, guess you need to talk to him. But like I said, he won't be in until nine." He points to a row of chairs by the door. "Feel free to wait if you like."

I bite my tongue to stop myself from saying something I'll regret, before finally retreating over to the line of chairs.

"Guess we could've slept in. Seems like everyone else in this town does," Zara says, plopping herself down and crossing her arms.

"You'd think with a killer out there they'd be taking this a little more seriously," I mutter. The chief has to know about the killings in the surrounding towns. So then why isn't this all hands on deck? It's like everyone here is acting like nothing happened.

We sit, waiting for more than half an hour before the door opens to reveal two patrol officers strolling through. They glance at us, then stop by the desk sergeant, all three of them talking in hushed voices. It's not hard to tell what they're discussing. Occasionally they look back at us, and each time they do, we just glare in their direction. Finally, one of the officers heads into the back part of the station while the other addresses us.

"You two from the FBI, huh?" he asks. "Aren't you a little young to be working for the government?" He's probably in his mid-forties, with a scruffy beard and moustache to match. My guess is he and his cohort were on patrol and are just getting off their shifts.

"Aren't you a little old to still be a beat cop?" Zara shoots back, causing his face to turn into a grimace.

"I don't know what you think you're doing here, but we

take care of our own in Collins. We don't need you here." He spits.

"Your new D.A. thinks differently," I reply. "But don't worry, we'll be very thorough. Unlike some places, we actually finish all our paperwork so that you'll be able to read about everything we're doing."

He sneers again, then removes his hat, revealing a mop of sweaty hair stuck to his skull. "Take the hint ladies and leave the difficult work up to the seasoned professionals." He turns and heads back into the station. I notice the desk sergeant eyeing us, but as soon as he sees me, he turns his attention back down.

"I want to humiliate that man like there is no tomorrow," Zara whispers.

"As much as I'd like to see that, we don't have the time," I say, as the door to the station opens again. A thin man in his sixties steps through the doors, his hat in his hands. From the rank on his uniform I already know this must be Chief Eastly. He glances at us a moment then stops when the desk sergeant motions to him. Zara and I stand to greet him.

"Chief Eastly?" I ask.

He furrows his brow and holds out a hand. "Yes. Are you—"

I take the hand and give it a solid shake. "Special Agent Slate with the FBI. This is Special Agent Foley. Were you informed we'd be coming?"

Eastly looks over at the desk sergeant again then back to us. "Yes, of course. I just—I didn't expect them to send someone so—"

Don't say it. For the love of God, don't say it.

"—fresh-faced."

I'll admit, that's a new one.

"You're aware of the other killings, correct? In the surrounding towns?" I ask.

"Graystone, Boone, and Highburg," Zara rattles off.

"Yes, yes, we know this isn't an isolated incident," Eastly says. "I've been in constant contact with the Adams County Sheriff and D.A. Rice." He seems put off by our appearance this morning. Like he wasn't expecting to have to deal with us, even though he knew we were coming. What, did he think we'd just not show up? "Are you…staying in town?"

"We are. Is that a problem?"

"Why?" he asks, as if it would be so strange we'd be staying where the most recent murder took place.

"Not that it matters," I say, doing everything I can to contain my frustration. "But since this is where the last murder happened, it seemed the most logical place to start."

"Right, right," he says, looking down at the other end of the station. "Where ya'll staying?"

"Chief," I say. "We have a very limited window here. Based on the killer's pattern, more than likely there will be another murder tomorrow night. Now we need your help to stop that from happening."

"You really think it's going to happen here again?" he asks. "Haven't we already had our turn?"

What is with this guy? "We're hoping we might find something that will give us some indication where they might strike next. Didn't you consider that?" Zara asks.

"Well, yes, but I figured…it's not like they can keep doing this forever, right?"

"Chief Eastly," I say, my voice firm. "We need to see your files on the Schmidt killing, right now."

He hesitates a moment, then turns and heads past the desk sergeant without a word. Either Eastly is one strange duck, or something else is going on here. I already don't like the implication. It feels like we're stepping into something, though I'm not exactly sure what.

Eastly leads us past a few open doors, one leading to an interview room and another that looks like a break room. The back of the station is about as glamorous as the front, and about what I expected from a small-town police station. From what I can tell, they probably have less than two dozen people on staff for the entire town, not that it matters.

"Is there any reason you haven't assigned this to your investigative division?" I ask as Eastly leads us into his office. It's plain, with little more than a desk and a row of filing cabinets. There aren't even any pictures on the walls, though a large window does look out on the back parking lot.

"Detective Schmidt was the victim's brother," he says. "The entire department knew him. I thought it would be better that they weren't involved. Emotions...and all that." He indicates we can take the seats on the other side of his desk, which we do. Eastly fishes around in one of the filing cabinets, pulling out a file folder from the "S" section.

"Poor Duncan," he says, gently sitting in his own chair. "I knew him as a boy. Always a shy kid. One of those boys you don't really notice, y'know? Hell of a thing to happen to a man, especially one in his prime." He hands the file folder over.

"How well did you know him?" I ask, taking the folder. "Other than when he was young?"

Eastly takes a deep breath. "Well enough. He worked over at the hardware store in town. Moved away for a few years but came back about a year months ago. Figured he'd come back married with kids but seems like he was the perpetual bachelor."

I flip through the file and Zara leans over so we can both look at what Collins PD has come up with. Unfortunately, there isn't much more in there than was in the file that Wallace sent us. "Haven't you done any follow up work since Wednesday?" I ask. "There's nothing in here we haven't already seen."

Eastly screws up his features. "There haven't been any new developments. Of course I've had the word out among all my people, but my guess is the killer is long gone by now. It's out of my jurisdiction."

I can't believe this guy. He has a murder right here in his town, the brother of one of his own detectives nonetheless, and he's just content to sit on it, betting the killer has moved on already? "Chief, I—"

Before I can finish, his door slams open, revealing a large man in a wool overcoat. His hair is disheveled and all he's got on underneath the coat is a wife beater and a pair of jeans. "Just what the hell is going on here, Jasper? You told me the feds weren't getting involved."

I glare up at the man who has come in here like a raging bull, his nostrils flaring.

"Rice called them in," Eastly says, absolving himself of any responsibility. "It's out of my hands."

Zara and I stand, mostly because I don't like the idea of a hulking man standing over me, especially one as wound up as this. "I presume you're Detective Schmidt."

The man huffs a few times, but doesn't respond, looking between us and Chief Eastly. The desk sergeant rushes in behind him. "Sorry, Chief, I tried to stop him."

Eastly holds up a hand. "Garrett, go home. Get your affairs in order. We got a funeral on Sunday, don't we?"

"I ain't doin' it with them here," he says, pointing to us.

"Good," I reply. "Because there's a good chance we'll need your brother's body for evidence after Sunday, so best postpone that funeral."

"You can't—they can't do that," Schmidt says, turning to Eastly. "Hasn't he been humiliated enough? The man needs a proper burial."

"And he'll get one," I reply. "As soon as we figure out who's out there killing these men. I would think that would be more important to a cop than postponing a funeral a few days."

"Don't you dare," Schmidt spits at me. "You feds think you know everything about everything, don't you? Think you can just waltz in here and point your finger at someone and be done with it. But we're a *community* here. We don't just go around accusing people 'cause it's convenient."

"Are you saying we don't know how to do our jobs?" I ask.

"Sure don't look like it. When did you graduate high school, last year?" he says, sizing us up.

Eastly stands. "Garrett, get the hell out of here and let me handle this, you're only making things worse." It's the most emotion I've seen from the man all morning.

"That's all right," I say, holding up the folder. "I think we already have everything we need. If you gentlemen will excuse us, we'll get out of your hair."

Schmidt doesn't move to let us by until a glare from Eastly changes his mind. Zara and I leave with the desk sergeant, and I notice Schmidt closes the door behind us, leaving just him and Eastly inside.

"I…uh…this way," the sergeant stammers, attempting to escort us out.

"Just a minute," I tell him and nod to Zara. Less than a few seconds later, I hear Schmidt's voice through the door, practically yelling at his boss.

"*How could you let them in here Jasper? They're goddamn teenagers! They don't know shit from shit, and they don't belong here.*"

"*What was I supposed to do?*" Eastly yells back. "*Rice is breathing down my neck on this one. Like it or not, but he calls the shots.*"

"*Last time I checked you were the police chief, not him.*"

"*Garrett. I won't tell you again. Get your ass home and stay there until all this blows over. I don't want to see you in this station again until those two agents are done, understand?*"

The door flies open, and Schmidt comes storming out, but stops short when he sees we've been listening right outside. He looks like he's on the verge of saying something else stupid, but manages to keep it to himself and storms out. I look back into the office and catch Eastly's eye. He clearly thought we were gone and for a moment I see a look of panic cross his face before he resets himself. I give him a brief nod then return to follow the grief-stricken desk sergeant back out.

As we make our way back out the front I hear Zara chuckle behind me. "That was beautiful."

"It was, wasn't it?" I say as we reach the car and slip inside. "Eastly is clearly hiding something, but the question is what? And why is he so hesitant to keep working this case?"

Zara shakes her head. "Man, you really do get the best ones. I need to tag along with you more often."

"Be careful what you wish for," I say, turning the engine over. But before I can back out, a Lincoln town car pulls in behind us, parking right next to our vehicle. A clean-shaven man in a dapper suit gets out, screwing up his features, then relaxing again before knocking on Zara's window.

She looks at me then rolls the window down. "If you're looking for the drive-thru we're all out of coffee."

The man smiles. "You must be the FBI agents from Washington."

"That's right," I say. "And you are?"

"District Attorney Rice. I'm glad I caught you. We need to talk."

Chapter Eight

AFTER A BRIEF CONVERSATION, we follow D.A. Rice out of town and over to the Adams County seat about twenty minutes away. The scenery is beautiful and picturesque, all the small farms and quaint little homes along the way. The county offices are a couple of low-slung modern buildings that are set in a little town called Ossippe, which is about a fifth of the size of Collins.

"Thanks for following me over, it's easier to talk here than to try and convince Eastly to use one of his rooms," Jim Rice says as we get out of the car, following him into the offices. He's younger than I expected for a D.A., probably in his early thirties. And his suit screams of an expensive designer label. No wonder Eastly hasn't taken to him. He probably sees Rice as much of an outsider as we are.

"He wasn't the most cooperative man," I say, entering the warm office building. Rice directs us to a modern-looking conference room off to the right.

"The chief is set in his ways, all right," Rice says, offering us a pair of chairs. I've brought the file from Eastly in with me. "He's been that way ever since I started working here. In fact, most people around here seem to be like that."

"What, distrustful?" Zara says.

"Careful," he replies. "The man who was the D.A. before me died in the position. Eighty-five years old. And he had a way of doing things. When I came in, I stirred up a lot of shit because of everything he'd let go. I think some people just get used to a way of doing things and before they realize it, they're pushing the boundaries of the law."

"The former D.A. was dirty?" I ask, incredulous.

"I wouldn't say intentionally so. He was eighty-five, after all. But he'd get a case on say, drunk driving. But because he knew so and so's father or went to school with someone's cousin's brother, he'd just write it off and close the case with little more than an apology. People had been used to getting away with a lot more. So when I came in, I faced a lot of backlash. Fortunately, Sheriff Dutton has been supportive." He looks around like he's forgotten something. "Excuse me for just a moment."

As soon as he leaves, Zara leans back, shooting me a look. "What?"

"Cute *and* righteous," she says.

"Thinking about dropping Raoul for a D.A. who lives a thousand miles away?" I ask.

She shrugs. "I wouldn't say it's completely out of the realm of possibility."

I frown, realizing she's serious. "I thought you and Raoul were doing good?"

She wags her head back and forth. "We're doing great. But it doesn't hurt to be prepared, right?"

I guess I can't blame her. Significant others who aren't in the Bureau often don't understand the kind of stress or hours we tend to keep. Which is what's nice about Liam. I hate how we left things. If I hadn't been so—

"Sorry about that," Rice says, coming back in, four folders under his arm. "I should have told your department to let you know to come here before interacting with any of the individual LEOs. Everyone's been on edge since the first killing and things are getting a little tense."

I push thoughts of Liam out of my mind and instead focus on my work. "Eastly didn't seem like he was in any distress. At least not until Detective Schmidt showed up."

Rice's face falls. "Oh god. Let me just apologize in advance. Like I said, things have been tense." He takes a seat close to us, close enough that I get a whiff of his cologne. I look over at Zara who folds her hands in her lap and winks at me. "Here's what we have on all the other cases. I've been working with Sheriff Dutton ever since the first man was killed."

"Do all four towns fall in the same county?" I ask.

He shakes his head. "Three do. One is in Jefferson county, a couple miles over. If you're looking for some connective tissue, I don't blame you. But so far, we have very little on these guys that connects them to each other." He spreads the files out in front of us, each with a different name. Robert Hainsworth, James Wheeldon, Nicholas Valentine, and Duncan Schmidt. Our four victims.

Rice then pulls out a folded map, spreading it out on the table before us. "Here are the towns where each man has died," he says. "As far as I can tell, there's no particular order."

I stand to get a better look at the map. "Can we hang this up?"

Rice looks over to the far wall where there's a whiteboard. "Um…yeah, hang on." He gets up, toting the map over to the whiteboard and clips it to the top so it's at eye level.

"First death was Hainsworth," Zara says. "Here in Grey-stone?" It's a small town south of our current position, about twenty miles from Collins.

Rice nods. We then go through the rest of the deaths, each in chronological order. There's no pattern that I can see. The killer starts south, then heads north to Boone, then back southeast again to Highburg and then northwest to Collins. "They're doing a lot of backtracking," I say.

He nods. "You'd think they'd move in some kind of systematic pattern. But so far it doesn't seem that way."

I let out a long breath. Without something to connect these men, finding our next victim is going to be next to impossible. "How many do you have on staff here?"

Rice looks at me, blinking a few times. "There's about half a dozen of us, why?"

"We need to dig into the victims' backgrounds to find what connects them to each other. Without that, we don't have a chance in hell of finding this killer, *or* where they're going to strike next." I glance back at the map. There are still half a dozen towns in the circumference of the ones where men have been killed so far. That's assuming our unsub stays within that circle. They could very well move outside it, which widens the possibilities considerably. "And that's going to take a lot of manpower."

He screws up his features again. "I'm sorry Agent Slate, I can't just pull people off their jobs to assist with this. We have an entire county to cover here, not just the towns affected. I have another four meetings today alone. The only reason I was able to squeeze this in was because it was first thing in the morning."

I exchange glances with Zara. It's a ton of work for the two of us. And I'm not sure we have enough time before tomorrow night. "We'll get started immediately," I tell him. "But given the scope of this—"

"I know," he says, interrupting. "I'm not expecting a miracle, and I know you're coming into this late."

"Why didn't you notify us earlier?" Zara asks. "You know, maybe after the second murder?"

"You have to see it from my side," Rice says. "I'm fighting a bureaucracy here that's steeped in good ol' boys. I didn't even know about the second murder until the third one happened, the chief over in Boone kept it quiet. To be honest, me and my team have been overworked. I thought the local towns could handle it, but the bodies keep piling up and none of them have made any progress yet. If it were up to them, you never would have been involved."

There's a knock on the door and it opens before Rice can answer. A middle-aged woman in a sheriff's uniform steps inside the door. "Jim? Oh," she says, noticing us. "Sorry, I know you're in the middle of something, but I've got Willows on the phone and he's raising hell about this arraignment. You know how he is, won't listen to anyone but you."

"It's fine," Rice says, heading for the door. "Tammy, this is Special Agent Slate and Special Agent Foley, from D.C. They're here to help us with our little problem." He turns to us. "You'll have to excuse me; I have a full day. You've got everything I have, feel free to use this office if you need it. In the meantime, keep me updated, and whatever you do, try *not* to make waves. It'll make things easier in the long run, for everyone."

"That's not exactly how we operate," I say, bristling at the idea of "toning it down" for anyone.

"Trust me," he says, almost out the door. "It's best." He leaves us alone with the sheriff.

"You must be Sheriff Dutton," I say. She nods and we shake hands.

"Thanks for coming up. Jim give you the rundown?" she asks.

"We pretty much did that on the way here," Zara says. "Is there anything you can tell us that *isn't* in these files?"

"'fraid not. Jim's too polite to say, but I've only been sheriff for about six weeks. The previous man in the job, Walt Cahill, he just up and quit. Said he couldn't work with Rice looking over his shoulder, suspecting him all the time."

"Is that what was happening?" I ask.

She shakes her head, a smile on her lips. "Naw. He was

just bein' an asshole. Cahill always was full of himself. I think he quit in protest; didn't like how Rice did things but was too proud to say."

"Seems like there's a lot of that going on here," I say. One look at Zara tells me she's thinking the same thing. There's a power struggle up here between the towns and the county that oversees them.

"Honestly, I think if he hadn't quit, he would have found a way to run Rice out of town."

"So then, do you know any of the local Chiefs very well?" I ask. I don't know how much help Sheriff Dutton will be, but at this point I'm willing to take whatever I can get.

"Wish I did. But I transferred over from Cain County, in Maine. Before that I'd only been through this area a handful of times. But it was a good opportunity, and I didn't mind the move."

"Then you don't know anything about Chief Eastly," Zara says.

She chuckles. "He's an odd duck, that one. But no. I've only met the man a couple of times."

I stare at the pile of case files on the table, along with the map up on the whiteboard, a pit forming in my stomach. How in the hell are we supposed to catch this guy before tomorrow night? "Sheriff, if you happen to have any off-duty deputies that might be willing to help do some research, we'd really appreciate it."

"Let me check the duty roster and call around," she says. "I'll let ya'll know if anyone volunteers, but I wouldn't hold my breath. If there's one thing you should know about Adams, it's that people take their free time seriously up here."

"Thanks anyway," I say. She gives us a nod and retreats out of the conference room.

Zara stares at the pile in front of us. "Where do we start?"

Chapter Nine

WE SPEND a good portion of the morning going over the files from Rice. Some of them have additional information that we didn't get from Wallace, but it's scant. As far as either of us can tell, these are just four random men who had no connection to each other whatsoever. They never worked together, never went to school together, never even met each other as far as I can tell.

"Em, we might have to face the fact that the killer might be randomly targeting people," Zara says, tossing Nicholas Valentine's file on the table and standing up for the first time in two hours, stretching.

"If that's the case, we're going to be hard-pressed to catch them, considering these cops found no forensic evidence at any of the scenes," I grumble under my breath. If we had been on the scene when the murders happened, I could have ensured that no stone was left unturned. I can't say for sure they're being negligent, but it seems like some of these cops don't want the killer caught, which only makes me more suspicious. "Why would Eastly be so cavalier about Schmidt's murder? Doesn't that seem contrary, especially considering he was the brother of one of his detectives?"

"Yeah. Unless he's afraid of something that might come out when the killer is caught," Zara says. I arch an eyebrow at her, motioning for her to continue. "Well, that makes sense, doesn't it? He's obviously hiding something."

"Something about Duncan Schmidt," I say. "Something that no one else knows. Or maybe they do, but it's something he doesn't want *us* to know. That's good thinking." Zara beams at me. Sometimes I forget it wasn't very long ago she was stuck in intelligence. But becoming a field agent has been the best thing for her, especially given how she likes to charge after cases. She's a natural; the kind of agent who doesn't let up until she's satisfied with the outcome. And if there's one thing I know about Zara, she's meticulous.

"I guess then the question is what don't they want us to know, and how do we find it?" she says.

"We obviously can't go to anyone on the force at Collins, not unless we manage to find some rogue who just happens to hate their job and everyone else there. Because if Eastly or any of them found out they had a mole, I'm sure it wouldn't be pretty. My guess is they're a solid unit, no one is willing to rat anyone else out."

"You never know," Zara singsongs. "There's always a chance." She sits back down and spins around in her chair.

"We'll make that the backup plan," I say. "What we need to do is dive into Duncan Schmidt's life. We need to find people who were close to him who weren't friends with his brother or anyone on the force. People who will tell us what he was really like."

Zara stares at me, incredulous. "You really think friends of his are going to open up to a couple of feds? In this community?"

I shake my head, giving her a wink.

"Wait a second," she says. The pitch of her voice goes up an octave. "Wait just a damn second. Are you saying what I think you're saying?"

"I dunno. Maybe."

She runs over to me, placing both her hands on my shoulders. "Emily Rachel Slate. Are you telling me we're going undercover to suss out this man's personal life?"

I nod. "I think it's the only way."

She practically squeals with excitement. "I have been waiting for this day ever since I got approved for fieldwork. What's the plan, how are we going to do it?"

I pull Schmidt's file and scan the pages inside. It's just some biographical information along with his employment record. No mention of any friends or acquaintances. "We need to locate his friend group in Collins." I check the time on my phone. "And we need to hurry. It's already lunchtime."

"How do we do that?" Zara asks.

"Remember what Eastly said? Garrett Schmidt has a funeral to plan. All we need to do is figure out who's planning on coming."

"Online guest book!" Zara says, running back over to her laptop. "Gimme just a second."

This is the thing I love about her; she seems to know exactly what I'm thinking without me specifically telling her. I think that instinct has only gotten stronger the longer we've worked together.

"Okay, I got it," she says, and I join her at the laptop. "There's only about thirty people who've signed the book, but it shouldn't be too hard to put a list together. Look, most of them sign with their full names already."

"There's one," I say, the fourth name down. "*Sorry we'll never be able to share another beer at the Stone. It was great having you back in town. RIP.* Landon Archer. Sounds like a promising lead."

Zara does a quick search on Landon Archer, pulling up his social media profile in a matter of minutes. He has the same profile picture on all the sites: one of him skiing, with a beer in one hand and a big smile on his face. Notably absent is a consistent significant other as Zara scrolls through the pictures. It appears Landon likes to date a lot. "Looks like a winner to me."

"Hang on, let me do my magic here," Zara says, and her hands fly over the keys, going back and forth between the guest book and the pictures on Landon's various pages. I have to take a step back because it's making me dizzy.

As she works my phone buzzes in my pocket. I take it out, looking at the text from Liam.

"How's it going? Timber has made himself at home and had a good day at the park."

I hesitate to send a text back, though I'm not sure why. It just feels like Liam, and I are in a weird place at the moment. I'm not sure what to do with that.

"Okay, check it out," Zara says, oblivious to my text. "See these two guys in this picture here?" She points to a picture of Landon with two other similarly aged guys, all decked out in ski gear with a white slope and blue sky behind them. "This one is Aaron Pewitt. And this one is Ian Adler. And look here." She switches back to the guest book. Both names appear a couple below Landon's offering similar sentiments.

"Bingo," I say. "Do we know that all four of them hung out?"

"Oh, you underestimate my power, young Emily." She scrolls down even further to another picture of all four of them in a selfie, a neon sign with the word STONE'S emblazoned on it behind them.

"Damn. That's it," I say.

"Am I good, or what?" she says, sitting back and crossing her arms.

"Oh, you're good." My phone buzzes a second time, but I ignore it. "What do you think the odds are that they'll be there tonight?"

She screws up her mouth. "I dunno. Fifty-fifty? It is Friday night after all. And they don't look like the family types."

"No, they don't," I say, staring at the picture. "They look like the trolling-for-dates types."

"The great American pastime of every single male on a weekend," she says. She sits up almost so suddenly that she comes out of her chair. "Wait a second. Does this mean I'm going to get you in an actual *dress?*"

"Hang on. Let's not go crazy here," I say.

"Oh, no, you gotta look the part." She stands, her grin a mile wide. "Remember what you said about undercover work?"

Ugh. I hate to admit it, but she's right. "It's too cold to wear a dress here," I say, hoping for a stay of execution.

"No ma'am, it is not. Not for a hot young woman on the prowl, which you need to be."

"Let's just try to keep the bare skin to a minimum, huh?" Outwardly I'm protesting, but really the thought of going undercover is more appealing than I anticipated. I haven't been under ever since the incident that almost ended my career. After that I thought undercover work just wasn't for me. That I'd leave it to the more professional agents, the ones with years of experience. But for whatever reason, I like the idea of pretending not to be me for a little while. Normally I'd be abhorred by the idea of something like this, trying to come on to a bunch of grown-up frat guys, but I dunno. It might not be as bad as I'm anticipating.

"Okay, first, we gotta get wardrobes," Zara says, packing her stuff up. "Finally, *finally,* I'm gonna get you in a pair of decent heels."

What have I gotten myself into?

WE HAVE TO DRIVE A FULL HOUR OUTSIDE OF COLLINS TO FIND a big box store that carries something other than skiing equipment and time is running short. We haven't even had a chance to stop for lunch yet. But Zara is adamant she knows what she's doing and after trying on a half dozen options, she says she's satisfied. All I know is that every one of those options squeezed and restricted me in every way possible. I'll be lucky if I'm able to stand up, much less walk straight. And forget about pursuing a suspect if the occasion arises. I have to admit I'm starting to rethink this whole undercover operation. It's been a long time since I've been in anything other than a comfortable blouse and jeans or slacks. I'm just not used to being on...display. My job is to blend in, or at least not call attention to myself.

This feels like doing the exact opposite.

We head back to the Mantokee but by the time we arrive it's already almost four. Our hope is to get over to the Stone bar, which happens to be on the far side of Collins, by around six-thirty so we can stake out the place and wait for our marks. From our research, it's *the* place where the locals all hang out and as far as I can tell, a prime location for Schmidt's buddies. Zara's right, we've probably got a fifty-fifty chance of them showing up tonight, but it's not like there's much else they can do around here. All the tourist spots are up on the mountain and with the pending funeral, I doubt any of them would have left town.

Somehow, Zara manages to squeeze me back into the black dress and heels and even does my makeup before taking care of her own. Once she's done, I feel like I'm back in college, when I would watch all those girls heading to the frat parties dressed to the nines, only to leave the next morning hanging on to their shoes with all their makeup smudged. I used to feel bad that they felt they needed to put on such a performance for a bunch of drunk guys, but I also have to admit it feels a bit empowering. Zara catches me looking at my ass in the mirror and about busts a gut laughing.

Even though I'm wearing less fabric than I probably have at any time in my life, it feels like a sort of shield. I'm not

Emily Slate, FBI Agent tonight. Instead, I'm someone completely different. Someone mysterious, perhaps even dangerous. It's an intoxicating feeling that I haven't felt in a long time.

Though my feet already hurt. I don't know how the hell I'm supposed to make it through the night with these things on. "Are you sure I can't wear flats?" I ask.

"No, you can't wear flats," Zara chides, swatting my hand away as I start rubbing my feet. "The whole point is they push up your calves and make that ass work. That's why they call them pumps."

"Yeah, but six inches?" I ask. "Isn't this a little extreme?"

"Hey, do you want to get these guys' attention or not? We gotta look better than anyone else in there," she says, applying her lipstick in the mirror. She's put on a shade of blue, which matches her dress and compliments her platinum blonde hair.

I stand, my legs wobbly at first on the things. I hesitate to even call them shoes, they're glorified accessories on my feet. "Okay, let's get this over with."

Chapter Ten

THE STONE IS short for *The Red Stone Inn and Bar*. It's a large building that's clad almost entirely of gray stone. I don't know where the "red" part comes in, but like most places around here, it feels very much like a building out of the 1700's. From what I can tell on the outside, the bottom floor is the bar, while the top two floors have rooms for rent, or perhaps for drunken patrons who can't make it home. Either way, I'm glad Zara got us in at the Mantokee; I'm not sure how anyone would be able to sleep in a place like this, given the ruckus coming from the front.

We approach, both of us in step with each other and making our way from the parking lot off to the side of the building.

"Stop pulling on your dress, you'll rip it," Zara says as we approach the front door.

"It keeps riding up," I say.

"It's supposed to ride up," she replies with a grin. "Hang on, I gotta get a picture of this. Stand by the door."

"No way," I tell her. "Next thing I know you'll shoot it off to Liam or something." *Shit.* Liam. I completely forgot to text him back from this morning. I'll do it once we're inside. I don't know if I should be worried or not that he hasn't tried to contact me again. At least I know Timber is in good hands.

"Yeah, that's the point." She's already got her phone out and is trying her best to snap a picture of me, but I open the door and get inside before she can get anything other than a blurry phantom.

Right inside the door is a large foyer, with large windows that look out on to the back of the property. Even though the sun has already set I can still see the last vestiges of light illuminating the mountains in the distance. I bet this place does a ton of business from the tourists.

Off to the right is a check-in desk and a sitting area, though all of these are already occupied by patrons, most with drinks in their hands. Over to the left through a double doorway is the bar, with a number of small tables and booths inside. The place is packed, and Zara and I have to squeeze our way past a few people to get inside. On the other side of the bar, through another double doorway is a large dining room, with yet another bar. This place really does seem like the heart of the town. There are people of all ages here, and from what I can tell, they're all enjoying themselves on a Friday night out.

"Evening," a young woman says as we approach the dining room. "Table for two?"

"Actually, we'd like to stick close to the bar," I say.

"Sure, not a problem," she says, her voice chipper. "It's first come, first serve, so grab a table or booth when you see one. But if ya'll would like the full menu, we still have a few spots here in the dining room."

"That's okay, we're just looking to get smashed tonight," Zara says, leaning past me. "We're here from Pennsylvania. Any good prospects in a place like this?"

The hostess smiles, she can't be long out of high school. "Oh yeah. Usually everyone ends up stopping by at some point or another during the night. I'm sure the two of you will have your pick." She winks at us.

"Thanks," I say and pull Zara back into the bar. "You are enjoying this way too much."

"It's a once-in-a-lifetime opportunity!" she says. "When am I going to get to see you like this again?"

"Z, we're not out looking for dates," I say, slowly. "We're here to do our job."

"And our job is to make it look like we're looking for dates." She makes her way to the bar. I notice a couple of guys catch sight of her and watch her all the way. I pull out my phone, double-checking the pictures we have of Landon and his buddies, but it's not them.

While Zara is at the bar getting us drinks, I look for a place where we can keep an eye on the place. There's an empty table in the center of the room, but it's too exposed. I need to be able to see both doors. I stroll around, squeezing past people and watching the crowd to see if anyone looks like they're about to get up. I spot an older couple with two empty glasses sitting in a booth at the back of the room, which happens to be right beside a window that looks out on the front of the property, right where we just came in. As soon as they begin scooting out of the booth, I make a beeline for it, and manage to slip in as soon as they're out. I gather their glasses and push them to the far end of the table for someone to come pick up. Unfortunately, I didn't realize just how short this dress was as it rides up even further now that I'm sitting.

"I'm gonna kill her. She's actually going to make me commit murder," I mutter, pulling it back down as best I can. Any semblance of armor has disappeared and now that we're out in the open, my discomfort levels are starting to peak. I don't know what I was thinking, putting on this stupid outfit. I'm starting to get that uneasy feeling in my stomach again, like there is something fundamentally wrong here, and it feels like it's coming from inside *me*. Like *I'm* wrong, somehow. I don't know how to explain it, but I have the sudden urge to get out of here, abandon this whole thing and get back into my normal clothes.

"Hey, great spot!" Zara says, placing two very bright drinks in martini glasses in front of us as she slips in the other booth.

"Z, I don't know about—what is that?" I point to the glass she's set in front of me.

"The bartender called it a blueball. It's on special."

"What's in it?" I ask.

She peers at the glass a moment. "Well, from the color, I'd say a copious amount of blue curacao. Probably vodka or rum for the rest."

"I'm not drinking that."

"Don't worry," she says. "It's just for appearances. Just pretend to sip on it every now and again. You never know how long we might be staked out here. Plus, I've got some waters in my purse."

I feel slightly better. I should have known Zara would have my back. Still, the urge to get out of here is almost over-whelming. "I'm not so sure about this idea."

"But it was your plan," she replies, taking a small sip of her own drink. "Gah! Yeah, okay, don't drink that. It's pure sugar."

"I know, but what are the odds we're actually going to see the guys we're looking for?" I ask. "In the meantime, we've barely got twenty-four hours until the killer will more than likely strike again."

"We could just go to their houses and knock on their doors. Do the whole gestapo thing," she suggests with a smile. "But I don't think that's going to get you the results you're looking for."

I sigh. She's right. I know this is a solid plan, it's just now that I'm actually here, in this ridiculous excuse for a dress with shoes I have no business wearing, all my confidence has fallen away. In all my previous experiences undercover, I was never *this* exposed. And I was usually armed, except for the times I knew we'd be searched. The last time I did this, I was in jeans and a heavy leather jacket, trying to expose an underground human trafficking ring.

"You know, I might actually end up getting something to eat here too," Zara says. "Do you smell that? Fresh north-Atlantic seafood. How can we not?"

My stomach is twisting itself into knots. If I eat anything now, it's going to end up back on the table post haste. I do everything I can to look away but accidentally meet Zara's gaze for a split second. "Em?" she asks. "What's wrong?"

"Nothing, I'm just…uncomfortable. I think it's this dress."

She shakes her head. "You're pale. I haven't seen you like this since…well, I guess you were a little pale the other night at your party too. What's going on?"

"Not the time or place." I nod to the entryway from the front door. Three men have just walked in. I don't even need to look at my phone to know they're the three we're looking for.

Her eyes go wide as she spots them. "Shit, here we go." She runs her hands through her hair, giving it a little flair and starts trying to make eye contact with them. At first they're totally fixated on the bar and the bartender. But as soon as they have beers from the tap in hand, they begin scanning the crowd. As much as it turns my already-in-knots stomach, I make direct eye contact with one of them, Aaron. He smiles when he sees me, and nudges his buddy, Ian. They're not terrible-looking guys by any means; they've obviously cleaned up for this evening. While Ian is a little heftier than his friend, they both sport nice button-down shirts and full beards that have been trimmed close. I also notice Aaron has an expensive-looking watch on his wrist. Zara has managed to capture Landon's attention, just as she planned.

The three of them seem to instinctually head in our direction. I have to keep smiling to encourage them, but inside I'm gritting my teeth. We just need a little info from these guys, to figure out what Duncan Schmidt might have been into before he died. At this point I'll take anything I can get, whatever it takes to get this over with as soon as possible and me back in my regular clothes.

"Hey there," Landon says as the three of them reach the table. "Haven't seen you two around here before."

"We just got in, from Pennsylvania," Zara says, sticking to the lie she told the hostess. "Heard the skiing is better up here."

"You heard right," Aaron says, grinning at me. It's a good thing he can't see my hands because they are balled into fists right now, my fingernails digging into my palms.

"We'd be happy to tell you all about it," Landon says. I can almost read the man's mind as his eyes crawl all over Zara. He's thinking he and his friends have just lost a good friend and they deserve a good night with some beautiful women. Women they'd rather not have to pay for.

"I've only been skiing a few times," Zara says, doing her best impression of a bubblehead. "Mostly bunny slopes." It's so convincing I want to throw up.

"Oh, it's not hard," Landon says, slipping into the booth beside her. Without invitation, Aaron slips in beside me and Ian grabs a free chair, putting it at the head of the table so he can stay part of the group.

"Hi there," Aaron says, his eyes locked on mine.

"Hey," I manage to say. It's like I've gone completely numb. How do people do this all the time? This was such a shitty, shitty idea. Why did I think I could seduce a man, I can't even tell when someone is flirting with me! Get me in a room with a bunch of drug dealers and I'll schmooze them all day long but make me try to try and entice a guy and it's like I've forgotten what words are. In a panic, I grab the blueball and take a sip. A sugary explosion of alcohol hits my tongue, and it takes all my willpower not to gag.

"What are you drinking?" Aaron asks.

"Blueball," I manage to say. "On special." I look down at his glass full of piss-colored water. "What about you?"

"Bud light," he says. Oh, this is going swimmingly.

"How long are you girls in town for?" Landon asks and I notice his arm is already across the back of the booth, ready and primed to wrap itself around Zara's delicate, exposed shoulders.

"Only a few days," Zara says. "We have to get back on Monday. There was an accident at work, a coworker of ours was killed and her funeral is that day."

Zara, you genius.

"Oh, that's terrible," Landon says. "Sorry."

"Sorry," Aaron offers while Ian remains silent, though he's looking down at the table.

"You're in good company," Landon adds. "We've got a funeral coming up too. A friend of ours recently died."

Finally, progress. "That's terrible," I say, turning back to Aaron. "What happened?"

He shrugs. "That's the thing, none of us know. The police won't tell us anything."

"The *police?*" Zara says, like it's the most shocking thing she's ever heard, still doing one hell of an impression of an airhead.

"Yeah," Ian says, finally breaking his silence. "They said he was murdered."

"Hey man, now we don't know that for sure," Landon says. His drink is on the table in front of him, forgotten. Though Aaron takes a long swig.

"Then why haven't they released his body to Garrett yet?" Ian asks.

"Who's Garrett?" I ask.

"Our friend—Duncan's brother. He's a cop here in town."

"You're kidding," I say, doing my best to act surprised. "Did they catch the guy who did it?"

Landon shakes his head. "We can't get them to tell us anything. Apparently, we're not important enough. Family only kind of thing."

"But we *were* his family," Aaron says. "Even when he moved away, we still kept in touch." He takes another long swig of his beer; it's already two-thirds gone.

"Oh, so it didn't happen here?" Zara asks.

Landon shakes his head. "No, it did. He moved back here to Collins a few months back. It was like we had the band back together again, and then this goes and happens."

"Must have been pretty recent," I say, looking at my glass and not meeting the gaze of any of them. I'm trying to pretend like I'm sad, but really I just don't want these guys thinking I'm trying to form a shared bond over tragedy.

"Happened last Saturday," Ian says. "Crazy thing was, we'd all just been out the night before. Here, actually. This is our first weekend without him."

"That must be really hard," Zara says. "You have Megan and my deepest condolences."

"Megan huh?" Aaron asks. "I'm Aaron. This is Ian and that's Landon. It's a pleasure to meet you." He holds out a hand and I give it a quick shake, repeating the process with Ian.

"I'm Jessica," Zara says. "Here's to those who leave us too soon." She raises her glass and the boys do the same. I'm forced to join in and take another sip of the disgustingly sweet drink. I'm going to need a shot of something a lot stronger to burn all this crap out of my mouth before the night is over.

Aaron drains the rest of his drink with the toast while Landon and Ian have barely made it halfway through theirs. "Welp, looks like I'm due for a refill." He slides out of the booth and heads to the bar. Ian spots his chance and moves into the booth beside me. Immediately I'm hit with the smell of body odor. It's faint, but it's there. Ian grins at me leaning on both of his elbows which are on the table.

"So you're commiserating," I manage to say.

"Seems like we all are," he replies. "What about your friend? What happened?" I look over to Zara for help, and see that Landon's arm is now wrapped around her. She's not putting off any negative energy about it either, like it's the most natural thing in the world. Damn, she's good at this. Better than I am, anyway.

"She—Becky—was in an industrial accident," I say; it was the first thing that came to mind. I realize now we probably should have pre-gamed some of our lies, so we didn't have to make all this up on the spot.

"Where do you guys work?" Landon asks.

"Oh, we work in an office," Zara says. "But it's attached to a factory that makes keys. Something happened with one of the machines and it malfunctioned, crushing her when she was fixing it."

"Jesus," Landon says. Aaron returns with a full beer and shoots Ian a particularly nasty look as he takes the seat at the head of the table. Ian shoots him a smirk before turning back to me; he knows exactly what he did.

"You guys must have some clue as to what happened to your friend," I add, trying to keep us on topic. "You don't really think he was murdered, do you?"

"Cops aren't talking, and they won't let us see him," Ian says. "What would you assume?"

"But he wasn't involved in anything…dangerous, was he? Like drugs or anything?" Ian furrows his brow, and I can tell that I'm beginning to push too far. But Aaron, who has had more to drink, glazes right over it.

"Nah, he was just like us. Straight as an arrow. I mean sure, he'd made a couple of mistakes in his past, who hasn't? But nothing worth someone killing him over."

I glance to Landon to gauge his interest in the conversation, but his attention is completely wrapped up in Zara. I catch him take a whiff of her hair and for a brief second her façade cracks before it's back up again. I don't know how much longer we can keep doing this.

"Did he say what he was doing the night he died?" I ask. "I mean that should at least give you some clue as to what happened. Then you could go to the cops or—"

"I mean, he was supposed to go on some date with a girl he met online, but that was it," Aaron says. I glance over to Zara. *That's* new information.

"You seem awfully interested in what happened to him," Ian says, eyeing me closely.

"Aren't you?" I ask, my question genuine. "I mean, if we found out Becky had been murdered, I'd be all over that. Do you guys ever watch *Unsolved Mysteries*?" Ian looks at me a few more seconds then I see him relax, which tells me my poor-ass cover story did its job. But it also means I can't ask who this girl was without completely blowing our cover.

"Let's talk about something else," Landon says. "This is bringing the mood down. Our friends wouldn't want us having a bad time when we've had the good fortune to just meet each other, would they?" Aaron raises his glass to that and takes another swig while Ian nods.

Shit. Now what are we supposed to do? Zara does a passable job of keeping the conversation going without committing to anything, but the longer I sit here, the worse I feel about all of this. I need to get out of this dress, and I want to get started on this date angle.

"Megan?"

I look over at Ian who is frowning at me. "Hmm?"

"I asked where you went to school. You look familiar."

"Oh, um...Virginia State," I say, absently. "Where did you go?"

He chuckles, and I notice it sounds a little like a growl. "No, I mean high school. You didn't go to James Madison

High, did you? I could swear I've seen you somewhere before."

"No, we're from Pennsylvania." I *was* on TV a couple of months ago about that big kidnapping case, but he wouldn't remember me from that, would he? I couldn't have been on the broadcast for more than a minute.

He nods to himself a few times. "Pennsylvania, right."

"You are effin' gorgeous," Aaron says, his words coming out slightly slurred. He's leaned over the table and it's clear he's already drunk.

"Thank you," I say, the pressure in the back of my head telling me to get out of here *right now.* "Excuse me, I need to use the restroom."

"So soon?" Ian says. "You've barely touched your drink." In that instant I feel his hand on my upper thigh and it's like something inside of me snaps. In one swift move I grab his hand, twist it, and force his entire torso on the table, knocking all the drinks all over the place.

"What the hell?" Landon says, jumping up while Aaron just laughs.

"Just what do you think you're doing with that hand?" I ask Ian, my lips right next to his ear.

"Nothing! I swear!" he says. A little pressure is all it would need for me to break his upper arm and keep him in a cast for eight weeks.

I look up and notice the entire bar has gone quiet, everyone staring at us. "Who was Duncan going to meet that night?"

"What?" Ian asks, the terror in his voice real.

"Who. Was. He. Going. On. A. Date. With?" I say, spelling it out for him.

"I dunno man, just some girl. He didn't tell us. What does it matter? Who are you?" I let him go and shove him out of the booth, where he falls on his ass.

"Welp, I guess that means the night's over," Zara says, getting out of the booth herself.

"Next time, keep your hands to yourself unless specifically and implicitly invited," I tell Ian, then shoot a pointed look at Landon, making sure he gets the point too. Aaron is still in his chair, laughing. I point in his direction. "And if you see something and don't stop it, you might as well be doing it yourself." That shuts him up.

"Hey, you can't just—" Another man begins as we make our way out of the bar.

"Can't what? Defend myself when someone puts their hands on me? Go ahead, finish that sentence." I can feel the anger radiating off me; it's the only thing keeping that sickly feeling from taking over. So right now, I'll take it.

The man puts his hands up and backs out of our way as we leave the establishment.

"Beautiful, just beautiful," Zara says, a big grin on her face. "Now *that* was worth it."

Chapter Eleven

"I CAN'T BELIEVE I just put myself through that humiliation," I say as Zara drives us back to the Mantokee.

"Humiliation? Are you crazy? That was badass! Did you see the look on that idiot's face when he realized he just messed with the wrong woman? He was practically crying."

"Doesn't mean he won't try it again with someone else," I say.

"I bet he'll think twice next time, though. They all will." I'm happy she's so confident in my ability to curtail a couple of assholes' behavior, but I'm just glad to be out of there.

"Let's just get back. I need to get out of this thing."

She seems to detect I'm out of sorts and doesn't say anything else until we've arrived back at the Mantokee. I get to our room as fast as I can and strip off the too-tight dress, and ridiculous shoes. In less than four minutes I'm back in my normal attire, despite the fact it's close to eight p.m. Those feelings haven't completely gone away, but I do feel a little better now that I can at least recognize myself in the mirror again.

"Did you really hate it that much?" Zara asks, unzipping her dress. I can hear the hurt in her voice.

"It's not…Z, it doesn't have anything to do with you. I just…I felt like an imposter in those clothes. They weren't me and it was almost like I was having an out-of-body experience. I know it sounds dumb, but I don't know how else to explain it." I'm frustrated with myself for not being able to maintain my cool, and at the same time I'm worried I've insulted Zara because this is the kind of thing she *loves*. But it's just not for me.

"Em, what's really going on?" she asks. I know this day has been coming, ever since Wallace assigned us both to this case. I figured she'd notice eventually, which was why I've been trying my best to keep it under wraps. Zara is my best friend in the world, and I don't want to lie to her. But at the same time, I don't want to go through everything with the letter and what it might mean. I've already had to do that with Liam and look what it's done to us. I don't want that to happen here. I can't afford to push her away right now.

"I…can't talk about it right now. But can you trust that I'll tell you when I'm ready? It's just…it's too hard at the moment."

She stands, her dress still hanging loose from being unzipped and comes over to embrace me. "Of course. You know I'm here for you, no matter what you need. You don't need to talk about it until you're ready. Just know that you don't have to pretend with me. Whatever you're going through, it must be tough otherwise it wouldn't be affecting you so much."

Suddenly I'm emotional and I feel tears fall as I hold on to her. I don't know why this means so much to me, but it does. We stand there for a few moments before I finally pull away, wiping at my eyes. "Maybe going undercover isn't my forte anymore."

She returns to the other side of the room to finish undressing. "You told me that in order to go undercover, sometimes it took weeks or even months of mental preparation. It's not always something you can just flip on, like a switch. You need to train your mental and emotional states to be able to handle it."

I rub at my eyes, trying to wipe away the tiredness. "Did I say that? I think past Emily must have been a smarter person than present Emily."

She throws an errant sock in my direction. "If you don't stop feeling sorry for yourself I'll have to show you some of those new moves I've been working on down in the gym."

This actually produces a laugh. "Just as long as you leave my brain intact. We still have a killer to find."

She pulls on an oversized sweatshirt and points at me. "That's right. The night wasn't a total waste. At least now we know Duncan Schmidt was out on a date before he was killed."

"Which means we need to find whoever he was out with," I say. "She could very possibly be the last person that saw him alive."

"Do you think she's a suspect?" Zara asks.

I reach down and grab her sock off the floor, tossing it back to her. "Until we have reason to believe otherwise, yes. We'll need access to his personal effects. I want to see his phone, maybe we can use that to figure out who he was out on a date with. There have to be text messages right?"

"In this day and age?" Zara asks. "Definitely. The question is, does Eastly have the phone? And if he does, how many of his teeth are you going to have to pull before he lets you see it?"

I take a seat on the edge of the bed to think. It's roughly eight p.m. All of the victims died around midnight on Saturday, which means we have a little over twenty-four hours to go. "I'm not sure we should even bother going through Eastly," I say. "I don't want him obstructing us any more than he already has."

"Then how do we get the phone?" Zara asks.

"We go directly to the source."

∼

BY NINE P.M. WE'RE BACK AT THE COLLINS POLICE Department, standing back in front of the same desk sergeant again. It seems like this guy keeps the same kind of hours we do. Either that, or they're so short-staffed that he's the only one available for the job. Before we can even get a word out, he stops us. "Chief Eastly went home for the night. You'll have to wait until tomorrow to speak with him."

"We're not here for the chief," I tell him. "Where's the evidence locker?"

"It's in the basement, why?"

"Because we need access," Zara says. "Why else?"

The desk sergeant looks around, though the place is mostly empty. "I can't just let you down there without an escort. We have policies and procedures here."

"We're not going to *steal* anything," I say. "This is regarding the Schmidt case. I don't have to remind you that federal jurisdiction supersedes local, do I? As soon as we arrived, this became our case, which means those are now *our* files." While not technically true, I'm using my intimidation voice on him, in hopes that he'll crack and get us the access we need.

He looks between us for a moment. "I'll need to check with Eastly first," he says, picking up the phone.

"Sergeant," I say, making sure my FBI badge is on display. "Are we really going to need to make this an issue?" He looks at me, then at Zara again, the receiver in his hand. "We're all trying to catch the same person here. Bothering Eastly at home will only slow down the process."

"B-but shouldn't he be involved in the investigation?" the man asks.

"He will be," Zara says, leaning over the counter as best

she can, given her shorter stature. "When he gets back in tomorrow. All we're doing is research. We're here, in your town. We don't have families to go home to right now. What would you rather us be doing, sitting in our hotel room watching Netflix? We might as well put our time to good use, right?"

"I suppose…" he replies.

"Look," I say. "We'll sign whatever forms we need to make sure everything is above board. We're just looking to get into Schmidt's evidence file." He continues to hesitate, but I can tell he's considering it. "We've barely got twenty-four hours before this killer strikes again. Do you really want to be the reason we didn't get to the information in time? If there's something in that locker that can help us and we're too late because—"

"Okay, okay, I get it," he finally says, setting the phone down on the cradle. "But you have to sign everything out, and I can't let you leave with any of the evidence. It all stays in-house."

"Fine," I say. "Point us in that direction."

"There's not anyone down there to help you," he says, sighing. He gets up, a set of keys in hand and goes to the front door, locking us in. "I'll take you down there to show you where everything is, but I have to stay up here."

"You guys really don't have anyone else on shift tonight?" I ask as he leads us down the hallway.

"Just Parsons and Harriman. But they're both out on patrol all night. It's just me here. The dispatcher works out of her home. Got everything she needs there."

"What's your name?" I ask.

"Sewell," he replies. "Martin."

"Well, thanks for your help, Martin. You're doing us a huge favor here."

"I just hope I don't regret it," he mumbles.

We follow him to the back of the station where we

descend a narrow stairwell into the basement, which is full of what look like library stacks behind a wire cage and a couple of desks. Martin leads us around the desks to a floor-to-ceiling wire door that's locked with a padlock. Pulling one of his keys out, he unlocks the padlock, opening the door to the files.

"Recent cases are in the front, so it should be up here, somewhere, probably on row one or two," he says. "There's a sheet on top of the box. Sign, initial and date in each location, and make sure your badge number is legible. When you're done, please return everything where it was when you found it, and sign the box back in, noting the time."

"That's it?" Zara asks. "No guard dogs we need to bribe with a steak?"

He shoots her a look. "When you're done, lock the stacks back up. I'll be at the front desk if you need anything."

"Perfect, thank you," I tell him. He hesitates a minute more before leaving us.

"You know I'll be noting this on the station log, *and* I'll be informing Eastly when he comes in tomorrow."

"As you should," I tell him.

Finally, he decides he's made his decision and now he has to live with it. He leaves us to our work, clomping back up the wooden stairs.

"I have a solid urge to mix up all the boxes, just to piss off Eastly," Zara says.

"Maybe if someone's life wasn't on the line." I head into the poorly-lit stacks and find I have to pull out the flashlight on my phone to read the case numbers on the side. There doesn't seem to be much rhyme or reason to how these things are organized; I'm not sure mixing them up would make any sort of difference.

"Here, I think I got it," Zara says.

I come around the nearest stack to find her hauling a small banker's box out. She takes it out of the cage and sets it on one of the desks, turning it so the front faces us. "Schmidt, zero-four-one-nine-eight-two-kilo. That's it." On top of the box is the sheet Sergeant Sewell mentioned. I make the necessary notations, then open the box to go through the evidence.

"Has none of this been processed yet?" I ask. Inside are evidence bags full of bloody clothes, along with other items of interest from the scene. Though I don't see a murder weapon anywhere. But as best I can tell, everything is still just as it was gathered. It hasn't been through forensic testing yet. "What are these people doing?"

"Participating in a cover up?" Zara suggests.

"But if it was all of them, Sewell never would have let us down here," I say. "This may just be the chief's doing. Him and a few accomplices."

Zara shifts behind me, pulling out a few of the evidence bags. "Then he's not going to be too happy to find out we looked in here."

"Which only gives us until morning before the shit hits the fan." Most of what else in the box are either things that caught blood splatter, or the film from the scene that shows how they originally found it. I take a minute to examine the pictures. "He was definitely put on display, look how the body is laid out."

"Looks kinda like Jesus, except he's missing his...bits," Zara says.

"Okay, so maybe we need to consider a religious angle here too." *None* of this was in the case files, from any of the towns.

"Cell phone?" Zara asks, impatience hinting in her voice.

I search through the rest of the box, but come up empty. "Not here." I pull the evidence list, which describes each item taken from the scene. "Wait...it's on the manifest." I look again, making sure I haven't missed anything. But there's no cell phone in the box."

Zara takes the top, looking over the information on the

sign-out sheet. "It doesn't show anyone removed it. At least, not officially. If they did, they didn't make a record of it."

"Dammit," I say. "Three guesses as to how many people have had access to this since last Saturday."

She shakes her head. "Only need one. Eastly."

Chapter Twelve

"Did you guys find everything you needed?" Sergeant Sewell asks as we head back down the hallway to the front desk.

"Yep," I say. "Everything looks like it's in order. Though we'll need to speak with Eastly in the morning about why some of those blood samples haven't been processed yet."

"I'll make a note so he can call you," Sewell says, jotting it down on the notepad in front of him. "Let me walk you out."

I snap my fingers. "Would you mind if I hit the restroom before we leave? The place where we're staying has the smallest bathrooms in human existence and I'd just like a little space for once."

"Sure," he says without hesitation. "Right down there, to the right." He points down the adjacent hallway.

"Meet you back in a second," I say to Zara, but she's busy leaning over Sewell's desk again.

"So tell me, what's the worst case you've had on this shift?" she asks, pouring on the sugar.

I smile as I make my way down the hall. Hopefully she'll be able to keep him distracted for a good minute or two while I go find what I need. I bypass the restroom and head straight for Chief Eastly's office. For some reason he pulled that phone from Schmidt's evidence box and I'm going to find out why. But I'm not about to wait around until morning so he can give me a line of bullshit about it not being him or whatever excuse he decides to come up with. There hasn't been something right about this case since we arrived, and it's time we got to the bottom of it.

When I reach Chief Eastly's office, I'm surprised to find the door already unlocked. Small-town cops. He probably didn't expect anyone to come sniffing around tonight. I don't know whether it's stupidity or hubris, but he has severely underestimated us.

The office is bathed in moonlight, coming through the blinds across the large window to the back so that they create a striped pattern across his desk and the floor. *This* is where I'm comfortable. Not sitting in some bar trying to ply a few wannabe alpha males for information. No, I belong here, following the clues that will lead me to the killer. I'm forced to consider that Easly might even be in league with our killer, though that doesn't make much sense. But I can't see why else he would be throwing up so many roadblocks, and even removing evidence. He's risking his entire career and for what? I *might* be able to see this if Schmidt were his own kin, but as far as I know, they only tangentially knew each other, through his brother, Garrett.

As I'm sure there are no warning systems in here, I take care to move quickly and quietly. I don't want to raise Sewell's suspicions, but at the same time, I have an entire office to search. But the first place I go is Eastly's desk. The top drawer opens easily, revealing nothing but a couple of file folders and some office equipment. The drawers on the right side of the desk open just as easily, though there is little of consequence in any of them.

The drawers on the left, however, are locked shut. There's a single keyhole that looks like it locks all three at once. Thankfully, though, it's not a fingerprint lock. Just a good old-fashioned key version. And from what I can tell, not even a special key. I pull a small lock pick set out of my pocket, courtesy of another one of the evidence lockers down in the basement. It was a closed case, used by a robbery suspect. Had it been an open case I wouldn't have dared mess with the evidence, but it had been closed for almost a decade and Zara even did a check on the man, he died in prison. And since we figured we'd need it to get into Chief Eastly's office one way or another, I decided it was worth the risk.

Wallace can rake me over the coals later. As far as I'm concerned, they're just tools that the Collins Police Department neglected to return to their owner's family.

Using the lock pick set, I manage to turn the tumbler in less than thirty seconds. It's an old desk, and an old lock, and not really meant as a strong deterrent. I gather up the tools and place them back in my pocket before going through each of the drawers in turn. In the second one, I find what I'm looking for: Duncan Schmidt's phone, still in the evidence bag, sitting in Chief Eastly's desk drawer. I pull out my phone and snap a few pictures, including a few more wider shots for context. A crime has been committed here, and I don't want to disturb anything.

Instead, I remove Zara's phone from my other pocket and search for the app she told me about. I finally find it, marked "clone.exe" on the last page of her apps. I activate the app, then hold it close to Schmidt's phone, but nothing is happening. Then I realize, the phone has to be on.

I know I'm running out of time, but I manage to hold the power button on the phone through the evidence bag, and I watch as his phone boots up. There's a droplet of blood on the screen that wasn't visible before with the phone off. Why did the killer leave this there? They took the murder weapon, but left his phone? Were they in a hurry?

I don't have time to think about it now, Sewell is probably already getting antsy. Once the phone is powered on, I hold

Zara's phone next to it and run the app again. This time it connects, and in thirty seconds I have the data I need. As fast as I can I replace everything as I found it, then use the pick set to re-engage the bolt on the drawers. I then make a hasty exit from the office. But before I can make my way back down to the front, I catch sight of Sewell heading in the direction of the bathrooms. I slip into another office before he sees me.

"Agent Slate, are you okay in there?" Sewell asks through the door to the women's restroom.

Damn. I knew I was taking too long.

"Is everything okay?" I hear Zara ask from a little farther down.

"I don't know, she didn't say anything."

Suddenly there's a crash from the front and I catch sight of Sewell running back to his post. I take the opportunity to dash down the hallway and slip into the bathroom. I flip on one of the faucets and let it run for a minute. Zara and Sewell are speaking, but I can't hear what they're saying. Just as I shut off the faucet, there's a knock at the door again. "Agent Slate?"

I take a deep breath, then open the door. He steps back, looking alarmed. "Sorry," I say. "I must have had something sour for dinner."

"Are you all right?" he asks. I notice him eyeing me carefully.

"I think I will be. I just need to lie down." I walk past him and head back to the front where I see Zara picking up pieces of a broken mug. "What happened?"

"I was admiring Martin's mug and it slipped," she says. "But I've promised to replace it."

"That's really not necessary," Sewell replies. "Accidents happen."

"I think we need to go," I tell Zara. "I'm not feeling my best."

A concerned look comes over her face, but I can tell it's all nothing but an act. She can do one hell of a performance when she needs to. "Okay. Let's get you in bed." She opens the doors to the station for me.

"I hope you feel better," Sewell calls after us.

∼

"Wow. Just wow," Zara says as we get back in the SUV. I hand her phone back to her. "Did you see that improv in there?"

"I saw it," I say, rubbing my hands together. Somehow the air temperature outside has dropped a good fifteen degrees since we were at the bar. "Nicely done."

"What took you so long?"

"Eastly's desk had a lock. Ironically, the door itself was unlocked."

"Another minute and I think he would have busted a gut," Zara says. "I can only keep a guy interested for so long."

"I just hope you didn't have to make any irrevocable promises," I say, starting the car and pulling out of the station.

"As if I would show up anyway," she replies. "That man is part of a dirty squad, whether he knows it or not. I'm not going to feel bad." She opens her phone and begins running through the data I pulled using her app. "Here we go. Just give me a minute to plow through some of this. It grabbed a lot of data."

"I didn't know you could do that without a hard connection," I say.

"Oh yeah, most phones these days keep one of several network connections always searching. All this app does is mimic an open connection and the phone just automatically sets it up. But even if it hadn't, there are other back doors we could have used."

"I don't think we would have had time," I say, turning down the street that will take us back to the Mantokee.

"What do you think will happen tomorrow morning when Eastly comes in?" Zara asks.

"Doesn't matter now. I have proof he tampered with evidence. He'll be lucky not to be in jail by tomorrow night."

"In *this* town?" she asks. She's right. I may have overestimated my clout here. How likely are any of Eastly's men to turn on him? Especially surrounding this case. Do I really think they're going to take the word of a fed over that of their own boss? Even with the pictures, it's going to be a stretch.

"I don't want to worry about Eastly right now. We can deal with him when we have our killer in custody. Did your phone pull the dating app data?"

"Sure did," she says, grinning at me. "And you'll never guess which app he was using."

"Surprise me."

"Holy Hands."

"A Christian dating app?" I ask. "There really may be something to this whole religious angle. Can you tell who he was most recently talking to?"

"What am I, an amateur?" She flips the phone around so I can see it. There's a text conversation in what looks like DOS green. It must be how the app is interpreting the data. She turns it back before I can read more than a few lines, though I really need to be keeping my eyes on the road anyway.

"For the week leading up to his death he was talking to a woman who was registered under the name *Julie Stanton*. But, the account is only a few weeks old, which means she—or whoever—created it right before they began talking to him."

"You're thinking he was catfished," I say.

"Makes sense, doesn't it? Guy looking to kill someone goes online, posing as a woman, a potential date. They agree to a meetup, and the killer gets the jump on the guy who is expecting a nice night out with a lovely woman." She bats her eyes at me as she says the last part.

"Please tell me you can find out who created Julie's profile."

"That data isn't stored on the phone. We'll need to call into Holy Hands and get them to give us the information."

I spot the Mantokee in the distance. "I'm willing to bet that's not going to go over very well."

"Plus, it's already Friday night. They're probably working with limited personnel as it is."

I pull up to the bed and breakfast, driving around the side like Andrea told us to and cutting the engine. I hang the little yellow tag on the rearview. "Well, they're going to have to. We're running out of time. Guess this means I finally need to call Wallace with an update."

"Good luck with that," she says without a hint of sarcasm. "In the meantime, I'm going to hunt down some snacks."

Chapter Thirteen

SLEEP DOESN'T COME EASY. My overclocked mind wakes me up every hour, hoping that I've missed a call from someone at Holy Hands. Zara spent forty-five minutes on the phone with them, trying to get them to comply to our request, but without a federal warrant, we have to rely on their good graces to actually call us back with the information we need.

Wallace was less than impressed by what we've found so far, even going so far as to say the pictures of the evidence could be nothing more than a clerical error, which is common in smaller departments with fewer resources. I tried to empha-size that Eastly is intentionally blocking our investigation, but he didn't seem to buy it. Not without more than a couple of pictures anyway. He also took the opportunity to remind me he didn't send me up here to sniff out corrupt cops.

I hate going to bed with a case on my mind, and this one is really irking me. There are so many unknowns, and the clock continues to tick down. After waking up the sixth time in two hours, I finally get up and silently pace the room. The old floorboards creak under my weight so I decide to head down-stairs rather than disturb Zara, who is snoring softly.

I grab my phone and enter the brightly lit hallway. It's

two-thirty in the morning, and as best I can tell, I'm the only one awake. Making my way downstairs, a thumping sound travels up to meet me. I freeze, unsure if it's another person or not. Every time we've come in or out of the Mantokee I've only ever seen Andrea. I'm not even sure she has anyone else staying here, though there was another car in the parking area when we pulled in.

When I reach the main floor and head into the kitchen, I hear the thumping again. It's coming from below me. The house must have a basement, though I can't imagine they've set up guest rooms down there.

My quest for something to eat forgotten, I instead start searching room by room, until I come to the only door that I'm sure isn't a closet. When I try the handle, it's unlocked, and I open it, the thumping coming more clearly now. My own heart is hammering; what the hell could be down there? And why is it making so much noise at two-thirty in the morning. Was this what I heard last night as well?

My mind runs through various morbid situations as I find myself descending into the basement. Are there people locked up down here, trying to get out? Or even worse, corpses? Am I descending into someone's sex dungeon? Or maybe I've stumbled across some kind of secret cult meeting.

I'm still in sweats and all I have is my cell in the event I run into trouble. It doesn't seem too unreasonable to go back up to the room and retrieve my firearm, but I'm already halfway down and my curiosity wins out.

I've seen enough horror movies to know this is how people end up getting killed. And yet, I can't seem to help myself.

But as I peer down below the ceiling of the basement, I'm taken aback. I definitely wasn't prepared for this, and never in a hundred years would I have suspected it.

An old man looks up, goggles over his eyes like some kind of mad scientist. He removes them, revealing young eyes that haven't quite caught up with the rest of his body yet. "I'm sorry, was I being too loud?"

"N-no," I say, still taking it all in. "I was already awake." Before me stretches a layout unlike any I've ever seen before. A model railroad, but not just any model railroad. There are towns, bridges, mountains, rivers, factories with smoke coming from the smokestacks, farms complete with livestock and even a little UFO "abducting" a cow. It's all been re-created at in model form, and the man stands in the middle of a cutout in the raised platform, a controller in his hand. A train runs past him but then slows and he smacks the controller a few times before the train starts up again.

"This thing has been giving me hell all night. I think it's got a short in it."

"Is all this yours?" I ask, reaching the bottom stair and taking a moment to soak it all in.

"I'm what you call a ferroequinologist."

"A ferro—"

"It means I like trains. I'm Matt, Andrea's husband. This is where she keeps me." I can tell he's joking, but at the same time there's an undercurrent of resentment there, I think. "I'd shake your hand if I could reach you."

"I'm Emily—Special Agent Emily Slate with the FBI," I say, correcting myself.

"I already know who you are, you are the only two guests we've got right now," he says, turning back to his trains. There are at least three different ones running, though I have no idea if they're all on the same track. The way the things wind back and forth it's impossible to get a complete picture of everything.

"What are you doing?" I ask.

"Just messing around. That's the thing about these damn things. There's always something to mess with. Something to make just a little bit better."

"It's very impressive," I say.

"Don't patronize. It's a hobby," he replies. "It ain't like it's the Sistine Chapel."

"Did you build it all yourself?"

He nods. "Once they made me retire. Needed something to do with all that time."

I take a minute to soak in a few more of the little details. Matt has gone to a lot of trouble to make his model look accurate. And I doubt many people get to see it down here. "So why are you messing with it at two-forty in the morning?"

"Andrea doesn't like me doin' it during the day. Says it disturbs the guests. But the guests are gone most of the day anyway, so I don't know what she complains about. She says I can work on it at night as long as I'm quiet. Guess I wasn't quiet enough."

"I heard the banging," I say. "Thought there might be a problem."

He nods. "Sensible. For a fed, anyways. Normal person would have left it alone. Coulda been an axe murderer down here." The way he says it makes me suspect he's had a career in law enforcement. Usually, I don't get that kind of attitude unless it's from local law enforcement.

"Let me guess, you retired from Collins P.D."

He gives me a wry grin. "Well look at that, she's smarter than the average fed too."

"Thanks," I reply. "I think."

"You workin' with Eastly on those murders?" he asks.

"We're getting there." I don't want to reveal anything about the case, seeing as it's an ongoing investigation. And even though Mr. Bale might have been on the force once, now he's a civilian, and married to someone who seems to me to be prone to gossip. I'd only be stoking the rumor mill if I confided in him.

"You watch that bastard," Matt says. "The man's smarter than he appears."

I arch an eyebrow. "Oh?"

"Let's just say he knows how to work the system to his advantage. Been doin' it twenty years."

"Is that right?" I clasp my hands behind my back and keep my attention focused on the model. It would be helpful to know something about trains right now. "Eastly seems okay to me."

"You're young. Probably haven't met a man like him before. Fact is, men like Eastly don't get where they are by playing by the rules. Things work diff'rent up here, people will look the other way for the right price. I've seen it." A train with a blue and gold locomotive goes gliding past in front of him. Matt's attention is on it, and his controller.

"You're saying he's broken the law?"

"I ain't sayin' nothing," he replies. "Except to watch your back. How d'ya think I ended up retired when I still had another two years on my ticket? Eastly found a way to fix it with the state. Still gave me full benefits and everything."

"Why would he do that?" I ask.

"To keep me quiet," he replies. "About what I know."

I lean down to look at the model's details and when I come back up, I catch his gaze.

"Is there something you want to tell me?"

A smile comes over his face. "You know, ask anyone in town about Eastly, and they'll tell you he's the most upstanding, good-natured cop this town has ever had. And they wouldn't be wrong. To everyone else, he's a saint. He keeps the community happy, and he does his job. Crime is low, people don't have to worry about locking their doors at night."

"But…"

"But if anything ever happens with one of his officers, you'll never hear a word about it. See, Eastly likes to keep things neat and tidy. And we all know that police officers are human too. They screw up. But you'll never know about it. You'll never hear about it in this town. Not as long as he's around."

"You're saying he routinely participates in coverups."

"All I'm sayin' is you try to find any record of police misconduct in this town, and you might as well stick your head down a well for all the good it'll do you."

"That's very interesting. I don't suppose you've spoken to D.A. Rice about this, have you?"

He chuckles as another train rumbles by. "Agent, I'm almost seventy years old. What do I need to go screwing up a good life for? If I went up against Eastly, I'd never be able to come back to this town. It protects its own. And I'm just not willin' to give up what little life I have left."

I sigh. Then it's all hearsay. But given what I've already discovered about the cell phone, this only further substantiates what I already suspect about Eastly. "You know Rice isn't like your old D.A. He won't stand for this."

Matt chuckles again. "Sure. I heard. More power to him, I say. Lotta people not happy with him being around, I can tell you that. I give him two years before he decides it isn't worth the trouble, or someone offers him a better spot somewhere else. Then things will go right back to normal."

It seems Rice may have more of an uphill battle than he thought. Which means he's going to need all the help he can get. "Well, thanks for showing me your model," I say.

"Come back anytime, you're staying until Monday, right?"

I pause. "It depends on how tomorrow goes."

"You mean if someone else gets killed." It seems like Rice's attempt to keep a lid on things hasn't been successful in the least. Instead of responding, I just give him another smile and head back up the stairs. Any lingering appetite I might have had is long gone, instead I can't quit thinking about what Mr. Bale told me about Eastly. I already knew he was crooked, but to know that he actively participated in coverups regarding his own officers? I wonder if that's what happened with Duncan. Maybe he wasn't on the force, but his brother is, and maybe that protection extends to him as well.

I need to find out what Eastly is hiding if I have any chance of catching this killer. At least now I know *why* he's gone to such lengths to protect Duncan. I just need to figure out what he's protecting him from.

When I get back into the room the first thing I see is Zara's face, lit up by the screen of her phone. She looks up, wiggling it at me. "Guess who just called."

I check my own phone. "At three in the morning?"

"I told them to get back to me day or night, it didn't matter when," she replies. "And believe it or not, but they have offices in India. Where did you go?"

"Couldn't sleep," I say. "Please tell me they complied with the request."

She turns the phone to face me. "Yep, meet Julie Stanton. Or at least her digital profile."

A woman with dark brown hair and piercing green eyes stares back at me. "Pretty. Does it show her address?"

She turns the phone back around. "The address she registered with is a warehouse about twenty minutes away. They store lumber."

I slump down on the other bed. "So Duncan Schmidt was catfished. You called it. What are the odds that's even her real picture?"

"About a hundred to one. All the IP information routes through a private VPN, which means I can't track the original person down," she says. "But this is only the top level of the data from Holy Hands. We could always run at them with a warrant."

I lay back on the bed, deflated. Another dead end. I should have known the killer would have been smart enough to cover their tracks. They've been systematically killing men every week for the past month. What are they going to do, leave us a trail to follow? This is someone who knows what they're doing. There's an emotionless mind at work here, someone who can see all the details without allowing their feelings to get in the way. Which is only going to make all of this harder.

"Did you at least find something good in the kitchen? I swear, this place has like zero late-night food options," Zara asks, gently changing the subject.

"Wasn't in the kitchen." I proceed to tell her about the man in the basement and his connection to Eastly. Though I neglect to mention the train setup because I know she'll hyper-focus on that until she can get down there to see it herself.

"Damn, it's too bad he won't go on the record," she says. "But I guess in a place like this that's social suicide."

"Doesn't matter," I say, sitting back up. "When we nail Eastly to the wall for tampering with evidence, everything will come out anyway. And given the online profile was a dud, I think the chief is our only chance at catching this guy."

She arches an eyebrow at me in the dark, I can just barely see it from the light of her phone. "Scorched earth?"

I nod. "Scorched earth."

Chapter Fourteen

"SLATE, I thought I told you *not* to make any waves," D.A. Rice says from across his desk. We booked an emergency appointment with his office first thing this morning, driving over from Collins.

"What did you want us to do, sit on it?" I ask, incredulous.

His face is flushed, probably from trying to figure out how he's going to deal with this mess. Zara and I have just related to him everything we know about Eastly, as well as the missing evidence bag I found in his office.

"No, of course not," he replies. "But you of all people should know that an illegal search won't have a chance in hell of standing up in court. In fact, Eastly could press charges against you for violating his privacy."

"He'd have to come to you to do that, wouldn't he?" I ask.

"Well, yes," he replies.

"And weren't you the one who told us this place was rife with *good ol' boys*? We just snuffed one out for you and you're worried about *his* privacy?"

"I'm worried about the law, Agent Slate," he replies. "Your antagonism will only get you so far. Our best hope is to make it seem to Eastly like he's got more problems on his desk than you searching through it."

"Funny," I say, my sarcasm dripping.

"What a mess," he says, looking at his desk, though I don't think he's really examining anything on it. His voice is full of trepidation; Mr. Bale was right; Rice isn't prepared to deal with this level of entrenched corruption.

"Look," I say, bringing him back to the present. "Whatever Eastly knows, it's the key to this case. He's hiding something for a reason, and I'm willing to bet as soon as we find out what it is, we'll find our killer."

"You think he's intentionally hiding this person?" Rice asks.

I shoot a glance at Zara, who has been quiet this whole time. "Not intentionally, no. But the man has an agenda, that much has to be clear. Or do I need to show you the pictures again?"

He waves me off, clearly frustrated. "You've made your point. Just…just don't go confronting Eastly until I've had time to devise a strategy," he says. He lets out another breath. "I was *supposed* to be golfing down in Florida with the governor this weekend."

"Sorry to ruin your vacation, but we've got less than twelve hours to go," I say, not a hint of sorrow in my words. "If you want us to catch this person before they kill again, we need to know what Eastly knows."

He bristles. "It wasn't a vacation. It was going to be an attempt to let him know we have the situation under control and that he didn't need to get anyone else involved. You've never met the governor, but he can be a bit of an alarmist. The last thing we need is the National Guard showing up, trying to force their way into a situation they have no business being in. I was hoping the two of you would have something by now I could give him."

"Sorry to disappoint," I tell him. "We're doing the best we can. Talk to Eastly."

"It's my top priority," he replies. "Give me a couple of hours. I'll call you as soon as I'm ready and you can meet me at Collins P.D."

Before I can get up, his phone rings. "Rice." A second later his face falls. "Yeah, put him through." He hangs up the receiver and puts the call on speaker.

"Go ahead, Chief," the woman on the other end says.

"Rice." Eastly's distinctive voice says. He's not asking, he addressing.

Rice glances at us, his face pinched and full of worry. "Good morning, Chief Eastly. What can I do for you today?"

"I need to file a formal complaint," he says. "Those two FBI agents accessed sensitive case information last night without my approval. They intentionally waited until I was off duty to do it, so they could tamper with the file."

Rice raises an eyebrow, then opens an app on his cell phone. I notice it's a voice recorder. "One second, Chief." He activates the recorder. "I'm recording this for my office. This is District Attorney Rice speaking with Collins Police Chief Jasper Eastly. It is Saturday, November 21st at nine-fifteen in the morning. Please, Chief, go ahead. You were saying the FBI tampered with case evidence?"

"Yes, sir," he replies. "The Schmidt murder case. Their signatures are on the box and the station's video feeds have them coming in and out at the late hours of the evening."

How *dare* he. We weren't the ones that tampered with evidence, he was! And now he's trying to accuse us of improper conduct?

Rice puts one finger to his lips when he sees me about to say something. "How do you know they tampered with the evidence?" Rice asks.

"There's an evidence bag missing," Eastly says. "It had

Schmidt's cell phone inside. They're the only ones who could have taken it."

I exchange an alarmed glance with Zara. He's trying to pin his own crime on us.

"Let me get this straight, Chief," Rice says. "You're saying the two FBI agents, Slate and Foley, assigned to this case by me have knowingly and willfully obstructed justice by removing evidence?"

"That's exactly what I'm saying. And I want them out of here, Rice. I don't care how you do it, but they need to be back on a train or bus or whatever out of this town. They have seriously compromised your investigation here."

"These are very serious charges, Chief," Rice continues.

"Don't I know it," he replies. "Do what you need to do. In the meantime, I'll monitor damage control here. We have to preserve what remains of the chain of evidence."

Rice looks at me as he finishes the call. "Chief, thank you for the call. I'll get right on this."

"Be sure you do. We respect the law up here, something I'm sure you can appreciate, coming here from Boston. You call me if you need anything." Eastly's voice is full of self-satisfaction and confidence. So much that it makes me want to reach through this phone and punch him.

"Thank you. Be in contact soon." Rice ends the call, then turns off his recorder.

"Talk about a snake in the grass," Zara says.

Rice folds his hands together. "Looks like Eastly thinks he just found his way to get rid of you two."

"But he couldn't have predicted we'd want to go look at the evidence box, especially without him around," Zara says.

"No. My guess is he's just using the opportunity as presented. He figures this is an easy way to get you out of his hair and seeing as he already removed the cell phone in question, he knows the evidence box has already been tampered with. This gives him a perfect chance to both cover his tracks and get rid of the two of you in the same blow." Rice plays part of the recording back, to make sure he got it. It comes through clear as a bell. "But combined with your picture, I have him on obstruction and conspiracy. Even if no one saw him remove the cell phone from the box, the fact that it was in his desk provides a reasonable assumption as to what happened to it." He stands. "Agents, I think we've just found the leverage you've been looking for to make him talk."

We stand as well. "What about the rest of the department? Won't they try to back him?" I ask.

Rice shakes his head. "Even if they do, they'll be hard-pressed to ignore what's in front of their eyes." He opens his phone line again. "Doris, where is Sheriff Dutton this morning?"

"I believe it's her day off," Doris replies through the intercom.

"Give her a ring at home then," Rice says. "We're going to need some backup."

As we're driving back to Collins, following Rice in his vehicle, my phone buzzes in my pocket. Immediately I'm reminded I still need to call Liam back, and when I check on the message, I see it's from him.

"Damn," I say.

"Boy trouble?" Zara asks.

"I just don't know what's going on with us," I say, putting my phone back before I can read the message. "Liam has been nothing but supportive, kind, loving…and yet my instincts are telling me to push him away. To put some distance between us. How does that make any sense?"

"Maybe your subconscious has seen something you don't like, and you're not allowing your conscious self to see it," Zara suggests. "Or you could find yourself falling hard for this man and you're getting scared. And every time you get scared, you push people away."

I don't have to ask her how she knows that; I've done it to her in the past. I did it when I first went on suspension, right after Matt died. I thought I deserved to be alone, that I would only bring other people around me down. And despite that, Zara stuck with me. But I'm not so sure Liam has that kind of patience. And he shouldn't have to. He's been through hell and back because of me; I wouldn't blame him if he just up and left one day.

"You know what we need once we nail Eastly's ass and find this killer?" Zara says, looking over at me conspiratorially.

"I'm afraid to ask."

"A spa day. Like they have at those mountain retreats? The kind where you sit in hot tubs surrounded by snow, or get massages as you're looking out at a beautiful vista? Cucumber slices and everything."

"Sounds nice," I say, though I know it's not realistic. Even if we manage to catch our killer, Wallace will want us back immediately.

"Either that, or we both just need to get railed really hard."

I sputter and almost swerve the car, causing her to cackle with laughter. "Oh, sweet innocent Emily, you are too fun to mess with." She giggles the whole way to the station.

Once there, we exit behind D.A. Rice and Sheriff Dutton, who has brought two of her own deputies to confront Chief Eastly. I always get a little nervous when we have to confront those I believe may be dirty. When backed into a corner, you never know what they might do. Sometimes they fold, believing that all attempts at fighting will be useless and want to minimize the damage as much as possible.

But other times, that's when the teeth come out. When they realize they've been found out and they no longer have anything else to lose. Eastly isn't a young man, he has more days behind him than ahead which tells me he'll do anything he can to protect the precious time he has left.

But before we head into the station, Rice hesitates. "I hate doing this here. It would be much easier to confront him at his home. Less likely to be a confrontation there."

I check my phone for the time. "These are the cards we've been dealt. We've got less than twelve hours before the next victim, assuming the killer sticks to their schedule."

Rice lets out a long exhale then looks at Dutton who just nods, her brow covered by her wide-brimmed hat. "Okay. But let's try to keep things from getting out of hand?"

"No promises."

As we enter the station, I notice there's a different sergeant on desk duty, and Sewell is nowhere to be seen. Looks like his shift ended early this morning. The sergeant looks up, his eyes going wide. "D.A. Rice. Can I help you?"

"We're here to see Chief Eastly," I tell him, taking the lead.

"He's…in his office. I'll let him know you want to see him."

"I'd prefer you didn't," I say. I nod to one of Dutton's deputies. "Stay here and make sure he doesn't give the chief any warning."

"Wait," the sergeant says. "What's going on here?" He reaches for the phone anyway and Dutton's deputy walks around the desk and hangs it up for him. I motion for the rest of us to proceed back through the station. Seeing it in the daylight only reminds me of how different it looked at night, without all the activity of a busy Saturday morning. It's like the station transformed overnight.

Eastly is sitting in his office, reading a local newspaper when we come in. Immediately the smile on his face falls and he drops the paper to his desk. "Rice? What—"

"Chief Eastly," I say, doing my best not to enjoy this too much. "You are under arrest for obstruction, evidence tampering and attempting to frame federal officers. Please stand up and put your hands behind your back."

"What are you talking about?" His face is flushed, all of that calm washed away in an instant. He turns to Rice. "You see what I mean? This is the entire reason I called you. They're unhinged, thinking I've committed a crime."

"Unfortunately, Jasper, I have good cause to believe them, or I never would have gathered the warrant. Now please, don't make this more difficult. You'll have your chance to explain once we get you back over to the county offices."

Dutton makes a move to round his desk and produces a pair of handcuffs from her belt.

"I knew ever since you were appointed you'd be trouble," Eastly says, allowing Sheriff Dutton to cuff him.

"I didn't want this, Jasper, I really didn't," Rice says. "But I have a job to do. And I can't just let things skirt by. That's not how I operate." He motions to Dutton's deputy. "Open his desk drawers."

Dutton escorts Eastly out of the way while the deputy opens the drawers that are unlocked. He goes through them, finding nothing of value. When he comes to the locked drawers he looks up at Eastly, who just turns away, defiant.

"The keys on his belt," Zara says. Rice nods and the deputy removes Eastly's keys, trying each one until one works and the latch retracts. As he opens the drawers I can feel my heart pounding in my chest. But when he reaches the same drawer I went through not more than eight hours ago, the evidence bag with Schmidt's phone isn't in there.

"Desk looks clean," the deputy says.

"What were you expecting to find?" Eastly asks, a satisfied look on his face.

"Sheriff, please remove the chief," Rice says. "We'll follow you back and then all of us are going to have a nice, long discussion." He shoots me a look, his face pinched with worry. The picture is helpful, but without the actual evidence bag, it's going to be a lot harder to prove the chief's guilt. He must have moved or disposed of it this morning before calling Rice. I still don't think he knew I went through his desk, but he's being too cautious. He really didn't want us finding what was on that cell phone.

But I know a picture of an evidence bag in a desk isn't going to be enough to convict anyone of anything.

As Sheriff Dutton leads Eastly through the station, many of the officers begin standing up, some of them even shouting at her and us, trying to figure out what's going on. Zara and I keep our gazes straight ahead, not making eye contact with anyone as we follow Dutton out. But as we reach the lobby again, we stop.

Three officers stand in our way. I check their nametags. Two of them are the ones Zara and I saw getting off patrol the other morning. The third is Garrett Schmidt, who has cleaned himself up and looks to be back on active duty. Funny, after his outburst yesterday I figured he'd be off duty for the next few weeks. But it seems Eastly has seen fit to get him back to work immediately, despite what he made it seem like to us.

"Just what the hell do you think you're doing?" Schmidt asks, his voice full of self-importance.

"Move aside, detective," I say. "This is a federal matter."

He shakes his head, a sardonic smile spreading across his lips. "You feds, you really do think you can do whatever you want." He looks past me to Rice. "And you. Chief was right about you; you don't know what it's like to be *from* a place like this. And nothing you can ever do will change that."

"Detective," I say again, warning in my voice. "Move aside."

"Not unless you take those handcuffs off him."

I have to suppress a laugh of surprise. "You have no authority over this matter. Move or I'll move you myself."

"Maybe not, *Agent*," he replies. "But that doesn't mean we're powerless." I notice more officers from the back have gathered to watch the show. This is exactly what I'd hoped to avoid. I don't look behind me, but I'm sure Rice is close to losing it right now. "Either explain yourself and get him out of those cuffs, or I walk."

As if that's going to stop me. "I don't owe you an explanation for my actions. You will be free to read the reports when they become public just like everyone else. But for now, get out of my way or I'll arrest *you* for obstructing an investigation." This is all getting too muddy, there are too many flared tempers in here, too many variables. It feels like that moment just before something irrevocable happens. Almost as if I can feel the paths some of these officers are considering.

"Fine," Garrett says, removing his badge. He places it on the counter where the desk sergeant sits. "I won't be part of a town that no longer prescribes to justice. And I invite any of my brothers or sisters who feel the same way to join me."

I barely keep from rolling my eyes until I see the two patrol officers beside him remove their badges and weapons, placing them on the desk beside his. All three men walk out without another word.

All the better. The less we have to deal with Schmidt right now, the better off we'll be. I'm about to take a breath of relief when out of the corner of my eye I see another officer step forward. He mimics the others and leaves without a word, just a pointed look. My heart begins to fall as more and more of the officers in the station join in.

When it's all said and done, close to twenty officers have left their badges on the counter, including the desk sergeant Dutton's deputy was watching. I take note of the remaining officers who broke rank. At least half of them are women.

"I told you, Agent, we respect the law around here," Eastly says, chuckling. "No one is going to help you falsely prosecute one of their own."

"C'mon," I tell Sheriff Dutton. "Let's get him through processing."

Chapter Fifteen

IT TAKES a good hour to get back over to the county offices and to get Eastly processed and into an interrogation room. The entire time I'm sipping on cold coffee while trying not to lose what little composure I have left.

Part of me feels like Eastly staged that little coup somehow. Like he knew if anything ever happened to him, he'd cripple Collins by getting over two-thirds of the police force to quit on the spot. It wasn't only the officers that were there, Zara is fielding calls from those left at Collins giving us a report on everyone else who is calling in to say they won't be in for their shifts, or they've quit entirely. It seems Eastly had quite the influence here.

Not to mention Eastly has already lawyered up. Before we could even get a word in edge-wise, he told us to get his lawyer on the phone and he wouldn't be speaking to us any further. Normally this would mean we wouldn't be able to get anything else out of him, but I believe it might actually work to our advantage. Once his lawyer sees we have some evidence on him, he may compel him to give us what we need to find this killer.

On the other hand, he could try to use it against us in an

effort to bolster Eastly's case. My strategy going in will be to try and remind Eastly that if he doesn't help us, another man will die tonight. The clock is ticking and I don't know how much time we have left.

But while I'm waiting on Rice to finish all of his paperwork, I pull out my phone and look at the messages from Liam. The man is a saint, full of more patience than I deserve. There are no accusations in the texts, no expectations, just someone who is reaching out. And I keep slapping his hand away.

I take a deep breath, set down my coffee and dial.

"Em?" he asks, his voice full of concern. "You okay?"

"Yeah...well, no. I'm not. I just...I wanted to apologize for not getting back to you sooner, and for everything that happened before I left. I'm just...I'm in a weird place and this case isn't going well." I pinch the bridge of my nose, attempting to fight of the oncoming headache.

"I know you've been under a lot of stress, especially ever since that...um...thing arrived. I just want to make sure you're okay."

I let out a breath of frustration. "Can't you just...I dunno, get mad at me for once or something? I've been treating you like crap and all you say is you want to make sure I'm okay?"

"Is that what you really want me to do? Get mad at you?"

"You should, you have every right to."

"But it wouldn't do you any good," he says. "You don't need people mad at you right now. You need people who are there for you. Tell me what's going on with the case, maybe I can help."

I smile, despite myself. "One of these days I'm going to find something wrong with you. I don't know when, but I'll find it."

"Oh, there's plenty wrong with me. First and foremost that I'm spoiling the crap out of your dog. He's going to be at least two pounds heavier when you get back."

"You know what that means then, don't you? The weather is perfect to start running again. All three of us will start hitting the greenways when I get back."

There's an audible groan on the other end. "Wait a second, I take all that back," he says, but I can hear the laughter in his voice. "Is it too late to get mad at you now?"

"Yes," I say, grinning. "Besides, running is good for you. It'll keep you in shape while you man that desk."

He laughs again. "You wanna tell me about the case? I'm happy to offer an ear."

I shake my head even though he can't see me. "It's a mess up here. We've got a corrupt police chief trying to pin his own crime on us, and he holds the only clue that might lead us to our killer, who due to his pattern, will strike sometime before midnight tonight. But we've got no leads, and no way to find this person. Oh, and two-thirds of the town's police force just quit when we arrested the chief."

"Woof," he says. "Did you tell Wallace yet?"

"I'm dreading the call. The D.A. who brought us up here already isn't happy. But what were we supposed to do? Ignore it?"

"As much as I wish I could give Wallace the news for you, I don't think that would be the best idea."

"Me either," I say. "Thanks anyway though."

"How about this? I'll be happy to have a homecooked meal for you when you come back." I can already see the gears working in his mind, trying to figure out what he's going to make. He's become a shockingly good cook in a short amount of time. I kind of think he missed his calling.

"Stop, you're already making my mouth water," I say. "I should go. I think this lawyer is due to arrive any minute and I still need to inform Wallace."

"Best of luck with all of it. If you need me, I'll be here," he says.

"Thanks, talk to you soon."

"Be safe."

Despite having been in a formal relationship for over a month, Liam and I haven't started using the "L" word yet. I know he wants to be sensitive to my feelings regarding Matt and I'm acutely aware that I'm not saying it, even if I've already begun to feel it. I'm not going to be one of those people who closes herself off to everyone she meets because she's been hurt. But at the same time I'm not about to go out and get myself into something I'm not ready for. Thankfully, Liam is giving me that time and space. I'm not so sure anyone else would.

Sighing, I scroll down my row of contacts until I find Wallace's number. Even though it's Saturday I know he'll be in the office. He always is.

"DAY OLD DANISH?" ZARA ASKS, HOLDING UP A BEAR CLAW AS I make my way to where she, Rice, and Sheriff Dutton are standing.

"No thanks." I turn my attention to Rice. "I just got off the phone with my SAC. He's about as happy as you are."

"Glad to know we're all on the same page." My call with Wallace wasn't as contentious as I thought it would be, and he agrees we're not being given a fair shake up here, though there's little he can do about it. Except the one thing I didn't want him to do.

"He's sending two more agents to assist with the investigation, and to help shore up the Collins Police Department, at least until we can get this sorted out."

Rice shakes his head. "No offense, but two agents aren't going to replace an entire police force."

"They're not meant to, I was hoping Sheriff Dutton might be able to lend a hand," I say, nodding at the sheriff.

Her eyes widen, as if she seems surprised to be addressed.

"Oh sure. I can pull in a couple of retirees, maybe a few who've moved on to other departments. Best case I can spare one or two of my own. I'd say I can contribute maybe five or more, in all."

"It's a start," Rice says.

I turn, looking at the doors. "Where is this lawyer? Doesn't he understand the urgency of this situation?"

"I doubt he does," Rice says. "I didn't speak to him personally, and if I know Eastly, he wouldn't mind waiting a little longer just to piss us off. We insulted his integrity back there. He'll want to make us pay."

"Sheriff, you *need* to find that evidence bag," I tell her.

She gives me an incredulous look. "That bag could be at the bottom of Lake Emerald for all I know. How do you expect me to locate it?"

"Em, was the phone still on when you cloned it?" Zara asks.

Rice puts up a hand. "Wait, you removed it from the bag?"

"No, I did it through the bag, never touched it," I say, turning back to Zara. "I think it was."

"I have the phone's unique signal then; I can ping it." She runs out of the station and comes back a minute later, hauling her laptop. "If it's on and within range of a cell tower, I can at least get an approximate location."

"And suppose you do," Dutton says. "Where am I supposed to get the manpower to search for a tiny thing like that?"

Before she can answer, the doors to the county offices swing open, revealing a full-bodied man in a dark gray suit. He's wearing a frown the size of Texas and glares at each of us, in turn. "Who's in charge here?"

I step forward. "I'm Agent Slate with the FBI. I was the one who requested the warrant for Chief Eastly."

He steps to me. "You are in big trouble, little lady."

My mood darkens. "Don't," I say, stopping him in his tracks. "I don't want to hear anything about how I look too young or too inexperienced to know what I'm doing. You're talking to a federal law enforcement officer. And if I hear another derisive comment out of your mouth, I will make you regret it."

He sneers at me before looking over my shoulder at Zara, Rice, and Dutton. Then he smiles, surprising me. "You've got some fight in you. This should be interesting. Where's my client?"

"Interview room two," I tell him.

"Then I best not keep him waiting." He walks off, as one of Dutton's deputies accompanies him to interview two.

"He's fun," Zara says under her breath.

"Constance Wilcox," Rice says. "One of those types who loves to play the game. Really doesn't care if he wins or loses, but he won't make things easy for us. Damn, I was really hoping it wasn't him."

"You've met?"

"In passing, with a few minor cases." He checks his watch again. "Even if he does get Eastly to talk, you think you can track down the killer before it's too late?"

"I honestly don't know," I admit. "We don't have anything else to go on, at least not yet."

"I'm going to try and track down this phone," Zara says. "By myself if I have to. If I can find it, at least you'll have some leverage against Eastly." She goes to work on her laptop, fingers clacking away at the keys.

This is insane. Eastly is supposed to uphold the law, not circumvent it. No wonder half the people in this country don't trust law enforcement. If they're willing to sacrifice the public trust for their own selfish needs, how are we supposed to make any progress? Even worse, Rice is right. I don't know how we're supposed to find this killer before midnight. They could be in any town within a two-hour radius, or even farther if they've changed their M.O. Not to mention Wallace sees the need to send additional agents up here to help. While I recognize it's probably prudent, it just feels like I've failed to contain the situation and keep things from spiraling out of control. It's as if everything is falling apart around me, and I'm at the center of it all.

"Agent?"

I look up to see Wilcox beckoning for us to join him in the interview room. "My client would like to have a word."

Chapter Sixteen

As DUTTON and I enter the interrogation room, we see Eastly sitting on the other side of the table, his expression calm and neutral. His lawyer has set up camp beside him and wears a similar expression. Already I don't like where this is going.

"Chief," I say, nodding. "Mr. Wilcox."

"Ah, I see my reputation precedes me," Wilcox says, smarmier than before. Dutton stays back while I take the seat across from the two men.

"I'm ready when you are," I say.

Wilcox gives Eastly a small nod. "Because my client has worked in law enforcement for many years, he knows that you must have some piece of evidence that has compelled you to take this drastic step of having him arrested. He would like to know what that is."

I hold out my hands. "It's no secret. Duncan Schmidt's cell phone."

"The phone that you stole from the evidence box," Wilcox replies.

"You know, that's funny," I say. "Chief Eastly keeps accusing me and my partner of stealing evidence, when he knows full well that evidence was already missing from the box when we got to it."

I see a flicker of unease cross Eastly's face, but it's gone an instant later.

Wilcox, however, doesn't miss a beat. "That's convenient. Especially when you and your *partner* signed the box in and out. And given that no one else has accessed that box since it was entered into evidence—"

"—if I was going to steal evidence, why would I sign my name to the box at all?" I ask.

"To provide yourself a cover," he replies.

"And what does stealing a cell phone do for me?" I ask. "How does that help me, in any way?"

Wilcox gives me a small shrug. "You don't like Chief Eastly, or his methods. You were put off by him yesterday when you arrived, and you don't approve of how he runs things here. Didn't you tell him yourself that you thought his people couldn't handle the job?"

"No," I say, glancing at Eastly. "We never said anything of the sort."

"Not everything you say is in words, Agent," Eastly says. Wilcox holds out his hand to keep Eastly from saying anything else.

"Agent, I must insist. I need to see what evidence you have on my client, otherwise I'll ask that you let him go. His absence from Collins is already having a widespread effect on the area. I've heard that without the police force in town, things will turn to anarchy."

"Stop being so dramatic," I tell him. "The FBI is sending reinforcements to help keep the community calm. And Sheriff Dutton is offering her services as well." I pull out my phone, hesitant to show Wilcox the evidence on Eastly. He strikes me as the kind of man who will take it and run with it, accusing me of an improper search. And he wouldn't be wrong. But right now, this picture is all I have that can clear up any confusion as to who exactly took that cell phone.

But before I pull up the picture, there's a knock at the door. Dutton goes over and checks the window. "It's your partner," she says.

"Excuse me a moment, gentlemen." I stand and retreat to the door. As soon as it's open, Zara looks at me with a huge grin.

"Guess what I found?"

I WRAP MY COAT TIGHTER AS THE WIND WHIPS THROUGH THE valley, blowing hard against all of us. I'm staring at a small river, probably no more than eight or ten feet deep at any point that cuts through a gorgeous plot of land. The trees all around us have lost most of their leaves and a bank of snow blankets both sides of the river. When the wind dies down, the only sound is that of the running water and the soft crunch of boots.

Sheriff Dutton has accompanied me and Zara, along with a search team out to the picturesque site. Sure enough, Duncan Schmidt's phone *was* still on, and Zara managed to use the local cell towers to triangulate its position. While not exact, it gave us enough of a starting point to begin looking.

But the sun is already beginning to set and in the back of my head that clock is ticking down, telling us we don't have a lot of time left. Dutton's team has brought out metal detectors and are going over every inch in a grid search, hoping to find the cell phone before it gets too dark. If we lose the light before they can find it…

"Hey," Zara says, coming up to me. "They just finished with grid nine. Moving on to ten."

"Is this really the fastest way to do this?" I ask. The ground isn't exactly even. It's littered with rocks and pebbles, though there is a small path that winds through the area, parallel with the river. It's a scenic hiking trail about a mile off the main road. Because the snow is so light, the path is still easily visible. Eastly must have come out here early this morning to dispose of the phone before returning to work. I've already checked the duty log. It has him coming in at six-thirty, going back out at seven, and then coming back in at eight-oh-five. My guess is he came in and saw we had been there overnight, then hatched his plan—half-baked as it were.

"Found something!" one of the searchers yells, holding up his hand. The three of us make our way over to him, though he's about ankle-deep in the river, wearing waders that come up to his chest. Before we stop I can already see the telltale red stripe of the evidence bag just underneath the water. It's been tossed there as carelessly as if someone were throwing away a piece of trash.

"That's it," I say.

Dutton waves her team and takes the necessary steps of gathering surrounding evidence, though there's little of it. As far as I can tell, there are no close footprints. The trail is littered with them, probably from hikers or tourists exploring the scenic beauty. I doubt we'd get anything to match his boots.

"Bag is bobbing," Zara says, pointing at it. I see that she's right. Since it's sealed with a little bit of air inside, it's made the bag somewhat buoyant. Not enough to bring it to the surface, but enough so that it didn't sink all the way to the bottom.

"I bet the chief didn't realize that when he threw it in," I say, pulling on a pair of gloves. When the team has finished with the photographs and gathering the necessary evidence, I reach in and pull the bag from the water, examining it. As best I can tell, it's still sealed, and the phone looks intact.

Ironically, we now have to put it in a *second* evidence bag, in hopes that we can get some fingerprints off it. I turn to Dutton. "I need this processed yesterday."

She nods. "We'll get right on it. Meet you back at the offices. I'm sure you'll want to speak with Eastly again."

"More than ever," I say.

~

"HERE'S THE DEAL, CHIEF," I SAY, STROLLING BACK INTO THE interrogation room. It's closing in on six p.m. and this man has wasted valuable time trying to save his own hide. I've run out of patience and I'm tired of playing this game.

"Whoa there, Agent Slate," Wilcox says. I notice he's gotten himself a cup of coffee in our absence. "You leave us sitting here for two hours, no explanation, and now you come storming in—"

"Can it." I turn back to Eastly. "First off, we know you removed the cell phone from the evidence box. We know because it was in your desk last night. We also know that after you came into work this morning, you curiously left for an hour before returning. An hour is just enough time to drive out to the South Moat Mountain Trailhead, get rid of the phone, and get back to work before calling Rice and informing him of your *discovery*."

Eastly looks visibly unsettled, though Wilcox isn't perturbed in the slightest. "That's a lot of conjecture, Agent Slate, how—"

"We have the phone, and the evidence bag it was in," I tell them both. "And despite being in the water for close to twelve hours, they managed to pull a partial print, which happens to belong to you, Chief Eastly. Strangely, none of my or my part-ner's prints were present."

"Well now, water can wash away prints, can it not?" Wilcox asks, though he shoots a look at Eastly.

"Sometimes. So now I have more than enough to charge

you with obstruction and conspiracy, not to mention evidence tampering."

"Agent, if you wouldn't mind, I'd like a minute to speak with my client, alone," Wilcox says.

I shake my head. "No deal. You've stonewalled us enough on this. I want to know what was on that phone that was so important you decided to risk your career over. What was so *dire* that it was worth attempting to implicate two federal officers?"

"Shouldn't have been able to find it," Eastly whispers.

"What he means is…uh…it's impressive the job you've done here, Agent, but—"

"Wilcox, I do believe your client just admitted to the crime," I say. "Now you've got two choices. You can either tell me what you're hiding and maybe I'll consider dropping the obstruction charge. *Or,* you go through the full brunt of the federal justice system. And believe me, they *hate* former cops in prison. Especially old, entrenched cops like yourself who think they're above the law. Cops who break the law when and how it suits them. And I'll make damn sure bail is off the table."

Wilcox whispers something in Eastly's ear, but he shakes his head no.

I want to reach across the table and strangle the man. He's been nothing but an obstruction since we got here. And now, even staring down the barrel of the gun, he *still* won't talk. "Don't you get it, Eastly? This isn't even about you. You've just decided to insert yourself into something for no reason. This is about the next man who is going to die out there. Tonight. How can you sit there and refuse to help us knowing someone's life is on the line?"

"Because it will ruin me," he says.

"Better check the mirror," I tell him. "You're already ruined. You'll be lucky if you ever take another free breath in your life."

He hangs his head, avoiding my gaze.

"Tell me what you were trying to hide. We already have all the information on the phone. Why are you trying to protect Duncan Schmidt?"

"Why couldn't you have just moved on?" Eastly asks, his voice small and weak. "Why did you have to set up shop in *my* town? The next murder isn't going to take place here. The killer hasn't struck in the same place twice. So why couldn't you have just saddled up with Rice? Worked from there?"

"I had *hoped* you'd be willing to cooperate with us," I tell him. "Given Schmidt was the most recent victim, it seemed prudent to start there."

"Duncan had already been dead five days by the time you arrived," he says, his voice pitiful. "You should have just moved on."

I take a seat across from him, making sure I catch his eye. "Something you should know about me; I don't just move on. I can't just throw up my hands and say 'oh well, guess this one's a cold case.' It's not how I work."

"You can't possibly solve every case you take," he says.

"Of course not. But I don't stop trying until every avenue is exhausted. And believe it or not, the more apathetic you seemed about this whole thing, the more curious it made me. Do you remember Matt Bale?" Eastly's eyes light up with recognition. "I spoke with him. And after I did, I knew you had to be hiding something."

"I'm sorry, who is this Bale person?" Wilcox asks.

"That man never could keep his mouth shut," Eastly says.

"What are you protecting Duncan from?" I ask again.

Eastly shoots another look at Wilcox, then back at me. "If I tell you, I want protection. I can't go into genpop."

"I can't make any promises, you know that," I tell him.

"Then I can't help you, Agent Slate."

On the inside I'm screaming. But somehow I maintain a calm façade. I've had years of practice. "If that's how you want it." I stand and make my way to the door.

"Agent Slate?" Wilcox calls after me, making me stop. I turn as he whispers fervently into Eastly's ear again. Eastly turns and says something back to him. It's a much longer conversation this time. Finally, they stop, and Wilcox turns back to me. "Can you at least guarantee if my client tells you what he knows, he won't face any additional charges?"

I hesitate. "I'm sorry?"

Wilcox nods at Eastly again. "You're already bringing obstruction, conspiracy and evidence tampering charges. The worst of those already carries a maximum of twenty years. My client is sixty-five years old. Allow him some dignity. He'll give you what you want *if* you agree no more related charges will be brought or revealed in the course of the investigation."

I walk back over to him. "Do you realize what you're asking me to do? I'll need to get a federal judge to sign off on an order like that, I can't just make that kind of promise out of thin air." I glare at Eastly. He doesn't deserve any dignity. Not after what he's done.

"Then I would hurry up if I were you," Wilcox says. "Like you said, you're on the clock."

Chapter Seventeen

"EASTLY STILL ISN'T TALKING," I tell Zara when I return to the conference room. Rice has set himself up in there as well, but there's no sign of Sheriff Dutton. "He wants immunity from any additional charges, which makes me think he's done something *really* bad."

"So then where does that leave us?" Rice asks. "It's seven-fifteen."

I nod. "I was really hoping the Eastly angle would pay off, but we're out of time. We need to narrow down where the killer will strike next. We know they target single men in towns within about a two-hour radius."

"Single men under forty-five," Zara amends. "And none of them have been younger than twenty-eight. So far."

"Okay, so then we just need to find every man out on a date tonight in the towns that fit that radius," I say, sarcasm dripping from my words. "Easy, right?"

"If the killer contacted Duncan Schmidt through a dating app, they likely contacted the other victims the same way," Zara says.

"But there's no guarantee the killer is using the same app

every time. In fact, I would be willing to bet they're switching it up, so as not to leave a trail."

"My thoughts exactly," Zara says, turning her laptop back to me. "I've put in requests with the five largest dating apps for information relating to anyone who has created a profile that's from this area within the last month. Of course, with it being Saturday night, I doubt I'll hear back from any of them anytime soon."

"We're looking at another five towns within that radius you mentioned," Rice says, going back over to the map on the wall. "Plus two villages, a township, and three municipalities. All spread out around here."

"Not all of these are in your district, are they?" I ask. "Some of them are across the state border, in Maine. We need to notify the local LEOs. Tell them to be on the lookout for—"

"—for anyone on a date?" He shakes his head, laughing as if he can't believe it. "I think we've just run out of time. I'm sorry, Agent Slate. It was too optimistic to expect you to find this person in two days."

"That doesn't mean I'm willing to give up," I reply. "We still have a few hours. Maybe with more patrols in these towns…" I trail off. Even I know that's nothing but a shot in the dark. Unless we decide to institute a mandatory curfew, though I doubt that would be effective.

Rice gives me a grim smile. "I appreciate the effort. But your original assessment was right. Eastly holds the key to this. And until he talks, I think we're dead in the water." He looks over at the map again, then heads for the door. "I'm going to get a coffee. Anyone want anything?"

Both Zara and I shake our heads.

Once he's gone, I flop down into one of the chairs and let out a frustrated breath. "I can't believe we know it's going to happen and there's nothing we can do about it."

"Are you going to speak to Wallace about Eastly?" Zara asks.

"I don't want to. Eastly doesn't deserve protection. But I don't think we have a choice here. He's our only lead, and he knows it. I just don't know if I'm willing to make a deal with that snake. What are these other charges he's so afraid of? If it were up to me he'd get multiple life sentences based on what he's already done alone. I don't know. Maybe. Even if I do, it won't come through until tomorrow morning, at best."

Why is he so insistent on protecting Duncan Schmidt? It's not like he's even on the force. He's the brother—

I bolt up, my eyes going wide.

"Em? You okay?" Zara asks.

"Garrett," I say.

"The brother?"

I nod. "The brother *on the force*. What if Eastly isn't protecting Duncan at all? What if he's protecting Garrett? Maybe this has never been about Duncan at all."

"Do you really think Garrett will talk to us?" she asks. "He made a pretty big show about not being cooperative this afternoon."

I start gathering up my stuff. "He will if he thinks Eastly has already spilled everything. Depending on what it is, he might even want immunity. He may be the only other person who really knows what's going on here." I was so focused on Eastly I forgot about the "other" Schmidt. Though, I'll admit, he's been highly antagonistic ever since we arrived. Getting something out of him is going to take some finesse.

We blow by Rice on his way back from the coffee machine. "Whoa, where's the fire?" he asks.

"We might have a lead," I call back. "I'll keep you updated."

"Okay," he calls back. "I'll just be here, I guess."

As Zara and I reach the SUV outside, I slide into the driver's seat. "We need Garrett Schmidt's address."

"I'm on it," Zara says, working her magic on her phone. "662 Windy Leaf Lane. About half an hour away, in Collins." I gun it, backing up so fast the tires screech. "Holy shit, I forgot you go into racecar mode when you get latched onto something," she adds, putting on her seatbelt.

"Sorry, but we're out of time, and Garrett is our last chance."

∿

It's closing in on eight pm when we reach Collins again. The posted speed limit in the town is twenty-five unless otherwise marked, but I'm doing at least ten over that. We pull up to Garrett Schmidt's house and I notice the porch light is still on. Hopefully that means he's home, sulking about his decision earlier today.

Zara and I hop out and make our way up the sidewalk, my mind going about a million miles per hour. The whole way here we talked strategy, and that going after him head-on won't be effective. We have to make him think Eastly has already told us everything and that it's in his best interests to do the same, otherwise things could get bad for him.

When we reach the door, I pull my coat back so that my badge is on display. This won't be easy, but hopefully a little visual reminder that he's dealing with the FBI will help temper Schmidt a little bit. I reach up and prepare to knock, but then shoot a look at Zara who is waiting with bated breath.

"You know what? Why don't you have the honors?" I step back from the door and her eyes go wide.

"Hell yeah," she replies and bangs on the door as hard as she can. I actually see it move in its frame a little.

"Nicely done," I say.

She smiles. "Learned from the best."

A few seconds go by with no response. "Garrett Schmidt. This is the FBI. Open up." Garrett has close neighbors on either side of him, close enough that they can probably hear us from their living rooms. At least that's the idea. If nothing else, we can try to shame him into coming to the door.

But the longer we wait with no response, the more I have to accept Garrett's not home. We knock a few more times, and I check the windows closest to the doors, but I don't see any activity inside.

"Nothing?" Zara asks. I shake my head.

"It's been a long day. Why don't we just go back to the B&B? There's nothing more we can do now. It's not like the killer is going to strike in Collins anyway."

As we're headed back to the car, the sound of a door opening behind us catches my attention and I turn, hopeful, only to realize that it's the house next to Garrett's. An older woman wearing a heavy overcoat and her hair in a cap. "Ya'll lookin' for Garrett?"

We close the distance between us. "Yes, ma'am, do you know when he'll be back?"

She shakes her head. "Sped off like the devil was chasin' him about an hour ago. Been makin' a ruckus all day long."

"What kind of ruckus?" I ask.

She leans forward. "Never could make it out. Just been yellin' and screamin' over there all afternoon. Sounded like he was talkin' to someone, but I ain't seen any other cars there all day."

I nod. "All right, thank you."

I get back in the car and slam the door, frustrated. "Great. Sounds like Garrett's stirring up a shit storm." I huff. "I just hate knowing the killer is out there and there's nothing we can do about it."

"Maybe we'll get lucky, and they won't strike tonight. Our presence here could have spooked them."

"If they even know we're here," I mutter. "Someone in this town has to know *something* about this. It's a small place,

gossip travels. Whatever Eastly is covering up for Schmidt…"
I trail off thinking.

"Em, come on, we both need some sleep," Zara says.
"We've been going all day and being up half the night didn't
help."

She's right. I'm already feeling the exhaustion seeping in.
And I don't even know when I ate last. I guess it was this
morning. After everything that happened with the Organization, I made a promise to myself that I'd stop doing this. That
I wouldn't let cases take over my life like this. And yet, here I
am, getting sucked right back into my old habits. Part of that
was just falling into routine. Yet I know another part of it was
an attempt to keep from thinking about what's waiting for me
when I get home.

I let out a deep breath, and pull the vehicle away from the
curb. I have a sinking feeling that this could end up being one
of those cases that ends up going cold due to lack of evidence.
But I need to exhaust all avenues before I let that happen. "I
guess I need to call Wallace again, let him know about Eastly's
demands. I hate giving in to that son of a bitch, but I don't see
we have any choice."

"There's still the dating sites angle," Zara suggests. "It's a
long shot, but maybe something will pan out."

Five minutes later I pull up to the Mantokee and park
around the side. Only one other car sits in the parking lot,
license plates tell me it's from Florida.

"Hey, at least you can't say I didn't find you a quiet place,"
Zara says. I know she's just trying to lighten the mood, but at
this very minute a man is out there, fighting for his life. And if
what we know is true, he's on the losing end of it.

As soon as we enter the Mantokee, Andrea greets us at the
door with a smile. She's sitting in a small chair near the door,
knitting. "Evening, Agents," she says. "Having a nice
weekend?"

"Not really," I reply, heading for the stairs. But before I reach them, I hear a thump from the basement.

"I'll swanee, that man," Andrea mutters, getting up. "I'm sorry. You both look tired. My husband unfortunately doesn't understand that people come here for rest and relaxation. Not to listen to his commotions all night."

Something tickles the back of my brain. "Wait," I tell her. "May I speak with him?"

She puts on a frown. "But...doesn't it bother you? I heard him banging around all night last night. I'm sure it woke you up."

I shake my head and make my way to the basement door. "No, it wasn't a problem at all." I motion to Zara. "Agent Foley, would you join me, please?"

She arches an eyebrow and moves past a confused-looking Andrea, then follows me into the basement. As soon as she sees the setup, she lets out an audible gasp. "Holy shit! You didn't say anything about a train set!" She barrels past me, her focus glued on the trains running around the tracks.

Matt stands in the middle of it all yet again, his goggles on, only this time he looks like he's working on taking apart one of his mountains. "Didn't expect to see you again so soon," he says.

"I wanted to speak with you again," I say. "After our illuminating conversation last night. Oh, this is Agent Foley, though you may not thank me for bringing her down here when this is all over."

Andrea appears at the top of the stairs. "Is everything okay down there?" she asks, coming down about halfway.

"We're fine," I tell her. "Just admiring your husband's setup."

"Why isn't *this* on the website?" Zara exclaims, her face about an inch from the model, looking at all the little details.

"Well...I...I didn't think anyone would want to see it," the woman replies.

"Are you kidding? This is great. You could charge *admission.*"

"How about that, Ann?" Matt says, removing his goggles to reveal a satisfied look on his face. "*Admission.*"

"Mm-hmm," his wife mutters, pursing her lips at him.

"So, what can I do for two FBI agents?" he asks.

"What do you know about the Schmidts? Specifically, Garrett?"

He raises his eyebrows. "Digging for dirt, Agent?"

"You were on the force. Did you know Garrett? Work with him at all?"

Matt nods. "Sure."

"I never did believe the rumors about those boys," Andrea says. "They've always been so nice and polite to me. The way people gossip in this town, it can ruin a person's reputation."

I turn to her, surprised. "Rumors?"

She turns up her nose. "It's not proper to speak about," she says. "Not in civilized company, anyway."

"Ann, would you please?" Matt says, indicating she should go back upstairs.

She huffs once, then turns, and heads back up. I return my attention to Mr. Bale. Zara has managed to position herself on the other side of the model, and though it looks like she's doing nothing but inspecting all the little details, I can tell in my periphery she's got an eye on him as well.

He removes his goggles and sets down the piece of mountain he was working on. "I told you Eastly had me removed from the force. Garrett Schmidt was the reason."

"Go on," I tell him.

"Turns out Garrett's brother had something of a...reputation with women," Matt says. "Started off mild, but then the accusations started coming in. The complaints from multiple sources."

"Complaints of what?" I ask.

"Abuse," he says, plainly. "I won't beat around the bush.

He was taking advantage of women when they were vulnerable."

"And Eastly didn't do anything about it?" I ask.

"Eastly didn't know. Not at first. Because Garrett had managed to destroy any evidence of the original complaints against his brother. He tried to make it look like they had never happened. But some of us knew. He couldn't sneak around that station without someone finding out." He takes a seat on a stool that sits in the middle of the setup with him. I'm just realizing that I don't see any way for him to get into the center. He must have to crawl under there.

"How many complaints are we talking about here?" I ask.

"Five that I know of," he says. "Probably more. Me and another fella took it to Eastly when we'd had enough." He drops his gaze. "I shouldn't have waited as long as I did, but I'd been a career cop. And you know the rule. Blue backs blue. But after a while, I just couldn't turn a blind eye anymore."

"So then what did Eastly say?" I ask, shooting Zara a look. Her attention is fully on Mr. Bale now, the trains forgotten.

"He said he'd take care of it. But the more time that went by and nothing happened to Duncan or Garrett, the more I began to realize he would never do anything. He was protecting those boys."

"Why?" I ask. "Why not just expose them, serve the justice and gain a little more public trust?"

He shakes his head. "You don't understand, Agent. People up here aren't like where you come from. They still believe in their police departments. They trust them to be shining beacons that can instill public confidence. If Eastly had admitted to a coverup, especially one like this, he would have been admitting he didn't have control of his own department, and that his own people were corrupt. Knowing what you know about him now, do you really believe he'd do that?"

He's right. Eastly would have done whatever was necessary

to save his own skin. That much I've seen in person. "So then what…he just perpetuated the coverup?"

Matt nods. "And the more I prodded him about it, the more he insinuated that I was expendable. Apparently, I'm not as valuable as a younger officer; I don't have the same stamina, or resolve."

"What about the women who made the complaints?" Zara asks. "Didn't they wonder what happened?"

"Of course they did," he says. "But without the reports they would just be setting themselves up for the hanging block. It's a he-said, she-said situation, and the police controlled the flow of information. They had no one on their side."

"You could have been," I say, heat rising in my cheeks. "You saw the reports being destroyed. You could have been their advocate."

He shakes his head. "Maybe. But like I told you, I'm too old to start over in another place. Not to mention Ann would kill me if we had to move."

"Even if it was because you were protecting innocent women?" Zara asks, incredulous.

"There's something you don't understand about getting old until you're there," he says. "It's a lot harder to sacrifice everything for what you believe in, because the odds it will destabilize your entire life grow by the day. Why do you think old people become entrenched in their beliefs, good or bad? It's because for us, it's too late to change. I can't afford to start over. I don't have that long left."

"So you just sit here, playing with your trains, while innocent women have to live out there, knowing their assailant is walking around free?" I can't believe this man. I thought there was at least one good apple in the Collins police force. But it seems like all of them come from the same stock. They just want to save their own skins.

"Well," Matt replies, giving me a somber look, "Not anymore. Someone took care of that for them, didn't they?"

Chapter Eighteen

"ARE you sure I can't convince you to stay?" Andrea says, following us out to the car. Both Zara and I have packed up our bags and have informed her we're cutting our stay short. I can't stay one more night in this place, knowing that her husband was okay with what he did. Somehow, I think he probably knew that too, which was why he didn't offer it up earlier.

"No, we really have to be going," I tell her, hauling my small bag and tossing it into the trunk of the car.

"But...you enjoyed the train set so much; I think I'll be taking your advice and adding it to the advertisements," she says.

Zara just gives her a quick nod before getting in the car.

"Isn't there anything I can say or do to make you change your minds?" she asks, almost pleading with us. I'm wondering now if they're hard up for funds. Mr. Bale did mention we were the only ones staying here since we checked in. Though I did see that car from Florida. Maybe Mr. Bale has already developed a reputation himself, despite his best efforts.

"No, sorry," I tell her. "But thank you for your hospitality anyway."

She gives us a sad, frustrated look as we drive off, but I'm not going to lose any sleep over it. I couldn't have stayed in that house one more night.

"Okay, next time, I'm going to do a detailed background check of the B&B owners," Zara says. "Because I did *not* see that coming."

"There's no way you could have," I reply. "You saw how reluctant he was. He probably only told us because he feels so guilty about it."

"Good, he *should* feel guilty. I hope he feels that for the rest of his life."

I pull out my cell phone, and dial Rice's number. "Agent Slate?" he asks. "Where are you?"

"Looking for new accommodations," I tell him. "But that's not important right now. Did you know that Duncan Schmidt was facing at least five sexual assault allegations?"

"*What?*" The tone of his voice tells me this is new to him as well. "That can't be possible. There was nothing like that in his file. How did you find that out?"

"Interrogating a former Collins police officer who just happened to be our B&B host," I tell him. "He told us that five different women had made allegations against Duncan, and that Garrett and Eastly had conspired to cover it up."

"No wonder Eastly doesn't want any additional charges against him," Rice says. "I had Dutton detain him at the county courthouse overnight and I went home, but this is a big break. Do you think you can still find the killer in time?"

I check the clock on the dash. It's already past nine. More than likely our victim is already in the crosshairs, if not dead already. "I wish I could say yes. But this at least gives us a direction to follow."

"What do you need from me?" he asks.

"Get a confession out of Eastly, see if you can't get him to tell you everything he knows about Garrett and Duncan. He just lost his last bargaining chip."

"What are you going to do?"

I exchange a glance with Zara. The FBI agents Wallace is sending are due to arrive tomorrow. I want to be ready by then. If we can't stop the next murder, at least we won't let it go to waste. I plan on hitting the ground running first thing, as soon as we find a new place to sleep. "Research," I say.

"Okay. Best of luck. I'll coordinate with Dutton and see if we can't squeeze Eastly for more information. Keep me in the loop."

I end the call as Zara searches on her phone. "I think I found a place."

"Not another B&B."

She shakes her head. "I learned my lesson from that one. Nope, this is just a simple, old boring hotel halfway up the mountain."

"And not a ski resort," I say.

"How does a Best Western sound? Simple and easy. Wallace won't have a heart attack over this one." She directs me to the hotel which is a bit of a drive out of Collins, closer to the Adams County offices, which will make coordinating with Rice easier. When we arrive, the hotel sits right along the ridgeline off the main road leading into Collins. I can still see the lights from the town below, but they're faint.

"Whoa," I say, looking up when we get out. The stars above us are as clear as I've ever seen them, though the air temperature up here has to be at least fifteen degrees colder. The snow is deeper too. I pull my jacket around me and gather my suitcase, following Zara into the lobby.

Ten minutes later we're set up in one of their two-room suites, which will give us enough room to work. Matt's revelation about Duncan Schmidt may have just given us the direction we need to find out who our killer is, though unless they're staying at this same hotel, I don't see how we're going to be able to stop them.

But...if my hunch is correct, and we're looking for someone who is out there serving retribution on men who have assault records, I'm not exactly upset at that idea. In many ways, I see sexual assault as the worst thing that can be done to a person. It violates them in a way that changes them forever and leaves them with lasting trauma that can take years to work through, if it's even possible. Thankfully I've never been a victim of it myself, but I know so many people, almost all women, who have been. If Duncan Schmidt really was a serial offender, then I won't shed any tears that he's gone.

"Okay," Zara says, getting her laptop set up on the couch in the second room. "Just so we're on the same page, we think that our killer is going after offenders?"

"Sexual offenders," I tell her. "Remember the condition Duncan was left in. His genitals had been completely removed. I thought it had been religious in nature, but now I see it was simpler than that."

"Right," she says. "Same condition for all the victims. So does that mean we're looking for a woman? Maybe Schmidt wasn't catfished after all."

"Maybe," I say. "There's not enough information to go on yet. We know Schmidt was out on a date with someone before he was killed. This 'Julie' person you found. If that ended up being a real date, insofar as he actually met up with a woman and brought her back to his place, then yes, I'd say she's our suspect. However, she could have just been a decoy, working together with someone else who actually killed him." Female killers, especially serial killers, are astonishingly rare. Odds are that she's still involved, but not committing the actual murders. Which means we might be looking at two or maybe even three unsubs. Right now, it's too early to tell, and this is still just a theory. "We need to figure out if all of the victims were sexual offenders or not. But I'm willing to bet they are."

Zara goes to work on her keyboard. "It wasn't in the original files, that much I know. We would have seen it and made the connection immediately."

"Which means it was either covered up, like in Collins, or the other men weren't predators."

"Or," she says, looking at me. "It wasn't reported. You know how these things go. For every report there's probably another five to ten who never say a word."

"Then how would the killer know who to target?" I ask.

She sits back, screwing up her face. "That's a good point."

"We'll need to do some deep research if we want to find out if this theory holds water. If this really is our connective tissue, we'll have a better chance of narrowing down future victims."

After gathering what little provisions I could from the hotel's snack machine, both of us get to work. I'd much rather have this theory either confirmed or thrown out by the time the other agents get here so we can all start fresh. I don't like the idea that we need backup, but even I can't deny this situation has spiraled out of control. We have a town on the verge of falling apart, all because one man decided to try and save himself rather than tell the truth. I don't know if I'll ever see Chief Jasper Eastly again, but if I do, I'm going to do everything in my power to make sure he gets the maximum sentence. He could have told us about Duncan's record, but instead he decided to play these little games in an attempt to save himself. And now it's going to cost him everything.

After over an hour of work, I haven't made much headway. I've been going through the socials of Robert Hainsworth, James Wheeldon, and Nicholas Valentine looking for any evidence of relationships gone bad or anyone complaining about their behavior, but so far it's been nothing. Obviously, they would have scrubbed anything that made them look bad from their own pages. Which means I'll need to start looking into friends and relatives to see if anyone knows anything. For the first time I'm grateful Wallace decided to send extra help. We're going to need it.

"Hey," Zara says, and I glance up. "So I had a thought."

"Yeah?"

"You know how Julie used Holy Hands to get a date with Duncan? She used some pretty descriptive stuff in her profile. Talking about her past, her home life, what she liked to do, all of that."

"Makes sense, the more detailed the profile, the less it would likely be a scam, right?" I pick up the last remnant of a cold pop tart.

"Yes, but these guys were catfished anyway. At least, sorta. But I was thinking that was a lot of detail in that profile. It would be a pain in the ass to keep re-writing that for each new social media site. Wouldn't be easier to copy and paste?"

I stop chewing. "Are you saying she used the same details on her profile pages, even if she used a different name?"

She gives me a slow nod and turns her computer to face me. On it is another profile on the biggest online dating site: Two Hearts. The name at the top says "Angela", but the picture in the profile is almost the same as Julie, except the hairstyle and color is different. "That's her."

"Yep," Zara says. "Found her on three other sites too, each under a different name, and each looking slightly different from this. Not enough to be strange, but enough so she's not identical."

"We need to find this woman," I tell her. "Are we sure she matched with our victims?"

"Still waiting to hear back from the dating site's customer service. I doubt we'll get anything back tonight. But I'd bet you my CD collection this woman is the one we're looking for."

"If nothing else it's suspicious," I reply. "Do you have any idea who she really is?"

Zara shakes her head. "I wish I did."

"We really need those victim backgrounds," I tell her. "This is looking more and more like a revenge-killing spree."

"I know, but without anything official, getting that kind of information is going to be next to impossible," Zara says.

I stare at the picture of the woman. "She found a way. Somehow."

Zara sits back and rubs her eyes, then looks at her phone. "Em." The way she says it stops me cold, halting my thoughts.

When she turns it to me, the digital readout clicks over to midnight.

That's it. We're too late.

Happy Birthday, Emily.

Chapter Nineteen

I AWAKE to the sound of my phone, vibrating on the desk that sits between our two beds. I sit up, realizing I fell asleep in my clothes again. My laptop is off to the side, the screen dark, though the lights in the room are still on. Zara is in the other bed, under the covers, though from what I can tell, she wore her clothes to bed too. The last thing I remember was we were still trying to track down information on all the victims, hoping to find out if any of them had histories of sexual misconduct.

I grab the phone, looking at the date and instinctively it hits me that I'm now officially twenty-nine, despite the party Zara threw for me a few days ago. It doesn't feel any different than any other birthday, but I'm already looking at the horizon to thirty. That one might be a little tougher.

"Slate," I say, my voice groggy.

"It's Rice," he says on the other end. Suddenly I'm wide awake. It's Sunday morning.

"Don't tell me."

"They found him this morning. You better get over here."

∾

After a quick shower and a reset, Zara and I grab fast food from the first place we pass on the way to Weton, New Hampshire. It's a small town about forty-five minutes from Collins, but only about twenty from the Adams County offices. Though it's still within the two-hour radius the killer has stuck to so far.

"Who found him?" Zara asks, her mouth half full of hash browns.

"His wife apparently," I say, relaying what Rice told me over the phone. He was brief and didn't provide a lot of detail, but it was enough to confirm the same killer struck again.

"There goes the predator angle," she says. "Most of those guys are single."

"Not necessarily. Some predators only act violent toward certain people. And given this guy was most likely out on a date with our killer, it already tells us he had no problem cheating on his wife. There are those men who will do unspeakable things with other people, but not those that they married." Though I have no proof of any of that, and right now it's still all supposition. But for some reason, this *feels* right. This could still fit our profile. Our killer could have decided to take justice into their own hands. But is it really justice? Or revenge? Are they getting back at all these men for something they did to her personally or is she just doing what the law never could?

I have to admit, I'm already conflicted about it.

Because at its core, this man died on our watch. Either from a series of bad luck or bad decisions—I don't know which—he was killed when we might have been able to save him. I don't like the implications of that. I don't like that we dropped the ball. And as we drive, I start to get that pit in my stomach again. The one that makes me want to shed my own skin because it doesn't really belong to me.

When we arrive to Weton, I'm still sick on the stomach,

but I down a big gulp of lukewarm coffee to try and stave it off. Zara and I get out, approaching the scene, with our badges on display. This will be our first opportunity to see one of these killings up close, before all the evidence is collected.

Rice meets us at the police line, still wearing the same suit from last night. "C'mon," he says, waving us through.

"This was one of the towns you mentioned last night, wasn't it?" I ask.

He nods, leading us into the house. Flashing red and blue lights reflect off the windows. "Honestly, this is the fastest anyone has found the victim. The wife wasn't supposed to be home until tonight. But she cut her trip short and came home early."

"How is she doing?" I ask.

"Physically, she's fine. But from the shock on her face, I don't think she knew her husband was seeing anyone else. She certainly didn't expect anything like this. I'm not sure anyone ever does." He trails off as we walk into the living room.

The victim is lying face up, completely naked, his arms crossed over his chest. His genitals have been completely severed, and there is a massive pool of blood beneath the body. There is also blood splatter all over the place.

"It's a massacre," Zara says.

"Here," Rice hands each of us a pair of booties and gloves which we slip on, careful not to contaminate the scene. Forensics teams are already on site, gathering up evidence, taking photographs, while the Weton police stand guard outside.

"Five," Rice says. "In the same number of weeks. If we don't stop this guy—"

"We think the killer may be female," I say.

"Female?" he asks.

"She could be the killer, or she could be working with the killer. Either way, she's involved." I crouch down to take a closer look at our victim. His eyes are still open, and the closer I get, the more pungent he smells. As I take a look at his neck,

I see a small hole right in the side where blood leaked out before coagulating. "What's the diameter of this?" I ask one of the techs.

"About three-quarters of an inch," she replies, then goes back to her job.

"We still don't know what's making these holes, do we?" I ask Zara.

She shakes her head. "But they've been present on each victim."

"Whatever it is, it's how she kills them, I'm sure of it. She probably catches them off-guard, either while their backs are turned or when they're not ready for it. And then once they're dead she goes about…preparing them."

"She better be wearing a hazmat suit for all the evidence she has to be taking with her," Rice says, looking around.

I have to agree. The level of carnage here is beyond what I would consider normal. This is someone with an agenda—something to prove. And she's not stopping until she's eviscerated every person she feels is responsible for her pain. I was wrong before. This isn't an emotionless killer. We're looking for someone who has an axe to grind and will stop at nothing to grind it.

"What about the victim's phone?"

"Here," another one of the techs says, holding out the phone in an evidence bag. It looks almost identical to the one Eastly tried to dispose of, except the phone in this one has been cracked and smashed.

"Looks like someone might be getting nervous," Zara says.

"Or smarter. She has to know the phones provide a lead back on her." That reminds me. I turn to Rice. "We need to examine the other phones from the rest of the cases. They may be able to provide us with more information about this woman."

Rice grimaces. "I'll requisition them this morning. But that's going to be a lot of driving."

"I'm not worried," I tell him. "We have backup on the way. What's the situation over in Collins?"

"Dutton and her people were on patrol all night. There was some civil unrest, but nothing that they couldn't handle. It's a small tourist town. The criminal element doesn't exactly thrive there. Though she did tell me she heard rumblings that some of the officers who quit were planning their own form of vigilante justice. But right now, those are nothing but rumors."

My jaw almost falls open. "What are they planning on doing? Taking over the town themselves? All for what, so we'll release Eastly?"

He holds up his hands. "I have no idea. I'm just telling you what she heard."

Zara comes up beside me, out of the earshot of the others. "Garrett might actually be planning something. He was out last night, remember? He knows his future is on the line here too, especially if we can prove he and the chief conspired to cover up his brother's crimes."

She's right. Hopefully Sheriff Dutton can handle the situation, at least until we have the evidence we need. I take one last look around. "I don't expect it, but let us know if you come up with any fingerprints or anything else solid. Maybe now that we're making her more nervous, she'll make a mistake."

"Do you think she'll keep to her timeline?" Rice asks.

"I wish I could say. But for someone like this, my bet is she's determined to finish what she started. And we don't know how many victims she's going after. If she feels like we're closing in or threatened in any way, she might panic and start killing more frequently."

My phone buzzes in my pocket before I can say anything else. "Slate," I say.

"Agent Slate, this is Agent Sandel. We should be in New Hampshire in the next few hours. Where should we meet you?"

I pause for a moment. Wallace sent Sandel? Zara cocks her head at me and I mouth his name. Her eyebrows go up in surprise.

"Meet us at the Adams County offices, off Route twenty-nine," I tell him after I've composed myself again. That couldn't be coincidence, could it?

"Will do. We'll see you in a few hours."

I slip my phone back in my pocket. "Did Wallace know they were at the party?" I ask Zara.

She shakes her head. "I don't think so. Maybe he's sending him because he didn't want to send anyone we were too familiar with. Given everything that's going on back home."

"Problem?" Rice asks.

"Just FBI stuff, not an issue," I tell him. I don't need Rice thinking we're anything but professional. "Zara and I are going to keep working on tracking down this woman. Get us those phones as soon as you can."

"I will, though I feel like the urgency of the situation has passed us by." He looks down at the corpse again.

"We can't afford to let our guard down. Especially not now." Rice gives me a resigned nod as we head back out.

Outside, Zara and I take a minute to walk the property. As best I can tell, the killer probably entered and left through the side door. It doesn't face the street and while not completely obscured, it probably provided enough cover for her to slip away unnoticed, especially that late at night. What I can't get over, though, is the amount of blood. She had to have been covered in it. And that should have left footprints, or marks or *something*. But as far as I could see, the inside of the house was clean, except for the murder location.

The outside is very much the same. No bloody handprints, footprints, nothing. It's like she wore a shield that prevented her from getting any evidence on her. If that holds, it's going to make proving she was here very difficult.

"Hey, you okay?" Zara asks. "You seemed a little…off in there."

I take a deep breath. She noticed after all. I thought I'd done a better job covering it. "I'm just tired. And hungry. We ran ourselves ragged yesterday and for what? We didn't stop the killer and right now we're no closer to finding her. We aren't even sure it is a her."

"Then let's go eat," she says. "I can treat you to a birthday lunch. We're driving ourselves crazy here. I say we go for some complex carbs, with some even more complex dairy items and we just pig out for the rest of the day. You can't tell me that doesn't sound like a good plan."

The thought of sitting down at an actual table to eat something does sound good right now. Whatever that was we had on the way over here wasn't filling at all.

"Fine. You wore me down."

"I knew I would," she replies, winking.

Chapter Twenty

WE MANAGE to find a cute little restaurant off the side of the road halfway back to Rice's office. It's a small, one-story diner, set back from the road enough so a few trees obscure part of it. Zara pulls us in, and parks off to the side. I realize, once we're close enough, it's another home that's been converted. The sign on the door simply says *Lottie's*.

Inside it's much the same as the Red Stone Inn. A countertop bar runs along the back of the large room, and freestanding tables take up the rest. About half of them are full and a waitress in a muted pink uniform comes by with a pot of coffee in her hand and a pen tucked behind her ear. "Just sit anywhere, we'll be with you shortly."

We take a table near the back and as soon as I sit down, I feel like I'm almost ready to collapse. I hadn't realized how much weight was bearing down on me in this case. It's been more than I was prepared for, especially coming off everything with the Organization. Without warning, it all comes flooding to the front, and I feel the sting of tears in my eyes. I look away quickly, hoping Zara hasn't seen, but I know she already has. Everything from the past month hits me, including my fights with Liam over that damn letter, and I can barely contain myself.

Before I know it, Zara is offering me a travel tissue package. I don't know where she produced it from, but it's a welcome relief. I know more than a few people are already staring at the woman who can't keep it together in the back of the restaurant.

I wipe my nose a few times, doing my best to compose myself when the waitress arrives.

"Two waters, please, and can you give us a few minutes?" Zara asks.

"Sure, hon. Just flag me down whenever you're ready." I see her sneak a look at me in my periphery and when I turn back to Zara her brows are drawn in concern.

"I know," I say, waving it off.

"I hate seeing you like this," she says. "But if you still aren't ready to talk about it, that's okay. We can just eat. You're probably exhausted. I know I am."

What am I doing? I'm sitting here, lying to my best friend and she's not even mad about it. Wouldn't I be mad if I were in her position? If she was this upset, wouldn't I be doing everything I could to help her feel better? And yet, here I am, pretending once again like nothing is the matter. It's like ever since that letter arrived I've just decided to close myself off, and I'm not even sure why. Maybe Wallace should have benched me after all.

"A letter came for me in the mail. From my mother." The urge to slap my hand across my mouth is so strong I actually hold my hand down with my other arm. I don't even know why I said it. It's like I'm fighting a war inside myself, and for the first time, the other side has shown up for the fight.

"What?" she asks, leaning forward. "Your *mother?*"

It's out now, I might as well tell her. Obviously, there's some part of me that wants to, otherwise I never would have said anything in the first place. I take a deep breath. "It arrived about a month ago, when I was still recovering after being abducted."

"By Hunter, right," she says. She was right there with me all during my recovery. She knows better than anyone, except maybe Liam.

"It just…arrived one day. It wasn't even by mail; it was through a delivery service. Someone paid to have that hand-delivered to me."

"Did it have a return address?" she asks.

"No return address, no idea of who paid for it to be delivered." I almost choke on the last word but manage to keep my composure. Suddenly my throat is dry, and I grab the water, downing half of it.

"So she must have mailed it before she died and set it up to be delivered to you when you were older. What day was it exactly?"

I shake my head. "No, it had my address on it. My address now, written in her handwriting. There's no way she could have known where I would be living seventeen years ago when she died. It doesn't make any sense." That's what I've been going over and over in my head. That's how I know it can't be from her. And yet, it carries all her hallmarks.

"What did the letter say?" she asks.

"In short, it said she would see me soon." I take another gulp of water. I'm terrified she'll think I'm crazy because none of it makes sense. "I think…I might need to go back home."

"Back to Virginia?" She makes the face she always makes when she's thinking hard. "And you're sure it's in your mother's handwriting?"

"I would recognize it anywhere," I say.

"Someone is obviously trying to bait you," she replies. "But why? Who would even know about your mother?"

"It's in my record at the Bureau," I say, glad that she's completely glossed over the fact that I kept this from her for almost a month. "Maybe Hunter leaked it to someone in the Organization, and they're trying to lure me into another trap. He had access to all my files and had plenty of time to do something with them."

"But what's the point?" she asks. "Why tell you to come home? And why do it in such a cryptic way?"

I shake my head. "Two very good questions."

"Did you bring it in for handwriting analysis? If someone faked it, the boys down in tech services should be able to figure it out pretty quick. We could even take it to Hunter, confront him with it."

"No, Liam insisted I should keep it. But right before we left I threw it away. It's what we've been arguing about the past couple of weeks."

"Why would you throw it away?" she asks. "It's the only clue as to who could be targeting you. You might have a stalker."

I let out a frustrated breath. "That's just it. After everything I've been through with the Organization, with Camille, with Dani and Chris...I just couldn't handle being the subject of another investigation. I can't deal with the idea that someone else out there might be watching me. I had to sit, night after night, worrying about what Camille might do, back before I even knew her name. Remember what that was like?"

She nods, watching me intently.

"I just...I can't put myself through that again. I don't even want to acknowledge it. I don't want to live like I'm back under a constant microscope."

"Emily," Zara says, reaching her hand across the table. "I know you don't want to hear this. But ignoring the problem won't make it go away. And you're allowing yourself to be vulnerable to someone who may want to hurt you. I don't want to alarm you; I know what you've been through. But you need to take this seriously."

I feel the tears prickle at the corners of my eyes again.

Deep down I know that. But I didn't want to acknowledge it. I still don't. I want to pretend like that letter never darkened my doorstep.

Reaching out, I take her hand. "You're right. I know."

"It could be nothing more than a simple prank," she adds. "You have been on TV a lot lately. Maybe someone took notice and wanted to mess with you a little. Though, I have to admit, that's the strangest way I've ever heard of doing that."

I give her a fake smile. "I don't know. I always do seem to attract the craziest people. What's one more?"

"What did Liam say about it?" she asks.

I pull my hand away and take another sip of water. "The same thing you did. He thinks I should have tech services analyze it to determine if it's even genuine. Then he thinks we should head down to Virginia, see for ourselves what's going on. It's been a whole thing."

"No wonder you were on edge the other night at your party. I thought you might just be anxious about turning twenty-nine. But then Raoul said you guys were arguing or something. I didn't think you would want to get into it during the party, and then this whole thing with the murder happened and…" She trails off. "I probably should have followed up sooner."

"You're worried you didn't keep an eye on me enough?" I ask, incredulous. "I've been lying to you for a solid month!"

"Yeah, but it's not like you didn't have a good reason." She glares at me under hooded eyes. "You had a good reason, right?" Somehow she manages to strike the perfect balance between joking and serious.

"You know that weird feeling I've been telling you about, the one where I don't quite feel like myself?" She nods. "It started when this letter showed up. I don't know what it is, but it's like it triggered something."

"Like a memory?"

I shrug. "Nothing conscious, at least not that I've realized. It's more like the memory of a feeling. And it's a very, very bad feeling. I just wish it would go away. I've never felt so uncomfortable in my own skin in my life."

"Em, we'll get to the bottom of it," she says. "You have me. You have Liam. You're not alone in this. Obviously, you're dealing with some kind of repressed trauma."

I chuckle. "Who are you, Dr. Frost?"

"No, if I were, I'd sound like this." She clears her throat. "You have to let yourself *feel* your feelings, Emily. You can't just shut them out forever. That will be a hundred and fifty dollars please. Also look at all my wonderful plants. Can't you see how much I like plants?" Her voice is a close-enough impression that I can actually see him saying it and I laugh, despite how I've been feeling.

"He does have a lot of plants in there." I take a second to wipe my eyes again. Already I'm feeling better.

"Yeah, I know. It's like, great, you've got a green thumb. Now put it away before someone gets hurt."

That gets an even bigger laugh out of me.

"Listen to me. We are going to sit here until we both add at least an inch to our waistlines, then we are going to go track down the rest of these victims, figure out if your hunch is correct and *then* we are going to find ourselves a killer, got it?"

I nod, more grateful than I can say. Work is the one thing that will help me keep my mind off things, and Zara knows it.

"Good." She waves the waitress over who gives us a suspicious eye as she approaches.

"Can I start you off with some coffee?"

Zara shakes her head. "Nope. We're celebrating. Two mimosas." She looks down at the empty table between us. "And two menus."

The waitress hikes up her eyebrows before she leaves. "I'm not sure they have mimosas here."

"They better have something. You need to calm your nerves and the odds of getting a whiskey on the rocks are pretty slim. Don't worry, when we get back home I'll take you out properly."

"Yeah, if this case doesn't kill me first."

"If it does, at least you'll be full."

Chapter Twenty-One

AFTER SPILLING the beans to Zara, I have to admit I feel marginally better. Probably because I'm not harboring this secret anymore. As we ate, she asked me more questions about the letter. Now I'm second-guessing my decision to trash it, though I can always fish it back out when I get home. I highly doubt Liam is going to take out my trash when I'm not there. It's a good thing he made me save it as long as I have, otherwise she's right. I would have lost the only piece of evidence I have that could shed light on who might be trying to intimidate me.

Still, that feeling deep in the pit of my stomach won't completely go away. What's even more aggravating is I can't seem to get a handle on it. It's just sitting there, a part of my past—or my perceived past—that I can't access, which doesn't make sense. I don't recall any traumatic periods in my childhood, things I would have blocked out. Then again, if I blocked them out, I might not even know I'm concealing them.

Man, Frost is going to have a field day with me when I get back. I just hope he doesn't recommend I go off duty. I know from experience that is the worst thing they can do with me. I *need* something to focus on, otherwise I'll start to spiral. It happened after Matt died and I'm sure it will happen again if I'm not careful.

Zara manages to convince me to eat an entire bowl of chicken alfredo, along with a salad and two breadsticks while she scarfs down the meatloaf. Turns out Lottie's does have mimosas after all, and after two each, we're both skirting the limit of how much we can take and still work effectively. All I know is after a satisfying meal like that all I want to do is go back to our hotel room and lie on the bed for the next fourteen hours.

Instead, we get started on the next phase of the investigation, heading to the nearest town, Highburg, to examine the victim's phone. Rice calls while we're on the way, letting us know they're expecting us there.

Thankfully, the Highburg police are nothing but helpful and cooperative. They already have the evidence box ready for us when we arrive, allowing Zara to get to work on Nicholas Valentine's cell phone. He was the victim the week before Schmidt, and found two days later by a neighbor who smelled something rotten coming from his house.

"Okay," Zara says, using her app on Valentine's phone. "This should just take a few minutes."

I turn to the town's chief, who was there to greet us personally. "Did you know him? Valentine?"

The chief, a heavyset man with a handlebar moustache and his hands hooked in his belt shakes his head. "Can't say I did. Never met him before we found his body. Though he'd been living in town about four years."

"Any idea of where he came from before that?"

"Somewhere out west, I think. Though I'm not sure."

"What about next-of-kin?" I ask.

"We tried, but could never find anyone," the chief says.

"That's because Valentine wasn't his real name." Zara looks up, after going through the data pulled from the man's phone. "It was a pseudonym. His real name was Charles Koss."

"How did you know that? We went through all his messages, emails—"

"But not his internet gaming history," she says. "The handle he uses: *Roxxor469* has its own history, and it was originally registered to a Mr. Charlie Koss, of Sacramento California." She turns her laptop so we can see it.

"How in the hell did you—"

"A gamer username is as unique as any person," she says. "And good ones are getting harder and harder to come by. Mr. Koss obviously didn't want to give up his, so he just kept it, thinking no one would ever look under his gaming history. Thankfully for us, I am fully invested in the world of online multiplayer games." She beams at us.

"She really is a genius at this stuff," I tell the chief.

"And the reason he changed his name was because Charles Koss is a registered sex offender in the state of California. Which means he would have had to notify you and all his neighbors when he moved to town."

"You're kidding," I say.

She shakes her head. "I wish I was. Here, look. Six reported assaults, two convictions, he even did some jail time. Looks like when he got out of prison he headed east, looking for a fresh start."

"And so he came up here," the chief says. "Dammit. Do I have to do a background check on every citizen that lives here?"

"I think this is a pretty unique case, Chief." I lean over Zara's shoulder to take a closer look at the information she's found on Valentine, or his alter-ego. But there's his picture, right on the sex offender website. Compared with the picture in the evidence file, there's no mistaking it's him.

"Fits your theory," Zara says.

"Anything on the dating apps?" I ask.

She transfers the information from her phone to her computer. For a minute I have a hard time reading it, seeing as it all looks like nothing more than code. Then I see a string of messages pop up. The header shows they're using one of the big dating apps. "There."

"Got it," she says. "Switching back to graphical." Another window opens to show the texts back and forth between Valentine and a woman named Ainsley. But the picture that accompanies the profile is undoubtedly the same woman that Schmidt went out with, though it appears she's wearing a wig.

"Damn. Both of them using assumed identities. Both of them lying to the other."

"That's online dating for ya," the chief says, his expression smug. "Can't trust people if you can't look 'em in the eye."

Normally I'd agree. But I've seen the statistics. People who match on these sites who are honest about themselves generally have a statistically better chance at staying together than people who don't meet online. "I think we have what we came for," I tell Zara and she begins to pack up.

"Anything else we can do for you?" the chief asks.

I give his hand a firm shake. "That's it. Thanks for all your help. It's nice to know not every local department out here hates us."

"Naw," the chief says. "Too much hate in this world for us to be spreading it around. You two take care."

We spend the rest of the afternoon driving to Boone and then on to Graystone. While we don't find anything on Robert Hainsworth, we manage to piece together from one of the officers who went to high school with James Wheeldon that he had a reputation back in high school with some of the girls. Nothing ever came of it, but by his senior year, girls had learned to stay away from him. Apparently, that had made him an angry young man and an even angrier adult. While it's not as solid as what we have on Valentine or Schmidt, I'm willing to bet Wheeldon's abusive behavior didn't stop in high school. It's enough that I'm confident in saying that our killer is specifically targeting men with histories of abuse toward women.

The question is, how does this woman know who these men are? It's taking the combined work of two FBI agents just to get basic backgrounds on these men. How would the killer know about them, especially like in the case of Valentine as he changed his name?

It's something I'm very much looking forward to asking her as soon as we find her. Unfortunately, we still don't have a real name for the woman yet. I'm tempted to put her face on the evening news to see if anyone recognizes her, but that would *really* spook her and there's no guarantee we'd get anything solid. Who's to say she doesn't go about her normal life using a different name and appearance?

By the time we get back to Rice's office, it's past eight. We had agreed to give him an update as soon as we had it, and given all the information we've learned today, I figured it was a lot easier to do that in person than over the phone. Also, I'm anxious to hear if he's made any progress with Eastly. I wish I could have been in the room when Rice told him he no longer had any bargaining chips.

This day has worn me down to the bone. Usually, I try not to work on my birthday. Not that I *need* to be off for any particular reason, I just like taking the day for myself. Last year Matt and I went out to the coast and just had a day on the beach. Unlike most people, I enjoy the beach when it's cold. Not to mention it's usually deserted. We had dinner at a nice seafood restaurant and then watched the sunset on the way back.

But this year I knew it would be better if I kept myself busy. So I wasn't perturbed when this case came along. Given that I still have a lot of conflicted feelings about Matt, it was better that I didn't focus on the day too much and just treated it like any other day. I think Dr. Frost would be proud of me, because that seems to have worked.

As we round the corner to the conference room, I see Rice is already inside. But he's not alone. Two other people sit with their backs to us, watching as he's pointing to the map he hung up on the wall of all the places the killer has struck.

I stop short. "Shit."

"What?" Zara says, then looks in on the conference room. "Oh. Right."

We'd been going so hard all day I'd completely forgotten. I trudge up to the glass door and push in, drawing the attention of everyone in the room. "Agent Sandel, Agent Kane. Good to see you again."

They both stand, though Sandel wears a dark expression. "Agent Slate. Glad you could finally join us."

"What time did you get in?" I ask, trying to keep the sheepishness out of my voice.

"Around four. We thought you'd be here to meet us," he says. Though I don't detect any animosity in his voice.

"We were chasing down a possible lead on our killer," I say, maintaining my composure. I hate that I dropped the ball on meeting them. It would have been more conducive for me to be here to introduce them to Rice. "How was the drive?"

Sandel exchanges a look with Kane. "Not bad. We got into Boston around eleven this morning and it was about a three-hour drive from there. Pretty. Never been up to this side of the country before."

"Wait, they *flew* you?" Zara asks.

"Of course. You didn't think we drove all the way up here, did you?" Sandel asks.

Zara shoots me a look. "I'm going back with them. You can drive your own butt home."

"Wait, *you* drove?" Agent Kane asks.

"It's a long story, I don't want to get into it," I tell them.

"I'm sorry we weren't here to meet you. But I think we've discovered something important about the case."

"I was just giving them the rundown on all the places the killer has hit so far," Rice says.

"Get anything from Eastly?" I ask.

He furrows his brow. "Unfortunately no. Despite no way out, he's refusing to talk. I informed him and Wilcox that they no longer had a leg to stand on, but Eastly still won't admit to anything solid. Wilcox said they'd get back to us later this week."

I shake my head. Some men are so damn stubborn. Fine, if he wants to go down fighting, that's his prerogative. In the meantime, I have a killer to catch. I can't waste any more time on Eastly.

"Who's Eastly?" Sandel asks.

"Local chief up here who was obstructing the case. But we got it worked out," I tell him. Is it weird that Sandel and Kane were at my birthday party a few days ago and now they're here? Yes. Should I be cautious around them? Also yes. I don't know what Wallace is planning or if this really is a matter of coincidence, but I can't afford to focus on that right now. We need to stop this killer before she strikes again and despite our gains today, we're still a long way off. Which means I can't afford to try and freeze Sandel and Kane out. Even if I could, I don't want to be like that, like Eastly. Zara and I have made a concerted effort to get the egos out of the FBI and if I were to stonewall them, it would only be taking us in the wrong direction. I just have to hope this doesn't come back to bite me on the ass.

"Did you get a chance to review the most recent murder?" I ask.

"Sheriff Dutton gave us the rundown when we arrived," Sandel says. "But we haven't seen anything official."

"Okay, then let me start at the beginning."

Chapter Twenty-Two

I'll ADMIT, it was a good meeting. Sandel and Kane listened intently, and neither of them tried to insert themselves into the investigation needlessly. After giving everyone all the data we had, I suggested that we start fresh tomorrow morning. Sandel and Kane followed us back up to the Best Western, where they got rooms of their own. I figured it would probably be easiest if we were all staying in the same place. Plus, for a budget hotel, it's got a great view.

"What do you think? Did that go okay?" I ask as Zara comes out of the bathroom; her face covered in moisturizer.

"Hell yeah it went okay. Have you *seen* our briefings back home? Half the guys in those rooms feel the need to interrupt every five seconds with either an unnecessary suggestion, a dumb comment, or a question that's already been answered. Compared to that, this was stellar." She hops on the bed, pulling the covers up around her.

"I just can't get over the fact Wallace sent those two, out of everyone else in our department. It just makes me feel like I'm being watched again."

"You kinda did go over his head with the whole Hunter fiasco. Maybe this is his way of sending a signal."

"That what? Sandel and Kane are here to keep me in line?"

She shrugs. "Maybe. Look at it this way though. What if they go back and there's nothing to report?"

"You mean I need to be on my best behavior for the rest of this case." I shoot her *the look.*

She laughs, shaking her head. "You don't need to worry; you've got nothing to hide. And you handled this evening great. Even if they're in their rooms skyping with Wallace right now, what are they going to say? You're professional and you're doing a good job of handling this case?" She pulls the covers up to her mouth. "*Oh, no. The horror.*"

"Okay, smartass. But when it's your butt on the line I'd like to see you this confident."

"I'm telling you; you're worrying for nothing. Sandel and Kane aren't the enemy. They're here to help."

I take a deep breath. "I hope you're right." I'm getting ready to get in my own bed when my phone vibrates. I check the call and see it's Liam.

"I'm going to take this out in the hall, so I don't disturb your beauty sleep."

"Tell that Irish hunk hi for me," she says, winking. "Oh, and Em? Happy Birthday."

I mouth *thanks* and then head out into the hall before answering. "Hey."

"Hey there," he says. "I'm glad I caught you before you went to bed. I wanted to wish you a happy birthday."

"How do you know I'm not already in bed?" I say, teasing.

"Because your voice would be more yawn-y," he replies.

"More yawn-y?"

"Yeah, when you get really tired you start yawning every other word and you can just hear it in your voice. But you still sound wide awake." Well, that's horrifying. I had no idea I did that.

"Yeah, we just got back from a wrap-up meeting with the

agents Wallace sent up. It's the same two from my party the other night. Do you think that's weird?"

"Who, Elliott and Nadia? Not really. They both just closed a series of small cases a few days ago. As far as I can tell, everyone else in the office is busy with other work, or still under investigation from IA, which means they can't leave. But since they weren't here when everything went down, they're not under suspicion. Wallace probably just chose them because they were available."

"I guess," I say. "I think maybe I'm just still a little on edge from everything with the Organization and Camille."

"You have every right to be," he says. I can just imagine him sitting on the couch, Timber right beside him, his head on Liam's thigh as Liam scratches behind his ear.

"How's my other boy doing?"

"Great. Sustaining himself on bacon, hamburgers, and waffles."

"Liam! You can't feed him that stuff all the time, it's not good for him."

He laughs on the other end. "I'm only kidding. He's been giving me puppy dog eyes every time I sit down to eat, but so far he's only managed a couple of pieces of sliced turkey." He waits a beat. "How's the case going?"

"Making progress, but it's slow. She's just out there, planning her next kill, and we're no closer to finding her."

"Maybe with the four of you things will go quicker," he suggests. I know he's just trying to be supportive, but I'm not so sure. This woman, if she really is the killer, has managed to conceal her identity enough that we still don't know who she is. And she's been smart enough never to hit the same town twice, which makes determining her future targets difficult. But at least now we know the types of men she's going after. That should help narrow the field a bit.

"Hey," I say, changing the conversation. "I told Zara about the letter."

He waits a beat. "What did she say?"

I scoff. "The same thing you did. And if you try to tell me *I told you so…*"

"What, do I sound like a man with a death wish?" he jokes. "I'd rather keep my head attached to my shoulders, thank you." I smile again, glad that we seem to be headed back to the place we left. The place that I tore us away from. I know what Dr. Frost says about my guilt, but in this case it's true. I'm the one who put up all these unnecessary barriers. I just don't know why.

"Keep me updated on how things go. Someone here misses you."

"Tell him I'll be back as soon as I can. This will have to end one way or another. She can't just keep killing these men, not without someone finding out who she is. I'd plaster her face all over the country if I didn't think it would just make her speed up her timetable."

"You'll figure it out," Liam says. "You always do."

I grin, looking at the ugly pattern of the hallway carpet. "Thanks for calling."

"Sleep well. As soon as you get home, I'm taking you out for a *real* birthday celebration."

After we say our goodbyes I head back into the room, only to find Zara staring at me from the edge of her covers. "What?"

"It's just nice to see you happy again. You were missing that for a long time."

I head into the bathroom and change into my sleep clothes. "He's a good person. And he puts up with more than he should have to."

"Em," she says, warning in her voice. Both Zara and Dr. Frost have talked to me about my underlying self-esteem issues.

"I know, I know. But he has. He was kidnapped and

almost killed because of me. What kind of person doesn't leave after that?"

"The kind who loves you?" I glance up again and see she's giving me that expectant look.

"You're probably right," I say. I flop back on the bed, my arms spread wide. "Why does this relationship stuff have to be so complicated? Why can't it be more like work? Victim, killer, that's easy enough to understand, right?"

"What are you talking about?" Zara asks. "You know better than anyone the relationship between the victim and the killer can range from simple to overly complex. In fact, a killer's relationship with their victim can be one of the most convoluted and involved types of relationships out there. Toxic, but ultimately complex."

I blow out a long breath. "I guess," I say, then I sit up. "So then what is our killer's relationship with these men? She's obviously drawing them in, trapping them. But to do that, she's…what? Catering to them?"

"Performing for them," Zara says. "It's an act."

I nod. "You're right. None of the victims share similar traits, tastes or interests. She's a chameleon, changing to fit each individual victim."

"She becomes whatever they want her to be, which immediately makes them attracted to her."

"And to do that, she'd have to be a pretty damn good actor," I say.

"Are you thinking she might have a theater or acting background?" Zara asks.

"Maybe not anything so formal. But she knows people, she knows how to cater to them. I'd say that at least puts her in the service industry, wouldn't you?"

"Definitely. But half the jobs out there are service jobs. How do we narrow it down?"

I give her a big grin. "What kind of service job caters

specifically to men? To their fantasies of what a woman should be?"

Her eyes light up. "Em, sometimes I think you're a genius."

Chapter Twenty-Three

THE FOLLOWING morning we update Sandel and Kane on our new theory and leave them to continue digging into the histories of the victims. Meanwhile, Zara and I drive an hour and a half down to Portland, Maine, to the closest strip club to the area where all the killings have taken place. My hunch is our killer decided to strike in remote places that aren't anywhere near where she lives. She could have specifically targeted those towns because they were so far away. This whole time we've been looking at a radius around a general area, thinking she was local to a specific location central to all the killings when in fact she may be making the trek out there each weekend.

When we pull up, the building is unmistakable. It's an all-black two-story converted warehouse called *The Kitty's Leash* and it advertises itself as the area's largest twenty-four hour-seven day a week strip club.

"You know what's going to happen as soon as we walk in there," Zara says.

"I know," I reply, resigning myself to what's coming. Still, I make sure my badge is easily visible, along with my gun. I'm in no mood for some asshole to jerk us around today.

A bouncer at the door notes our badges, but doesn't offer

any resistance to us heading in. Once inside, we're assaulted by a collage of pink and purple neon, along with a bass-heavy soundtrack that makes it almost impossible for me to hear myself think, much less try to talk to anyone. Seeing as it's Monday morning I don't expect the place to be very busy, but I'm wrong. There are dozens of patrons inside, and the place seems as raucous as it would on a Saturday night. Then again, I don't normally frequent strip clubs, so I have no idea if this is the norm or not.

Right past the door a young woman sits in a small alcove, playing on her phone. She looks up when she sees us and points to the sign beside her which declares the entrance fee for men is thirty dollars. Women get in free.

"Looks about right," I yell to Zara. I wave my hand in front of the girl to get her attention again. "We need to see the manager."

She hooks an unhelpful thumb into the main room. I motion for Zara to follow, maybe we'll have better luck at the bar. The base is so loud it's like someone is hitting a drum right beside my ear. I catch a few furtive glances from some of the guys, as well as the scantily clad waitstaff, but seeing as I have all my clothes on, none of them pay me any attention for very long.

"We need to see the manager on duty!" I yell to the bartender. Her hair is fire-engine red, and she's got at least four piercings in her nose alone.

"You looking for an application?" she yells back. "I got them here behind the bar."

I hold up my badge hoping that will make my meaning clear.

She shoots us a wink of understanding and reaches up under the bar. I assume there's some kind of panic switch under there, so she can notify management quickly in the event something gets out of control.

A few minutes later, a man in an immaculate Gucci suit

approaches. The top button of his dress shirt is undone, and he isn't wearing a tie, but I can already tell this is a man who takes care of his appearance. He's trim, though not so much that I don't believe he spends a lot of time at the gym.

Before he even reaches us, I feel his eyes crawling all over both Zara and me. But before he can utter a word, I show him my badge and his face falls, though he retains a smirk. He motions for us to follow him, and we circle around the large room, staying close to the wall beside the left-most stage. As soon as we're through the large black door he holds open for us, the noise level drops considerably.

"Usually it's not this busy this time of week," he says, his voice is smoother than I'd anticipated. "But there's some sort of fisherman's congregation going on all week. It's been like this since Friday. I had to bring in some extra girls from Boston just to cover all the shifts."

"And you are?" I ask.

"Malcolm Stipes. Co-owner. I run this place with my cousins and brother." He holds out his hand.

I give it a quick shake. "Agents Slate and Foley, FBI," I tell him.

"I saw the badge. Too bad. You two would fit right in here. And you can't beat the tips." He turns and trots up a few short stairs to a hallway with three doors, opening the first one for us. "So what does the FBI want to do with us? Looking to go undercover?"

It takes all my willpower to ignore the smarmy comment. "We're looking for someone. Possibly a former employee." I pull up the picture on my phone and show it to him. Once we're all inside the office he takes a second to study it.

"Yeah...that looks like..." he rounds the desk, sitting in the only chair in the room which faces a computer. A few seconds later he has an employee file pulled up. "Sammie."

On the screen is the same girl we have from both Schmidt's phone as well as Valentine's. Except in this picture she's blonde, and her hair is much shorter, styled in a pixie cut.

"Samantha Morris," I say, reading the file. "How long has she been employed here?"

"She was with us about six months," he says, reading the file. "Sweet girl. Had that girl-next-door vibe, if you know what I mean. Customers loved her."

"When did she quit?" Zara asks.

He shakes his head. "Didn't. We had to fire her. About two months ago." He turns back to us, giving us a placating smile. "One of the customers tried getting a little too close. Some other clubs, they'll put up with that stuff, even allow the girls to take on after-hours work, if you catch my drift. But it's strictly forbidden here. We don't mess with that."

"You wouldn't happen to be saying that because you're talking to two FBI agents, would you?" I ask.

He shakes his head. "No, I'm serious. I don't want this place getting shut down for prostitution. We find out it's happening; the girl is gone. Zero tolerance policy."

I glance back over his shoulder at Samantha's profile. "Is that what happened with Samantha?"

"No, she...well, she kind of went off on the guy. Started scratching him, biting him, doing anything she could. Even when Lenny—that's our head bouncer—when he pulled her off him, she was still going after him. I've never seen anything like it. She must have taken something before her shift that night."

"Taken something?" I ask.

"Yeah, you know. X or whatever. Something that made her go off her rocker."

"As if being sexually assaulted wasn't enough." I glare at him.

He holds up both hands. "Now wait a minute. Being touched inappropriately comes with the job. All the girls know it. And we do everything we can to keep it to a minimum. But if you expect to work here and think no one is going to brush up against you or make suggestive comments, you're in the wrong business, sister."

"So what did the guy do?" Zara asks, though from her tone I can tell she's as annoyed as I am.

"I dunno, grabbed her butt or something, I wasn't here that night. I only heard it from Paddy. He was on duty. But I did watch the security footage."

I lean forward, placing both my hands on the desk. "Do you still have that footage?"

He's still wearing that damn smarmy grin. "Nah, we erased it a few weeks later. After we were sure we weren't going to get sued."

"And Samantha?" I ask.

"Haven't seen her since. Obviously we had to let her go. She said she understood. Her last paycheck is still here, in fact." He turns to a filing cabinet, rifling through the first folder. "Yeah, here." He holds it out so we can see. Her address is printed right below her name.

"Why not mail it to her?" I ask.

"Tried. But it got returned. Said the address was no longer valid and we didn't have a forwarding address for her."

"Do you have any information on the man she attacked?" I snap a photo of the front of the paycheck, so I at least have a record of her information.

"Yeah, hang on," he says, huffing and turning in his chair again.

"And we'll need a copy of her employment record," Zara says.

"Jeez, what did she do? Rob a bank?" He goes to work on his computer for a minute and I hear the printer on the other side of the room warm up. We finally have a name. And an address, even if it's no longer valid. It at least gives us a starting point. We also may finally have a motive. But right now it's nothing but supposition. I don't want to get ahead of myself.

"Name is Lazlo. Dermont Lazlo."

"He a local?" I ask.

"I've seen him in here a few times, but I don't know where he lives if that's what you're asking. We banned him from returning after what happened, but given the damage she did to him, I was surprised we didn't get hit with a lawsuit."

I grab the printout of Samantha's employment record from the printer. It's basic stuff, but at least it finally gives us some solid information. "Was anyone that still works here good friends with Sammie? Anyone who might have spoken to her since she was fired?" I ask, motioning back to the main room.

He leans back in the chair, locking his hands behind his head. "You can try Shawna, or maybe Monique." He leans forward again. "They go by Diamond and Ariel out there though. Diamond is due up on stage in about five minutes if you want to speak to her before her performance."

I hand him my card. "If you hear from Sammie, call me immediately. I don't care what time of day it is."

He takes the card, that same smile still plastered on his face. "Sure. Whatever you say, beautiful."

I shoot Zara a look and we leave the office, headed back down the hallway. We pass a young woman who can't be older than nineteen and is trying her best to get the back of a very skimpy bra attached.

"Excuse me," I say. "Where can we find Shawna?"

She looks up at me with huge brown eyes. God, she's just a kid. "She's probably in the dressing area, getting ready," she says.

"Here," Zara says, taking hold of the bra straps. "Let me get this." She has the complicated piece of "clothing" sorted and fit in only a few seconds.

"Thanks," the girl says. "I'm so nervous. Today's only my second day at work."

I'd like to ask her more about the conditions here, but she probably hasn't even had time to fully acclimate to what she's doing. Though I hope Shawna will be able to provide us with some more information. "Good luck," I tell her. "You look great."

She beams at us. "Thanks."

I try to think back to what I was doing at that age. I was in college, working at the local sandwich shop. And when I got back to the dorm, I'd always smell like mayo and salami. It's a very different life, but I can see the appeal to a young girl, right out of high school. Flashy outfits, lots of attention, and a ton of cash. And as long as it's all above board, I don't have a problem with it. It's when places like this try to employ underage girls or start their own side businesses, like Stipes was saying back there. That shit won't fly.

"How did you know how to fix that?" I ask Zara as we make our way to the dressing area.

"What, you've never worn an Agent Provocateur Rubi corset with matching bra and panties?" she asks, a sly smile on her lips.

"And you have?" I ask.

"Now I know what to get you for Christmas," she laughs. "Although I guess that's really more of a present for Liam."

Despite everything, Zara still manages to surprise me sometimes.

We reach the dressing area, which only has eight different stalls, of which two are occupied. "Shawna?" I call out.

"Yeah?" A dark-haired woman sticks her head around one of the mirrors, her eyebrows drawing close when she sees us. Her eyes are the most turquoise blue I've ever seen in my life, so much in fact that I'm caught off-guard by them.

"May we have a moment?" I ask.

"I don't have time right now," she says, impatience in her voice. Stipes did say she was due to go on in a few minutes.

"It will only take a second. We just want to ask about Sammie."

She sticks her head around the mirror again, and I can see she's attached a black collar around her neck. "What about her?"

"Have you spoken to her since she was fired?" I ask.

She pulls back, muttering curses under her breath until she emerges again, wearing a silk robe. "Look, I have to get on stage in like three minutes. Can't this wait?"

"We just want to know if you've spoken to her or had contact with her at all since she was fired. Do you know how we can get in contact with her?"

"Why?" Shawna asks. "What's this about?"

"We just need to ask her a few questions," Zara says.

Shawna shakes her head, and I can practically feel the distrust rising up in her. She's had a bad run-in with cops before, I don't even need to ask to know she's already made us. This woman has put up with her fair share of it before. "I'm sorry, I really need to finish getting ready." She turns and disappears behind the mirror again.

I let out a frustrated breath and motion for Zara to follow me back to the hallway.

"She's hiding something," Zara says.

I nod. "My bet is they're still talking. But if Samantha Morris is our killer, I doubt she's going around telling her friends about it."

"Who knows?" Zara asks. "Shawna made us pretty quick; she could be a lookout of sorts. And she might warn Sammie we're on her trail."

She's right. We may have just inadvertently sped up Samantha's clock. "Let's try to find Monique, maybe she's more willing to talk to us."

We're forced to head back out into the main arena, which

has become even more raucous since we left. I return to the bartender and mouth the name *Ariel*. She points me to a young woman serving drinks on the far side of the room. She's decked out in a gorgeous green outfit that's more tasteful than I would have thought in a place like this. The bartender catches her attention and waves her over to us.

"Can I help you?" she yells over the music.

"Monique?" I ask.

"What's this about?" Just like Shawna she's immediately guarded, on edge. Like she's been through this all before.

"We just need to ask a few questions about Samantha Morris," I yell.

She purses her lips, then looks over my shoulder at the bartender, then back at the stage where a new song has begun as Shawna comes trotting out, looking every bit like a million dollars in heels. Finally, Monique motions for us to follow her to the right side of the room. She leads us through a doorway where another man stands, his hands clasped in front of him. These must be the private dance rooms. We pass a few that are already occupied until we come to an empty one. The room doesn't have a door, just the hint of a curtain that only halfway covers the opening. But it's quieter in here, though the music is still being pumped in through overhead speakers.

Monique sets her tray down and takes a seat on one of the couches. "You here about the fight?" she asks.

"Which fight would that be?" I ask as Zara, and I take a seat on the opposite couch. I try not to think about the men who've sat here before me.

"The one that got Sammie fired," she says.

"Have you spoken to her?" I ask. "Since it happened?"

"A few times, yeah," Monique says. "She had to move because she couldn't afford her apartment anymore. This place was keeping her afloat."

"Where'd she move to?" I ask.

Monique shakes her head. "Don't know, never said.

Look, Sammie didn't do nothin' wrong. That guy was all over her. He deserved to have the shit scratched out of him. If I didn't need this job so badly, I would have cut him up myself."

"What did he do?" I ask. I'm willing to bet Monique knows more than Stipes is willing to investigate himself.

"Put his hand down her g-string," Monique replies. "I told her she needed to file an assault charge, but she refused, saying no one would ever believe her. And even if they did, she couldn't afford the court fight. The john was some bigwig. Owns a yacht or something."

I lean back. So the truth comes out. Of course Stipes would chock it up to a drug like ecstasy and gloss over what really happened. A woman was assaulted on their watch, and they fired her for it. "Monique, we really need to find Samantha. Do you have any idea where she might be? Is she still living in town?"

"I think so, but we haven't talked much over the past month," Monique says. "And every time I've called, the line has been busy. I just hope she's doing okay."

"Could you give us her number?" Zara asks.

Monique lets out a long breath. "You're just going to question her? You're not going to arrest her?" she asks.

I have to stop myself from wincing. Given everything we've found out, Samantha is our primary suspect. So I will be arresting her as soon as we find her. But at the same time, I'm getting the feeling we don't have the whole story. "I promise we don't mean Samantha any harm. We just need to ask her some questions, get her side of the story."

I can see she's fighting with herself to trust us or not. And if Sammie ends up in cuffs, she'll never trust another cop again, federal or otherwise. "Okay," she finally says, and rattles off the number. Zara copies it down. "If you find her, please let her know I'm worried about her. I just want to make sure she's okay."

"Did she give you any reason to make you think she wouldn't be okay?" I ask.

"Just…Sammie used to be a really outgoing person, really happy. But after what happened here, she just lost some of that sparkle, you know?"

"Once we talk to her and get all the details, we'll make sure the right people pay for this," I tell her. "Thank you for speaking with us."

She stands, taking her tray with her. "Just don't make me regret it." Once she's gone, Zara turns to me.

"She didn't even ask for our ID. Do you think she knows we're feds?"

I shrug. "I doubt it matters. To her, a cop is a cop." I nod to her notes. "Let's see if you can't use some of that technical know-how to track her down."

Chapter Twenty-Four

"YOU KNOW, if I didn't have to talk to people all night long, I could be a stripper," Zara says as she works on her laptop in the club's parking lot.

"What?" I ask.

"Yeah, I mean the pay's great, fun atmosphere. The only downside is you have to cater to a bunch of creeps."

"You're telling me you'd actually get up on stage and work that pole," I laugh.

Zara shoots me a look under hooded eyes. "If I can sing Ace of Base in a room full of half-drunken people, I think I can dance half-naked to it too."

She's got me there. Zara is one of those people who has no problem performing in front of others, even though it's all very much a show. She's like an introverted extrovert, if there is such a thing. But I'm often in awe of her ability to leave it all out there and go for broke. I'm much too reserved for that; I often end up trying to predict how a certain scenario will play out before it happens, so that I might be better prepared for it.

It only ends up working a small amount of the time. But still, I keep doing it.

"Okay, well, bad news, the phone is off," she says, trying to use the same software to triangulate Samantha's phone that she used on Schmidt's. "I can't get a pingback, which means it's either been turned off or destroyed."

"And would explain why all of Monique's messages are going to voicemail," I say. "Is there no way we can track her down?"

She closes her laptop. "Not without a lot of legwork."

"Sounds perfect for our new friends, don't you think?" I ask.

She only shakes her head. "You're terrible."

I pull out my phone. He answers before it even rings a second time. "Sandel."

"It's Slate. How are things going over there?"

"We've managed to find out more about one of the victims. Bobbie Presley. It turns out his first wife left him because of abuse. Changed her name tried to erase her own past. It took some clever work on Nadia's part to figure it out, and we've even managed to confirm it with the ex-wife, who wasn't happy that we'd managed to find her. Apparently, she'd changed her name so he couldn't find her anymore, moved to Idaho of all places." His words come across succinct and clear, very little emotion attached to them, which makes it difficult for me to get a read on him. He sounds something like a robot reading a book report. "So far everything fits your theory that each of our victims was abusive in some way toward women. I'd say we definitely have our pattern."

"That's good work." I relay everything we've found out about Samantha Morris to him. "Finding Morris has to be our first priority. There was another woman at the strip club, someone who might still be in contact with her. We're going to wait until she's off shift. It's a long shot, but she might lead us right to her."

"Or it could be a waste of time," Sandel says.

"Maybe. But I want you and Agent Kane to look into Morris's background. Go through her social media, anything that might tell us where she could be."

"Very well," he says. "I can also update Wallace, if you like."

I hesitate a moment, looking at Zara. "Sure. That would be helpful."

"We'll let you know if we find anything." He hangs up without another word.

"Huh," Zara says. "I thought maybe he was being stand-offish at the party because he didn't know anyone and felt out of place. Turns out that's just his default setting."

"I still don't understand why you invited them," I tell her, settling into the seat and keeping an eye on the club's employee entrance.

"Well, they seemed nice enough," she says. "And to be honest, you could use a few more friends at the Bureau. You can't keep antagonizing everyone you work with. First there was Nick, who was put on leave and eventually fired. Then there was DuBois who turned out to be a double agent and tried to kill you. And let's not even talk about your problems with Wallace. Ever since Janice was promoted you two have been butting heads like two mountain goats. I just thought it would be nice to have a few people over from work who didn't want your head on a pike."

"Thanks," I tell her, sarcasm seeping from my lips. "But I'd like to point out Nick tried to blackmail the two of us, so he doesn't count. And neither does DuBois. Those were not my fault."

"Okay then," she says. "How many people came to back you up when all that went down?"

"You, Liam, and Janice. Who else do I need?" I ask. What is she getting at here?

Zara holds up three fingers. "Your best friend, your

boyfriend, and your former boss. You need more people in your corner. It's not going to hurt you to have more friends."

"I know," I say, drawing out the last word. "But people are just so much work."

Zara laughs. "Tell me about it." We both watch the back entrance for a solid minute before she speaks again. "Do you really think Shawna is going to lead us right to her?"

I shake my head. "She'd have to be pretty stupid. But I wouldn't be surprised if she gave her a call or text after she was off work."

"But her phone is off," Zara says.

"The phone *Monique* knows about is off. No twenty-something is going to be walking around today without a phone of some kind, I don't care how wild it is up here. She's using a phone; we just need to find out which one."

"Damn," Zara says.

"What now?"

"If I'd known we were going to be here a while I would have peed when I had the chance."

STAKEOUTS REALLY ARE THE WORST. YOU'RE SITTING THERE, doing absolutely nothing as you wait for something that may or may not happen. And I'm not the kind of person who does well with sitting around. Especially not with everything going on. My mind can't seem to stop running all over the place when it doesn't have something to focus on, and I find myself thinking more and more about that stupid letter.

Zara is right, I need to find out who sent it and why. And if it has something to do with either the Organization or Hunter then all the better. It will just give me more ammo to take them down with. I'm sure whoever is left is looking for some retribution. And now that I think about it, I should have anticipated some blowback. I think I was just so relieved for it all to be over with that I didn't allow myself to see the possibility. But I've fought too hard and too long to give up now. That's what they want, and they're not going to get it.

After over four hours in the car, we finally see Shawna emerge from the back door, bundled up in a stylish white coat, her dark hair cascading over it.

"Finally," I say, watching as she walks over to Green RAV4, getting inside. She pulls out of the parking lot without even a glance in our direction.

"Do your thing," Zara says, hitting the button to sit her seat back upright.

I keep a close distance, but not so close as to be noticeable. Shawna is unlikely to go to Samantha, but I'm hoping if we catch her off guard, she might be willing to share more than she did at the club. She knows something is going on, and I'm going to find out what.

We follow her to the dry cleaners where she picks up a large amount of clothes, storing them in the back of her car, then to her bank, probably to deposit all her cash tips. More and more this is looking like a wild goose chase. She's obviously not in a hurry and wasn't spooked by our appearance. I guess she really was just anxious to get out on stage. I imagine it's probably a lot like speaking in front of people where it's probably terrifying for the first solid minute, and then you finally relax and lean into it.

Finally, she parks at what looks like an upscale shopping area. Even though it's chilly, plenty of people are out, buying gifts and enjoying the upcoming holidays. Shawna parks her car in the nearby parking garage and heads down to the mall area, which is mostly outdoors. It's one of those places that is probably teeming in the summer, with movie festivals out on the lawns and kids playing on the gated playgrounds. But today, despite the cloudless sky, it's a bit too cold for people to just sit outside. Shawna heads into the local coffee shop and I spot her take up a seat halfway back, a to-go cup on her table. I'm not sure if she's meeting someone inside or not, but this is the best chance we're going to get.

"Let's do it," I say.

"You're the boss." Zara and I make our way across the open area, headed right for the coffee shop. The wind whips at our jackets, and a sharp chill comes in, dropping the temperature what feels like ten degrees. I can't imagine what it's like up here in January and February. Do people even leave their homes?

Inside the coffee shop, we make it halfway to Shawna's table before she looks up and sees us. Her eyes grow wide and the phone drops from her hand, like she's been frozen to the spot. "Hi, Shawna," I say. "How's the coffee here? Any good?"

"What are you doing here?" she asks. She's stopped blinking, which is never a good sign.

I take the chair across from her while Zara sits at the table beside us. The last thing I want to do is cause some kind of panic. But I need to shock this woman into talking. "Well, we didn't get to finish our conversation from earlier. I was hoping we could do that now."

"Have you been *following* me?" she asks. Even though her voice is hushed, it's loud enough for other patrons to hear and one looks over at us.

I pull out my badge. "My name is Emily Slate. I'm a Special Agent with the FBI," I say.

"The FBI?" she asks, her voice smaller than before.

"Yes. As we told you, we're looking for Samantha Morris. Have you had any contact with her since she was let go at the club?"

"I…" She looks around, trying to figure out her options. I know what she's doing: looking for a way out. But Zara and I have her backed into a corner. "Um…why?" she asks.

"We just need to ask her a few questions, and your boss

and coworkers don't seem to know how to get a hold of her. We thought you might," Zara says.

"But, I mean, what do you want with her?" Shawna asks and I detect a slight waver in her voice. She's scared. Of what, I don't know. But I feel like we're finally on the right track.

"We can't discuss the details of the case with anyone but her," I say. "If you know where to find her, I suggest you tell us."

Shawna's eyes flash down to her phone and back up again, betraying her.

"Do you have Samantha's number? Her *new* number?" I ask.

"I…um…"

"Shawna, let me be very plain. By not helping us you are impeding in an investigation. A *federal* investigation. Now you can either help us locate Samantha right here, or we can drive down to the FBI office in Boston." Technically I can't do anything with Shawna, but I'm betting she doesn't know that. She's as young as I was when I first started at the Bureau, maybe a little younger. And while it would be great if she would help us, I can't compel her to.

"I'm…not supposed to say," she finally says.

"Say what?" Zara asks.

"Anything. Sammie told me if anyone came asking about her, that I hadn't heard from her."

"When did she tell you this?" I ask.

"A couple of weeks back, when she moved out of her apartment," she replies.

"Are you still in contact with her?" I ask.

She bites her lip, then I see something in her break, and she lets out a breath like she'd been holding it for a month. "Yeah. We've been talking."

"What's her number?" I ask.

She shakes her head. "It doesn't work like that. She doesn't pick up when I try to call. Most of the time it goes straight to voicemail. If I want to talk, I send her a text, then she texts back a time and place where she'll call. But the weird thing is the texts back never come from the same number. And the places she calls are always pay phones and never the same one twice. One time I had to drive all the way down to Biddeford. She's been super paranoid ever since she got fired; I don't know why."

I turn to Zara. "Never the same place twice." She nods. It fits our killer's pattern. If Samantha is being that careful with her phone calls, then it's likely she's adopted the same strategy for her kills. Never kill in the same town twice and don't follow a discernable pattern.

"Still, give us her number anyway," I tell her.

"Here," she says, turning the phone around. I see she's in the middle of typing out a text which reads: *Two cops in the club looking for you earlier. Need to talk?* I make note of the number at the top. There's no name attached to it.

"Send that to her," I tell Shawna.

"You want me to send this?" she asks. "But—"

"Em, do you think—" Zara begins, but I stop her.

"Yes, and when she texts back with the callback information, I want you to call us." I hand Shawna my card. "Agent Foley here is going to be tracking your phone, so if you decide *not* to call us back, we'll know."

"You can do that?" Shawna asks.

"Sure," Zara says, shooting me a dirty look.

"So you're going to be the ones at the pay phone then?"

I nod. "Like I said, we just want to talk to her."

Shawna looks at us again, then finally relents. "Okay. Sent."

I stand, Zara following my lead. "Thank you. Don't forget, let us know as soon as she texts back."

We leave her to finish her coffee, but once we're back outside I already feel Zara's eyes on me. "This is tactically unsound. How do you expect to bring her in? All you're going to do is send her into the wind."

"How long will it take to put a trace on a payphone?" I ask.

"About three minutes," she says. "But I'll need to call Caruthers back in D.C. He can set it up from there." She shoves her hands in her pockets as she walks. "But do you really think you can keep her talking that long? And given how paranoid she is—"

"—more than likely she'll be calling from a burner," I say. "You're right. But at the moment this is our best chance at tracking her down. At least we'll know her last known location."

"But, Em, what's going to stop her from just bolting? If she thinks we're on to her she'll disappear, and we'll never find her again."

"Unless her compulsion to finish her mission takes over," I say. "You're right. Ideally I'd prefer to interrogate her, get a solid read on her before attempting something like this. But she is going to extreme lengths not only to protect her own privacy, but to kill these men. This is not just a weekend spree for her; she's preparing for this. Which tells me she might not be willing to give it up so easily. I mean, even if she knows that we're looking for her, it would only be blind luck that would allow us to find her before she kills her next victim. We're talking about virtually anywhere between here and Collins and beyond. And the way she's drawing these men in is impossible to stop. What are we going to do, put a moratorium on all dates until we find her?"

We get back to the car and I'm grateful to get in and out of the cold.

"I guess, I just wish there was some other way to get a bead on her," Zara says. "Or at least her next victim. I mean, yes, they're all abusers, but that doesn't really narrow the field a lot."

"I'd be willing to bet if the strip club kept all its video we'd see each of our victims on that footage at least sometime in the past six months," I say. "I'm guessing that's how she's choosing her targets. But she can't be going after all of them. She's picking 'special' ones, and I'm going to find out why."

Chapter Twenty-Five

"ABSOLUTELY NOT," Wallace says.

"Sir, this is the best way to get an idea of where she's operating," I tell him. I've just finished explaining my plan to him and to no one's surprise, least of all my own, he's completely rejecting the idea.

"Slate, I'm not about to rest the entire outcome of this case on your belief that you'll be able to convince this woman to turn herself in over the phone," he says.

I blow a frustrated breath out my mouth. "Okay, then our other option is to wait until Saturday for another corpse to show up."

"You need to find another way to track her down, letting her know we're on to her is no better than releasing her picture to the media. Which, if I might add, would give us better odds of finding her than what you're proposing."

I clench my fist. "Sir, there is something about this woman, something driving her to do this. This isn't some random murder spree; she has an *agenda*. And she's the only one who can tell us who her next victim will be."

"And you think you can get her to give up her entire plan so that you can stop her," he says, humor in his voice.

My mind flashes back to all the conversations I've had with Zara ever since we came up here. We've had time together that we'd been missing ever since Liam and I became serious. I'd missed her counsel, and despite all my time with Dr. Frost, it was my conversations with *her* that have helped clear my mind on this matter. "I think I can at least understand her. At least empathize with her. I want to know *why* she's doing this. Maybe if she had someone she could talk to, it might make things a little easier for her."

"You've been spending too much time on Frost's couch," he replies. "I wouldn't let the Bureau's best psychiatrist take a crack at this; I'm certainly not going to sanction you to do it. Find another way to track her down or we'll release her picture to the media. By *tomorrow.*"

"But sir, that'll just—"

"That's the order, Slate. Get it done." He hangs up before I can protest any further.

"You know, we should have invited *him* to your birthday party," Zara says. "One Jell-O shot, and it would have been over. There's no way that man can hold his liquor. I bet you anything his pants would have been on his head within the hour."

"Ugh, don't put that image in my head," I say, half laughing.

She pulls a leg up into the passenger seat, leaning off to the side. "So, what now? Shawna already sent the message."

I check the time. It's almost four p.m. and the sun will be setting soon. "I guess we need to reconvene with Sandel and Kane. Figure out a new strategy."

"Still think they're nefarious?" she asks, a glint in her eye.

"Like you said, even if they are, I have nothing to hide. Obviously, I'm not keeping anything from Wallace."

She smiles. "See? It's like I said. Just a coincidence."

"I suppose," I say, dialing Sandel's number again. Just like last time he picks up on the second ring.

"Sandel."

"Are you close to Agent Kane?" I ask.

"One moment." I hear the phone click and more ambient noise over the speaker. I put my phone on speaker as well. "Go ahead, Agent Slate."

I give them the full rundown of what happened with Shawna along with Wallace's response to my plan. After I'm done, Zara fills them in on the technical side of attempting to trace whatever phone Samantha may be using.

"I can't disagree with the SAC's assessment," Sandel says. "Exposing ourselves like that would almost guarantee we'd lose her."

"Unless Emily is right," Agent Kane says. "What if she's on a personal vendetta? She might not stop, no matter what." I glance at Zara. That's the first time either of them has spoken up in support of us. "I thought you should know; we tracked down the man Samantha Morris attacked at the club. Dermont Lazlo. It turns out he's a real estate magnate who likes to sail his yacht up and down the east coast for the winter. In the summer he takes it over to Europe, but right now he's down in Boston's harbor."

"Two hours south," I say.

"Thinking about paying him a visit?" Zara asks.

"Yeah," I say. "I want to know why he's still alive and all these other men are dead. After all, he's the one who allegedly assaulted Samantha."

"That's a good point," Sandel says. "If she's enacting some kind of vendetta as you suggest, you'd think she'd start with the man who kicked this whole thing off."

"She could be saving him for last," Kane adds. "Sort of like a capstone to the whole endeavor."

"If that's the case, then we'll need to get eyes on him anyway," I say. "Good thinking. At the very least that should help us get close enough to him that we'll be able to interrogate him."

"Agent Slate, shouldn't we stay here and focus on this aspect of the investigation? Men are dying *here*. Not in Boston," Sandel says.

"We can do both at the same time," I tell him. "I want you and Nadia to say where you are, keep things calm in Collins, let us know if there are any developments with any of the other victims. In the meantime, Zara and I will see if we can't get an audience with *his majesty*, the real estate magnate." I can almost see Sandel's hard stare through the phone, but he doesn't protest.

"Very well," he says. "We'll keep working up here."

"And see if you can't uncover any more background information on Samantha Morris," I tell them. "Now that we know who she is, maybe we can find something that will help us predict her next move."

"I'm on it," Nadia replies.

"Thanks," I say, and I'm struck by just how much I appreciate them working with us. Having four of us on the case is a lot better than two, and a hell of a lot better than one, which is how I thought my career would be going at this point. Thankfully, that's not the case.

After we hang up I turn to Zara. "Ready for a road trip?"

She grins. "Just keep it under eighty."

BY THE TIME WE REACH BOSTON IT'S ALMOST SIX AND THE SUN has already set. Damn time change. I swear, by this point you'd think we could figure out how to get along without it. I wouldn't care if we stayed in one time zone or the other, just as long as it stayed consistent. A few weeks ago when the time changed over, Timber had the hardest time trying to figure out why he wasn't being fed at his normal time. It took me a solid week to get him reacclimated. And we get to go through it all again in the spring. Yay.

Thankfully, Nadia has sent us everything she has on Dermont Lazlo, including his yacht registration number, which makes locating him in the harbor slips as easy as a call down to the Charlestown Marina identifying ourselves as FBI agents.

We pull into the parking garage by six-thirty and then it's just a short walk down to the slips themselves. While not as bitterly cold as New Hampshire, the wind coming off the harbor whips at our jackets, causing me to pull mine tight as we make our way down the primary dock. Rows and rows of ships line the sides, most of them already shunted for the winter with covers on them and all their equipment stowed. Though there are a few that haven't gone into hibernation yet; it takes a brave soul who will still take them out even on these cold days for a taste of the open ocean.

Lazlo's yacht sits at the end of one group of slips, the ship too big for it to park alongside the sailboats and speedboats. While not the largest yacht in the harbor, it's certainly a contender. At least three decks high and lit up like a Christmas Tree, the yacht seems to be where the action is happening tonight. While all the other ships are dark and quiet, bobbing softly on the calm water, loud music and voices are coming from our target.

When we reach the ship itself, there's a double-wide plank which allows access on and off the ship. A large man stands before us, bundled up in a thermal coat, his face dark and his arms crossed.

"Sorry, ladies, closed party tonight," he calls out before we've even reached him. Seeing as the ship is at the very end of the dock and there's nowhere else to go, I'm sure he's expecting us to turn back.

I pull out my badge. "FBI, we're here to see Dermont Lazlo."

His face twitches and he taps on the Bluetooth device in

his ear. "FBI agents. Here for Mr. Lazlo." He waits a moment, then addresses us. "What's this regarding?"

"An open case," I tell him. He relays the message and I have no idea if he's talking to Lazlo or another one of his lackeys.

"Sorry, but Mr. Lazlo is entertaining this evening. You'll have to come back tomorrow," the man says.

"We don't have time for this," I mutter. I step onto the bridge connecting the dock to the ship and the man puts an arm out to stop me.

"Now wait a—" Before he can finish the sentence, I've got his arm and it's behind his back, the large man is on his knees.

"Don't touch me," I tell him. "I don't care what *Mr. Lazlo* is doing tonight. This is a matter of some urgency, so we are going to talk to him right now, do you understand?"

"Mm-hmm," the man says, nodding. I can tell he's biting the inside of his lip to keep from crying out, as the pressure I'm putting on his arm is enough to make it feel like it's going to snap out of the socket. I let him go and he falls to the side, then takes a moment to stand back up, moving out of our way.

"Thank you," I reply. "Please tell your boss we'll be with him shortly."

The main points up to the deck above us with the arm I didn't hold. His other one will be sore for a day, but he'll be fine. "He's up there."

I nod my appreciation as Zara, and I navigate our way down the side of the ship to the closest narrow stairway.

"I think that's the best part about this job," she says. "They *always* underestimate us."

I couldn't agree more. And that gives us an edge that not many other agents have. Especially some of the older, more seasoned ones. Everyone expects them to be hardasses who look like they could take a bear in a fight, but people don't necessarily expect that from a five-four brunette who looks young enough to still be in college.

When we reach the second deck the music is slightly louder, but still muffled as it's all coming from inside the deck itself. Bright windows reveal a spacious gathering area. Two large couches that face each other dominate the space, and there's a large TV on the far wall. The other side of the room has a full bar, and there are at least a dozen people inside. Some watching TV, a couple of others are dancing to the music. From the notes Nadia sent me, I spot Lazlo right away. He's sitting on the couch, his hand wrapped around a forty. I note at least three diamond-encrusted rings on his fingers. Apparently his man downstairs didn't warn him we were coming. Maybe he decided he didn't get paid enough to be manhandled like that.

Zara and I approach the sliding back doors that separate the interior space from an outdoor hot tub, though it's covered up at the moment. Even as we enter no one pays us any attention, most of them either focused on the Football game on TV, or too involved with their dance partner.

"A-*hem*," I call out, and a few people look back. I hold up my badge and the entire party stops, as if frozen.

Dermont stands, pinching his features. "What the hell is this?"

"Dermont Lazlo," I say over the music. "We'd like to have a word."

He hops the couch and approaches us, pushing through the people dancing. "Just who the fuck do you think you are coming on my ship—" But as soon as he sees my badge reads FBI, he stops short. "FBI?"

"Let's have a chat."

Chapter Twenty-Six

"LOOK, there's a game on and I've got about fifteen grand riding on it, so make this quick." Dermont leads us into an office on the deck that we came in on, after taking us down a set of interior stairs. He's full of bluster and an inflated sense of self-importance, like he doesn't have time to deal with the FBI. It doesn't surprise me, given the kind of lifestyle he leads. He's not used to someone coming in, telling him what to do or how to act. The office itself is paneled all in wood and there are a couple of shelves filled with books; most are books on success, or from self-help gurus. His desk matches the rest of the office, though there's only one chair behind it, and a lone laptop sits on top, closed.

"We're investigating the incident that happened about six weeks ago at *The Kitty's Leash*, up in Portland," I tell him.

Lazlo literally stops moving, like he's frozen to his seat. Where there had just been bravado and annoyance, now there is only stillness. I almost think he's gone into shock. "W-why would I want to talk about that?" he finally asks. "It's over."

"For you, maybe," I tell him. "But let's revisit, shall we? Care to tell us what happened that night?" Whatever advantage I have here, I can't waste it. I need to push while he's vulnerable.

I can see he's trying to regain his earlier confidence and swagger. "Yeah, it—I mean, I uhh…"

"Having trouble remembering?" I ask.

"No, just. Okay, look. I made a mistake, all right? I was drunk, and I got a little…too friendly."

My stomach turns at his description of it. But I'm going to make him say it. Admit to it. "How?"

His eyes go to Zara, who is standing behind me with her arms crossed, then back to me and then out the window to his right. He's panicking, like he knows he's been caught in a trap. "I…uh…look, I know it was a stupid thing to do, okay? But I haven't even been to a strip club since. Like I promised. She said that if I kept my hands to myself that I'd never see her again."

I lean forward. This is new. "Who said that?"

"The girl, the strip—the woman I…uh…touched," he finally says. A bead of sweat runs down his brow. He's panicking, but this seems like more than just being intimidated by a couple of FBI agents. He's scared. No, he's *terrified*.

"Dermont, I need you to tell me exactly what happened," I say.

"I didn't mean anything by it!" he yells. "I was just drunk! Haven't you ever done anything stupid when you've been drunk?"

"I sure as hell haven't put my hand down a woman's underwear," Zara mutters.

He holds up both hands, swallowing hard. "Yes, okay, yes. You're right. I shouldn't have even been there that night. I'd had too much to drink, and I wasn't myself."

"I don't give a shit about your moral character," I tell him. "I just want to know what happened."

He takes another deep breath. "Okay. After…um…after it happened, we had an argument—"

"Do you call her scratching your arms and face an argument?" Zara asks.

He pauses, looks down, wets his lips and starts over. "You're right. I...touched her, when I shouldn't have. And almost immediately she went off on me." He holds his hands up again. "Completely justified. I deserved it. She scratched my arms, my face, everything. If that bouncer hadn't been there, I'm pretty sure she would have clawed my eyeballs out."

"Then what happened?" I ask.

"They banned me from the club, so me and the crew, we came back to the ship to sleep it off. But I had to stop by the minute clinic first. They wrapped up my wounds." He shakes his head again like he's afraid of something. "Again, no lasting harm done. All healed up now, see?" He pulls his sleeves up and I don't see any trace of any scratches. Nor do I see any on his face. They must have just been superficial from Samantha's nails. "That was it."

"What about the part where she told you to keep your hands to yourself?" I ask, leaning forward so my hands are on the desk.

"Oh, right," Dermont says, like he's just remembered. "So...um, a few days later she came by the boat."

"She came here?" I ask.

He hesitates. "Yes. She told me never to touch another woman again. Then she left."

"Just like that?"

Another hesitation. "Pretty much."

I stand back up, working my jaw. Obviously he's hiding something. Something big. I take a look around the room, it's filled with plaques and awards, for what I couldn't even guess, but it's clear to me Lazlo has no problem showing off his accolades. And knowing what little I know about his business, courtesy of Nadia, he doesn't strike me as the kind of person who just gives up on something.

"You're telling me that a woman attacked you, physically

injured you, and you just walked away without so much as a shrug?" I ask. "And then this woman confronted you again, and you immediately complied with her request."

I watch him squirm out of the corner of my eye. "Well, I mean, I didn't think I should rock the boat, you know. She seemed pretty serious."

I turn back to him. "Dermont, do we look like idiots to you?"

"N-no. No, ma'am," he replies.

"Then I need you to be honest with me. What *really* happened?"

He swallows again, then opens a drawer in his desk. For a brief second I think he's going for a weapon, but instead he pulls out a very expensive bottle of bourbon. I recognize it immediately. It's one I've never had the pleasure of tasting seeing as a single shot costs a couple hundred bucks. He removes the cork and pours two fingers in a glass, downing them both immediately before doing it again. The man literally just downed a grand worth of alcohol in twenty seconds.

"Okay, but you gotta protect me," he finally says. His eyes go up to the ceiling and I can't help but wonder if he thinks the people still above us can hear us.

"Protect you from what?" I ask.

"From *her*," he says, his hand with the empty glass beginning to tremble. "She showed up here, the day after the thing at the club. I had my lawyer on the phone, ready to sue the ass off those guys. I was determined to own that club by the time it was all over. At first, I thought she came looking for a fight, like she wanted me to pay her off or something, I dunno. But then...it was like...nothing happened. She pretended like everything had been fine at the club. Even offered me a private session."

"And how could you say no to that?" I ask, sarcasm seeping from my lips.

"Okay, yeah, I was probably thinking with my dick and

not my brain. I started out thinking it couldn't be as easy as that. I thought maybe she was here for a shakedown, but she just made it so...effortless. It was like nothing ever happened; she was being super nice and flirty and I just...uggghh." He leans his head back and I can feel his frustration. "I let my guard down when I said I wouldn't." He points a finger in our direction. "But this was after she started dancing, okay? I mean, she had nothing on! She was standing in front of me, buck-naked. How was I supposed to know she was a threat?"

I exchange a look with Zara. "I don't understand. What did she do?"

"One second she's dancing, and I can just feel the vibe, you know? Like, I know things are happening. She was sending all the right signals. The next thing I know, I have a blade to my throat and she's whispering what she'll do to me if she ever finds out I've touched another woman again. And it wasn't normal. It was like this woman had gone into some kind of psycho-killer trance. I've never heard *anyone* talk like that before."

"Where did she get the blade?" I ask.

"It was part of her heel; I saw it when she pulled away. She made this icepick-looking thing into the heel of her stiletto, then covered it up with what looked like a normal heel. I didn't even have to barely breathe before I felt it cut into my skin."

That could explain the holes we've found on the victims' necks. "She threatened to kill you?"

"Yeah, but not before she cut everything off and made me watch myself bleed out. Don't no man need to see that." I have to turn away to hide the smile on my face. I know it's morbid, but there's a certain appeal to what this woman is doing. Using men's own libidos against them. And from what I can tell, she's only going after men who have hurt other women. She's taking out her revenge on these men and stopping them from hurting anyone else. *That's* how she sees it, I'm sure of it.

I shoot a look at Zara who has strategically positioned her hand over her mouth, telling me she's thinking along the same lines I am. But that still begs the question, why did Samantha leave Lazlo alive and instead go after all these other men?

"Did she say anything else?" I ask, turning back to Lazlo when I'm sure I've composed myself.

"Just that as long as I kept my hands to myself, I'd never see her again."

"You haven't seen or heard from her since?" I ask.

He shakes his head. "And I hope I never do. That bi— *woman*—is crazy. I could see it in her eyes."

I look around the room some more, frustrated that we seem to have hit another dead end. *How would she know?* I have to assume she's not keeping a constant eye on Lazlo; she doesn't have the capability to come down to Boston or wherever he happens to be parked for the week and watch him all the time. Is she just relying on her own intimidation to keep him in line, or does she have a more direct way of watching him?

"Did she go anywhere else on the ship? Anywhere without you?"

He blinks a few times. "I don't know…maybe? Once she got dressed and left I didn't think it would be smart to follow her."

"Was there anyone else on the ship at the time?" Zara asks.

"Nah, just me. I think she planned it that way."

We don't have the time or resources to search the entire ship for anything that Samantha may have planted here. And unfortunately it still may not get us any closer to her, with as careful as she's being. I have to give her credit; she's managed to cover her tracks well. Even assuming that we'd track her down eventually, she's left us no other avenues to follow.

I motion for Zara to follow me back out to the deck outside. "What do you think?" I ask her as soon as I'm sure Lazlo can't hear us anymore.

"Ingenious," she says. "Concealing the blade in her stiletto? I wish I had thought of that. This woman has some serious skills if she made a weapon like that."

"Still doesn't explain why she left him alive, though," I say.

She shakes her head. "I'm not so sure she's coming back for him either, like Nadia suggested. Kind of seems like she's done with the guy."

That could go either way at this point. We don't know enough about her master plan to determine whether she'll be back here or not. "Still, I'm going to call the office here in Boston. I want to get someone keeping an eye on Lazlo just in case she does show back up." As I pull out my phone to make the call, it vibrates before I have the chance. I check the screen and see it's Sandel calling.

"This is Slate," I say.

"You better get back here," he says. "There's been a development."

Chapter Twenty-Seven

As we approach the toll station, I slow and head to the *authorized vehicles only* lane. A cop with an orange vest steps out from one of the tollbooths but I already have my badge out. As soon as he sees it, he moves out of the way, motioning us to continue on. I slam my foot on the gas and the tires spin for a second before catching, rocketing the car back up to speed with the rest of the traffic.

"Jeez, Em, we're not gonna be able to confront them if we don't make it back to Rice's office," Zara says.

I grumble, not really saying anything, instead going over what Agent Sandel relayed to me on the phone right before we left Boston and Lazlo behind. Like Lazlo, I shouldn't have dropped my guard when I wasn't looking. And now I've got a mess of shit to sort through.

My phone buzzes again and Zara grabs it before I can. "Emily Slate, Formula One Racer's phone. Please make this brief as we may find ourselves wrapped around a tree in the next five seconds."

I let out a breath and take my foot off the accelerator. She's right, I'm overreacting. But I tend to do that when someone comes after my reputation and my job.

218 • ALEX SIGMORE

"I'm glad I caught you," Nadia says on the other end. "Elliott is in with Rice and Sheriff Dutton right now, going over the paperwork."

"What paperwork?" I ask. "It's a formal injunction. What else could there be?"

"Chief Eastly is alleging personal and psychological harm in addition to invasion of private property," Nadia says. "His lawyer says you intimidated Eastly to the point where he couldn't do his job correctly."

"That will never hold up," I say.

"But this improper search might," she replies. "I know you were just covering your ass, but they have a valid claim here."

"I guess it doesn't matter that Eastly tried to immediately frame me and Zara the next morning?" I yell, furious that he and that jerk of a lawyer are even attempting something so ludicrous. There is no way any of this will lead to any actual charges, but it is enough to gum up the works, to get me and Zara out of commission long enough for Samantha to strike again. And honestly, I think Eastly is just doing it because he can. Out of spite. Per the injunction, we've been recalled to Collins to defend ourselves in front of a local magistrate, who Sandel has informed me is a friend of Eastly's. Rice wasn't kidding when he said it was a network of corruption up here. People who are used to doing things one way and one way only, and have a real problem when a newcomer steps in. I have no doubt this is as much an attack on us as it is on Rice, seeing as he's the one who brought us in.

"I'm just relaying the information. Have you spoken to Wallace yet?" Nadia asks.

"No," I reply. I don't want to get him involved. At least, not until I've had a chance to straighten all this out. The last thing I need him thinking is I need him to come up here and save me. Which is why I haven't called Janice, or Liam either. I'm not about to let these bastards think they can pull one over on us. But this is coming at the worst possible time. I felt like we were finally starting to close in on Samantha Morris, even if we don't have a concrete idea of where she is yet. At least now we understand her process more, and hopefully we'll be able to use that to figure out where she's planning on striking next.

"If you want me to call him and give him and update—" she begins.

"No, not until we've had a chance to sort this out." I shoot a look at Zara. *Spies* I mouth. She only shrugs.

"Okay, if you're sure. I'll hold off until I get the green light from you. But I still think we should keep him apprised of what's going on."

"I appreciate that, Agent Kane, thank you," I say. Now we'll just have to wait and see if she keeps to her word or not. Regardless, Eastly is about to find out just how nasty I can get. He hasn't seen anything yet.

"You two have a safe drive back up. We'll try to make sure everything is ready to go as soon as you get here."

"Our ETA is nine-twenty-three," Zara says. "Or, you know, if Emily manages to break the sound barrier, sooner."

"See you soon." Nadia hangs up and Zara puts my phone back in the rocker.

"Em, you gotta calm down," she says. When in the history of anyone saying that has it actually worked? I *don't* need to calm down. I need to put a fist-sized dent in Eastly's skull. "Why are you letting him get under your skin? You know these charges are baseless. Even the improper search one, after everything that Eastly was hiding about Schmidt comes out. It's plain as day."

"I just don't like people questioning my integrity," I say.

"No, I'm aware of that. But you seem to harbor some kind of special hate for Eastly."

I draw in a deep breath and let it out, reminding myself I have to keep breathing. That's the best way to stay in control. "It's probably because of the way he's using the office. Everything is for his own benefit. If it doesn't help Eastly, he doesn't do it. And if he can twist the situation to help himself, he will. He may seem all meek and unassuming, but he's cunning and manipulative. And he's been doing it for decades. It's this kind of behavior that makes people not trust the police."

"Which, ironically, doesn't seem to be a problem in Collins. Small town, mostly homogenous population. Everyone seems to get along."

"And Eastly is using that to his own advantage, to cover up crimes by his officers. You saw how they all quit when he was arrested. It's because they know he's not there to protect their lawlessness anymore. If there's one thing I can't stand, it's someone representing themselves as one thing while being someone completely different."

"Like James Hunter," Zara says. "And Chris and Dani. And…Matt."

She's right. All of these people presented themselves to me in a certain way, when in fact they were just playing a role. And while I think I can forgive Matt for his part in it, seeing as he was actively trying to dismantle the entire thing, I can't forgive the rest of them. It reminds me that I need genuine people in my life more than anything else.

"Damn," I say, regaining control of myself before the tears fall. "You really *are* Dr. Frost."

"Hey, I'll take the job if they want to pay me double," she says, leaning the seat back and locking her hands behind her head.

We're about halfway to Collins when my phone buzzes again. Zara grabs it but doesn't answer.

"Who is it?" I ask.

"It's a text, from Shawna. Samantha returned her text and sent contact info."

My heart rate picks up. "Where?"

"A town called Sanford. It's about forty-five minutes outside Portland."

"How far from here?" I ask.

"Em," Zara says, warning in her voice. "I know what you're thinking. We can't go off-book. Not again. Don't give Wallace a reason to bring the axe down on you. If you deliberately disobey orders and she disappears, I don't know that even Janice could do anything."

"I know," I say, staring straight ahead. I also know that if we lose this chance to speak to Samantha, we'll find another body in less than five days. I know what everyone is thinking, if I were in their shoes I'd be thinking the same thing. Maybe it is crazy, and then again maybe not. It's impossible to know until I speak with her. I think she at least deserves a chance to explain herself.

Zara sits back in her seat, her lips drawn in a line. "Okay, fine," she says. "We're doing this, then."

"No," I say. "I'm going to drop you off. Tell them you tried to stop me. You're doing so well at the Bureau; I can't risk your career too."

She scoffs. "Drop me off where? It's the middle of nowhere and dark out. What am I supposed to do, hitchhike to the closest town?"

"We'll find somewhere. Call Sandel or Kane, get them to come get you. I'm not going to let you torpedo everything you've built over the past year because I'm making a risky call." It's late, yes, but I'm sure I can find somewhere safe to drop her.

"Emily Rachel Slate," she says, using *the voice*. "Who gave you permission to make my decisions for me?"

"Well, I—"

"*You* don't get to decide what I do or don't do. Like you said. This is *my* career. And if I'm going to lose it backing you up, then so be it. I sure as hell am not leaving you alone in another situation, especially after what happened with the Organization."

I'm touched. But that doesn't negate the danger. "Z, look

at what happened to Rodriguez. I can't put you in that position. If I get a bead on Samantha, she's not going to go quietly. Unless I manage to convince her to come in." I think we're all aware of the odds on that one.

"*You're* not putting me in that position. I am," she replies. "Don't you dare slow down or look for a place to 'drop me'. Cause you're going to have a hell of a fight getting me out of this car."

I smile. "Damn, you're stubborn."

"Learned from the best," she says, leaning back in her reclined seat again. She looks over the details from Shawna. "It's a payphone at the Sanford bus station. It says she'll call between ten and eleven pm. The town is about twenty-five minutes away."

I push the accelerator harder. "When did the text come through to Shawna?" I ask.

"Looks like around nine. That would have given her enough time to get out of Portland and over to Sanford."

"But it doesn't leave us very much," I say. Shawna held on to that message for over twenty minutes. I don't know if it's because she sent some kind of emergency code to Samantha, or because she was still weighing the consequences of what she was about to do. She's not a stupid girl; she knows we're interested in Samantha for more than just a talk. And if it turns out Shawna knew anything about these killings, then we'll bring her in as well. As much as I may agree with the spirit of what Samantha is doing, I can't condone it.

The dark highway stretches before us, and despite everything going on with this case, my mind goes back to the letter. In some ways, the sender is very much like Samantha: working behind the scenes, anonymous, not wanting to be seen, but also disrupting lives left and right. It takes a clever and calculating mind to work from the shadows like that, someone who is focused on a long-term goal. Someone with patience and self-control. Samantha doesn't strike until the time is right. I have a feeling whoever sent that letter won't either.

"Coming up on Sanford," Zara says. We first see the glow over a distant hill, and as we draw closer, the small town comes into view. It can't be much bigger than Collins. I see a smattering of homes, a couple of strip malls, and, strangely, the lights from a small airport runway in the distance.

"Where's the bus station?"

"More like bus stop," she says, looking at her phone. "Take a right on 109—Main street. We're going to follow it halfway down until we reach the station."

I glance at the clock on my dash. Nine fifty-two. If Samantha calls right at ten we might miss it. As we get closer to the town, I get stuck behind a pickup truck going about thirty. Despite the fact there are no dashed lines on this side, I swerve around the truck, earning me a honk for my trouble.

"We really need lights and a siren," I say.

"Cause that wouldn't alert her or anything," Zara replies.

"You think she's watching the pay phone?"

"If we know anything about this girl, it's that she's careful. If I got a text for contact from my friend and it wasn't at her normal time, I'd be very interested to see who shows up to take the call."

"Good point," I say, turning at the light onto main street. The town is a sleepy one, not a lot of traffic out as there's nowhere to go around here. The few businesses in the malls that line the street are already closed, except for a couple of restaurants.

"There it is," she says, pointing ahead of us.

"Get ready," I tell her. "This might be our only chance."

Chapter Twenty-Eight

THE TOWN of Sanford's bus station reminds me of a convenience store without gas pumps. It's a small, one-story cinder-block building with large windows on one side and a sign out front designating it as the bus depot. There are two lanes for buses to park and inside the building are four rows of plastic chairs, though all of them are empty at this time of night. There's also a ticket station inside, where the convenience store clerk would normally be, but the window is shuttered with a metal gate. Even though all the lights are on, it looks like the last bus has already come through for the night.

"Cheerful place," Zara says as we pull up.

I park in the small lot beside the building, noting that there are no other cars around us. As we get out of the vehicle, I can't help but take a look around, though it's pretty much black in all directions, except for the streetlights that led us here. Tall pine trees prevent us from seeing into the wilderness. If someone is out there watching us, they probably have a pretty good view and know there's no way we can see them back.

Above us, a full moon bathes the forest in a bluish-green

hue. The temperature has dropped again, making me wish I had my gloves.

"Here," Zara says. The left side of the building has three pay phones, though one of them looks like it's been ripped from the wall and the receiver is missing. The other two are covered in stickers or graffiti. Before we reach the phones, I pull out a nitrile glove and slip it on. I'd rather not touch those receivers if I don't have to.

Zara looks at her phone. "Ten-oh-four. Think we missed it?"

"I doubt it," I say, looking around again. "I think you're right. She's probably out there, watching. Waiting for us before she calls." A chill runs down my back. This is too familiar. Camille did something similar, though she was a trained assassin. As far as I know, Samantha hasn't had any formal training of this sort. Which, in a way, makes her more frightening. She's doing all of this of her own accord. It's making me want to re-evaluate the profile again.

A cloud of vapor escapes Zara's mouth. "I wonder—"

Before she can finish the thought, the phone closest to us rings. I glance at her, then pick up the receiver, making sure not to touch it to my ear. "Hello?"

"Who are you?" a female voice says on the other end. Zara was right. She knows Shawna isn't here. Either she's keeping tabs on her friend's phone, or she has eyes on us right now.

"Someone who wants to help," I say.

"I don't need help." Her words are clipped, and I can already feel her slipping away. This isn't someone who is willing to waste their time.

"Samantha, we know about the men." I look at Zara, who nods. "We know what you've been doing to them. And we know you spared Dermont Lazlo."

"Let me guess, you're a detective with one of the police departments investigating them?" she asks.

"FBI, actually."

There's a pause on the other end. "I didn't anticipate you becoming involved so quickly. You must be looking to rise up the ranks."

I let the snide comment pass. "We were brought in by the District Attorney who serves the communities where the men have been found." I'm hesitant to call them victims because of their nature, but also I don't want to put her more on the defensive than she already is. "I'm being honest and open with you, Samantha, because I just want to help you."

She laughs. It's a high-pitched sound, and from what I can tell, genuine, not sardonic at all. "You want me to stop killing people, that's what you want."

"True. Help me understand what you're doing. We already know that each of your targets is a predator of some kind. Whether that be a past, current, domestic, et cetera. You're sending a message to these communities. You want them to know you won't put up with it." I notice Zara is on her phone, speaking with someone. My eyes go wide, and I motion with my free hand for her to put the phone away.

She mouths *Caruthers*. I shake my head. If I'm going to gain this woman's trust, we can't be stabbing her in the back in the same breath with a phone trace. Zara purses her lips, then says something, ending the call.

"I don't care about these communities," she spits. "They're the ones who foster these monsters. All I want is to stop them from ever being able to hurt anyone ever again. And I'm doing that. Can you say the same, Agent? Can you guarantee me that when you arrest someone for rape, hold them in jail for ten years and release them that they'll never do it again? Because I can. I can *guarantee* they won't."

"Samantha, what happened? Why start all of this?"

"You talked to Lazlo. You know what happened."

"No," I say, my voice stronger. "There was something else. He was just the tip of the iceberg."

"Oh," she says, and I can hear the smile on her lips. "You want my life story. Sorry, but I don't have time for that." She's about to hang up. And I'm going to lose her forever.

"I agree with what you're doing," I say. Zara's eyes go wide.

"No, you don't. You're just saying whatever you need in order to keep me talking. Do you think I don't know how phone traces work?" she asks.

"I've already asked my partner to kill the phone trace," I tell her. "But somehow I don't think we'd find you even if we did manage to trace the phone. You're using a burner, and once this call is over, the phone will be destroyed, am I right?"

"Okay," she says. "But don't lie to me and tell me you believe in what I'm doing."

"That's just the thing, Samantha. I do. I've never been a victim of sexual abuse myself, but I know so many women who have. I have sat with them, as they've recounted the worst nights of their lives, sometimes being unable to escape their tormentor. I've seen domestic abuse situations where women have no choice but to stay because he controls all the money in the house, who she speaks with, who she sees. I've seen the desperation in their eyes as they try to tell me they need help without actually saying anything. I've watched as they've tried therapy, drugs, alcohol, support groups, anything they can to dull the pain, and fail. And I've been there the next mornings, when we find their bodies after they've decided they just can't take it anymore. I get it, I understand what you're doing. You're doing what we in law enforcement can't."

"Then you shouldn't be trying to stop me," she replies, though I hear the edge in her voice soften.

"Do we look like we could stop you?" I ask. "We have no idea who you're going to attack next. You've been clever enough to cover your tracks. We have no idea where you are right now. For all I know you have a remote camera set up in the woods and are watching us from a hundred miles away."

228 • ALEX SIGMORE

She chuckles, and it's the first joyful emotion I've heard from her. "I'm not *that* crazy."

"I don't think you're crazy at all, Samantha. And I understand why you're doing what you're doing. But you know this can't go on forever. There will always be more victims out there, more predators. You can't single-handedly wipe them all off the face of the Earth."

"So I should what? Just quit, and turn myself in?" she asks.

"No," I say. "I just want you to talk to me. You already know we can't get to you. I'm offering you a chance to be open and honest with someone, maybe for the first time since you've started doing this."

"I don't need to talk about it," she says.

A hint of a smile touches my lips. "I used to think the same thing. My husband was killed. By a rogue organization working to undermine certain parts of our society. I spent months tracking them down, finding the truth. And when I finally did, and the people who were responsible for his death were finally in jail, I thought it would all be over. I thought I could move on with my life, that I would finally have peace. But do you know what?" I wait for a response, but none comes. "I found myself pushing away people who cared about me. Because they could see what I couldn't...that I was still hurting. Finding and punishing my husband's killers wasn't the end of my trauma. It was just another step in the process. I still have a long way to go. And I wouldn't have known any of that if the people who cared about me hadn't forced me to sit down and examine what was happening around me."

When she responds, her voice isn't as strong. "Not all of us are as lucky as you. Not everyone has people like that in their lives."

"What about Shawna?" I ask.

"Shawna was my coworker. She just lets me know if people come looking for me, that's all."

"Are you sure about that? Because when we spoke with her, she seemed concerned about you. It took us a long time to convince her to contact you for us. She didn't want to betray you." I look off into the distance, no clue if I'm looking in the right direction or not. She's out there...somewhere.

"Yeah, well, look how that turned out," she says, anger clouding her words. "If she was such a good friend, she would have said she hadn't spoken to me since I quit."

"Unless she's worried something might happen to you," I tell her. "Help me see your side. I'm offering you an ear. No strings attached. I'm here, willing to listen, if you're willing to tell me your story."

She barks a laugh. "It won't make any difference. I've killed five men. No story in the world is going to keep me from spending the rest of my life in prison. Which is why by the time I'm done; it will already be too late." My heart picks up speed. She does have an exit plan after all. A permanent one.

"Samantha," I say, my voice softer. "I'm not asking you to relive your trauma. I have seen what that does to people. I just want to know *why*. Why these men, why now? What's your endgame? I know how hard it is to hold all of that in, to allow it to eat away at you. Please, at least give it a try."

She hesitates again, and I sense she's really thinking about it. But I can also feel the resistance in her words. She's afraid that if she opens up about it, she might decide she's made the wrong choice after all. And she's come too far to turn back now. I know that feeling.

"You make a good argument," she finally says. "But this only ends one way. My way." The line goes dead.

"*Dammit*," I say, slamming the receiver on the handle.

"Em," Zara whispers, holding her phone up but close to her jacket, not making any sudden moves. On the phone is what looks like a radar ping. A bright white dot appears in the upper right-hand corner, and I realize we're at the center of the ping. A second later the dot disappears.

"She's right here," Zara continues. "About two hundred yards west of us."

"She just destroyed the phone," I say. Zara nods. She's close. Closer than I would have guessed. We need to go, now.

"Stay low, stay quiet, and keep your safety on." She nods. We don't make any other sudden moves, instead, make it look like we're heading back to our car. As soon as we're on the other side, effectively putting the car between us and where we think she's perched, we drop down low and rush into the darkness of the woods.

We're in uncharted territory now.

Chapter Twenty-Nine

IT's pitch black out here. The only light is what little filters through the trees, and that's barely enough for me to see a couple of feet in front of me. Still, I can feel Zara beside me as we attempt to circle back around to the place where we suspect Samantha was watching us. I've always had a good internal compass; usually I'm able to orient myself without much trouble. But I have to admit this is a challenge. Fortunately, since all the trees are pines, leaves under are feet are nonexistent. Instead, there is the light blanket of snow, with nothing but a bed of discarded pine needles beneath it, which helps conceal our location. If we don't move too fast we can keep the sound of our approach to a minimum.

I have no idea if we're going to catch up to her or not, all I know is Zara was right, I wasn't able to talk her back down. I was barely able to get anything out of her, other than the fact that she's been hurt in the past. And she's angry. Angry enough to start killing men she sees as a threat, not just to her, but to every woman out there. It's a noble idea, but I can't condone her actions. If we do manage to catch up with her, we'll have no choice but to take her into custody.

I feel a hand on my shoulder, and I almost jump until I

realize it's Zara, who has closed the distance between us. She points off to my right, where we can just barely see the lights of the bus stop through the trees. We've managed to come up on a small rise, which would give us a great position to watch the bus station from. But from what I remember on Zara's phone, I don't think we're quite far enough into the woods yet to have reached Samantha's location. There's also no reason why she would stay put after our conversation. I'd expect her to move, unless she wanted to watch us drive away, in which case she might still be out there, wondering what we're doing. I just hope she doesn't have a pair of binoculars otherwise she'll know we're not in the car as we tried to make it appear.

I nod as we continue deeper, parallel now to the bus station. Her position should be somewhere right up ahead of us and I'm doing everything I can to keep quiet. But I already feel the frigid night air seep into my skin, chilling me to the bone. At the same time my heart is pounding so loud I'm sure it will echo among the trees, but it's silent out here. It seems there's not a living thing around us.

After another hundred feet, I slow, holding out my hand so Zara won't go on without me. The bus station is behind us now, just slivers of light visible through the trees. But I can see a clear line to the parking lot and the phones. I take a moment to listen for any sound around us, but there's nothing. Vapor escapes my mouth, partially illuminated by the moonlight coming down and then I hear it: a soft padding sound from somewhere behind us.

I crouch down, turning as I do to try and see through the trees, but it's impossible. The darkness takes over not more than twenty feet away and the blanket of snow is free of any tracks. Instead, I close my eyes and tilt my head, attempting to shut everything else out so I can hear her. She's still out here and she may know she's not alone anymore.

My breath stills and I hear it again, very faint, moving away off to my right. I tap Zara's shoulder and point in that direction. We both move as fast as we can while still staying quiet, though I'm sure if Samantha stops for a moment, she'll manage to hear us just like we heard her. Somewhere in my brain I wonder if there are bears in Maine and for the first time start to worry that it might not just be humans out here. Samantha could be long gone, and we could be tracking a very dangerous animal.

My hesitation causes me to slow, allowing Zara to get out in front of me. I'm about to reach out to let her know to slow down when I see her go down, crying out in pain.

"Z!" I yell and move to rush forward. At the last second I see what tripped her up, and I manage to stop myself from running into the strip of razor-sharp barbed wire strung up between the trees. Zara, on the other hand, is tangled up in it, beginning to thrash around.

"Hey, hey," I tell her. "Just calm down. The more you jerk about the deeper it's going to cut into you."

"What the hell," she says, wincing. "I'm all caught up in it and it's cutting me to shreds."

I have to physically put my hands on her shoulders to stop her. "I'll get you out, just give me a second, okay?"

But before I can untangle her legs from the mess of sharp metal that has her all twisted up, I feel a sharp blade at my neck.

"Drop the weapon," Samantha says.

I slowly lower the weapon to the snow-covered ground, the blade staying on my neck the entire time. My bet is Zara lost hers when she got tangled up.

"Now stand back up, hands up."

I do as I'm told. I can't look down to see it, but this blade feels a lot bigger than one that could come out of a stiletto. "Samantha, you don't have to do this. We're not your enemies."

"Yeah, then why did you come after me? If you believed in what I was doing, as you claimed, then you should have just let me do it. Go back and tell your boss you couldn't find me. I only have a few left. It would have all been over soon anyway."

"As much as I may agree with the spirit of what you're doing, I took an oath," I say. "I can't let you continue to kill people for your own personal vengeance."

"Why not?" she asks. "Cops do it all the time. Didn't you hear about the cop who got killed in a training exercise by the very men he was investigating?" I don't reply. "Law enforcement has a blank check to kill whoever they want. They just have to come up with a convincing story so the public doesn't lose its mind. And yet, here I am, doing some *good*, changing this world for the better, and you're trying to stop me. I bet you'd shoot me right now if you could, wouldn't you?"

Her voice is ice cold. From what little I know about Samantha Morris, she doesn't have any formal military training, but you'd never know it from the way she's acting. "Did you set up the barbed wire?" I ask. "That was quick."

"As soon as I knew you weren't leaving, I realized I needed some backups. I'd hoped to get away before you caught up with me, but it seems you knew my exact position. How do you think that happened?"

"I did it," Zara says, still on the ground, tangled up in the barbed wire. "Emily told me not to, and I did it anyway. I managed to get a ping on the burner before you destroyed it." I can hear the pain in her voice.

"Emily, huh? Nice to put a name with the face." The blade is pressed so close to my throat I can't risk moving. She'll cut my jugular and I'll bleed out before I even have a chance to strike her. Now I understand what Lazlo was talking about.

"What's your endgame now?" I ask. "You're either going to have to kill us or let us go, and I don't think you want to kill us. That's not part of the plan, right?"

"It wasn't," she says, anger in her voice. "But you made it part of the plan. I won't let you stop me."

"Samantha, I know you think you're doing the right thing. I know it even feels like the right thing. But this isn't the way. Killing these men is only inviting more pain."

She grunts. "You're delusional. These men only hurt people. Removing them from the equation will make the world a better place. It already has."

"Then what's the plan? Kill a certain number of men, and then kill yourself? Is that really how you want the rest of your life to go?"

"It doesn't matter anymore," she says.

I have to press her. Not knowing how badly Zara is injured could mean we don't have a lot of time. Especially way out here. "It does matter. Tell me. I'm still willing to listen."

"Talking won't do any good. It never does."

"Why not?" I ask.

"Because no one ever listens!" The blade presses up against my neck again and I close my eyes, waiting for it to be over, but it doesn't come. Instead, I can still feel the cold steel pressed against my skin. "No one ever listens," she repeats.

"Samantha, what happened?" I ask.

She pauses, then lets out a breath. "You've been to the towns around here, you know what they're like," she says. "Either you end up working at some menial service job for the rest of your life, or, if you're lucky, you get hired by one of the resorts on the mountain, and you get to serve rich assholes all day long. The people who are born in these towns, the ones who hold them up on their backs, they're the ones that get screwed. And the people who come in on the weekends in their fancy cars are the ones who reap all the rewards."

I don't recall anything about any of the victims being rich. Except for Lazlo, but she didn't kill him. "You're saying the tourists are exploiting the working class. That they aren't appreciated in these towns."

"I'm saying they can come in, do whatever they want, then leave, with no consequences."

"Something happened to you, didn't it?" I ask.

"Not me. My friend. Charlotte. She worked at the club too. We went in together, determined we weren't going to fall into the trap of everyone else in our town. We were going to make our money, then get the hell out of here. Go down to Boston or New York. Start somewhere fresh, away from these insulated communities. Do you know how infuriating it is to have everyone you know go to the same school, same church, same restaurant, same everything? No one here ever thinks any different."

I shoot a glance in Zara's direction. I still can't see her very well, but I can see enough that she's still tangled up on the ground. "But you do. You found a way out."

"Yeah, 'cept I was stupid and didn't know what really went on at those places. Charlotte found out the hard way. Men would buy her drinks, get her nice and drunk before they would—" Her voice catches.

"Assault her," I say, finishing her thought.

"It started happening so often she got used to it. Said it was no big deal, but I could see the light in her eyes slowly dying."

"Your boss, Stipes, was adamant they didn't allow that kind of thing," I say.

"Stipes didn't know," she replies. "It never happened at the club. It was always after hours, once the shift was over. Word got around. Men would come in and seek Charlotte out, waiting for her shift to end. But before they did, they'd make sure she'd had plenty to drink. And then they'd take her back to a hotel or apartment. Sometimes she got paid, but most of the time she didn't. They'd just have their way with her and be done."

"Didn't you ever try to stop them?" I ask.

"Of course I did," she spits. "But Charlotte would insist she was fine, that she knew what she was doing, all while being three sheets to the wind. And she'd come back to our place the next morning. I'd hear her in the bathroom crying, sometimes for hours. Then we'd go back to the club, and she'd do it all over again. I tried to get her to stop, to get another job somewhere else, but she insisted she was fine and we were still going to get out together."

"Where's Charlotte now?" I ask.

Samantha hesitates. "They found her, six months ago. Half-naked in the woods. She'd been disposed of like a piece of trash. There were rumblings of a suspect, but nothing materialized."

"There had to have been evidence," I say. "Someone had to know something."

"If there was, the police didn't do jack about it," Samantha says. "So I decided I needed to."

"How?"

"At first I wanted to stick a knife in the belly of every man that walked through those doors," she says, speaking through her teeth. "But I realized it was better to play the long game. So I kept dancing. I kept *acting* for them, pretending to be their best friend, their dream woman. As time went on I recognized familiar faces that came into the club. Men who had preyed on Charlotte. And I kept a list. I did my research. And I found out everything I could about them. Anyone with even a hint of abuse went on that list. By the time I was done, I had ten names in total."

"How did you get their names?" Zara asks.

"They told them to me." Suddenly, her voice is like honey, and it's like she's transformed. "Men will tell you anything if they think you're interested in them. But I never let them buy me drinks. And I never went back with them."

"So you think one of these men murdered Charlotte," I say. "Why not just take this information to the police?"

"It's as I said. You can't trust the police. They'll kill their own if it's in their best interests. And if they don't, they'll certainly protect them. Up here, there's a code."

I think back to Eastly and how far he was willing to go to protect Schmidt. And what Mr. Bale said. "I've seen that for myself."

"Then you already know why telling them would have been pointless," she says.

"Why not kill Lazlo?"

"He never touched her," Samantha says. "But he made me realize I'd waited long enough. I knew if I stayed there much longer, the same thing could happen to me. And I wasn't going to let that happen. I had my names. There was no sense in waiting any longer. You could say he was the spark that lit the dynamite."

"If I can find out who killed Charlotte," I say, going out on a limb. "Will you stop your rampage?"

I feel the knife slip away from my throat. She's no longer on my back. Keeping my hands up, I slowly turn around. But what I see surprises me. She's no taller than I am, though she's decked out in full military camo fatigues, complete with combat boots. In the dim light I catch sight of her emerald green eyes. They're so bright they almost sparkle. She's got a pack of some sort strapped around her back, and her short hair is slicked back. She holds a KA-BAR at arm's length between us. Its blade is a good seven inches long. Definitely not a stiletto.

"It won't matter," she says, though this is the first time I've heard her voice waver. "These men, they pretend to be all nice and good-natured. They're *nice guys*. But the truth is they're all liars. And I'm going to put them all in their graves."

"It's not up to you to make that decision," I say. "Answer me. If I can find out who killed Charlotte, will you put a stop to this?"

She shakes her head. "I'm already halfway done. Five down, five to go."

"Listen to me, Samantha. I know you're smart. You wouldn't have made it this far if you weren't. You have a choice. There's still a possibility you can have a life beyond all this, especially if Charlotte's killer is already among the dead. But if you go out there and murder five more innocent—"

"*They're not innocent!*" she screams. In the split second when her attention breaks, I grab her hand holding the knife. Immediately she tries to yank it away from me, but I hold fast, pushing it up into the air as I try to get her arm around behind her. But she's stronger than I anticipated, and she pushes back, managing to knock me away enough so that I stumble back. She charges me with the knife in hand, ready to cut me to ribbons. I manage to dodge the first swipe, then land a kick squarely in her midsection, causing her to cough and hit the ground on her knees. I score another kick on her hand holding the knife and it goes flying. There's enough light for me to see her struggle with the thought of looking for it or going after me again, but she doesn't get a chance to do either because I tackle her before she makes a decision. With a few well-timed hits I manage to incapacitate her enough to pull her arms back behind her and secure them with a zip tie. She might have been quick with that knife, but she definitely hasn't had any martial arts training, otherwise I would have had a much more difficult fight on my hands.

Fairly sure she's not going anywhere, I run over to Zara, pulling out my phone. I dial emergency services, giving them our approximate location, then turn the light of my phone on her legs and the barbed wire. Fortunately, it doesn't look like anything too serious, but we're going to need some bolt cutters to get them off.

"Looks like you're going to need a tetanus shot," I tell her.

"You can't do this!" Samantha yells from a few feet away. "I have a promise to keep! I have to make them pay." Even though I can't see her very well, I can tell she's yelling through tears.

"Em," Zara says, looking up at me. "This is a mess."

"I know," I tell her. "But we're going to get it cleaned up."

Chapter Thirty

"HERE," I say, throwing down a file on Rice's desk.

"What's this?" he asks.

"Charlotte Keener's case file," I say. "I had Sandel and Kane run the DNA collected from each of the victims so far and compare it to the DNA found at the scene of the murder. We got a match on Duncan Schmidt. He killed her, then dumped her body in the woods near Portland."

Rice takes the file, flipping through the reports Kane and Sandel just spent the last three days putting together. I was under no obligation to investigate Samantha Morris's claims, but when I tell someone I'm going to do something, I do it. And I wasn't about to let Charlotte's murder go unsolved. The good news is we can put her case to rest, instead of filing it down in the cold cases of the Portland Police Department where I found it.

"Did Eastly know?" Rice asks.

"I have no idea. But I'd be willing to bet his brother did. Or he at least had an inkling."

"I'll get Dutton to bring him in for questioning," Rice says. "We also still have that matter of the civil unrest that just happened to take place in the days following his resignation from his job. I think we have enough to charge him with civil disobedience. If I can add a coverup to that too? It will be all she wrote on Garrett Schmidt."

"Good," I say. "You've got your work cut out for you up here."

"Don't I know it?" he asks, standing. "How is Agent Foley?"

"Hasn't slowed down, despite both of her legs being covered in bandages for a week," I reply. "We'll be headed back tonight along with Agents Sandel and Kane. I just wanted to bring this to you personally. I thought Samantha deserved to know."

He nods. "She's still not talking. And despite a search of the hotel she was living in, we still haven't found any list of potential victims, so we have no idea who her other targets were. She's refusing to talk to anyone, including her court-appointed lawyer."

"I could take another swing at her," I suggest.

Rice stops himself from laughing. "You're the *last* person she wants to talk to, seeing as you're the one she blames for ruining her plans."

I glance down at the file. "Maybe that will help soften her up a little."

He nods. "Thanks for the background profile on her. Growing up a military brat seems to have given her a hard edge. Even tougher when both your parents are dead before you get out of high school."

I feel a familiar pang of pain. That's one thing Samantha and I share in common. I know how hard it can be to feel alone. She and Charlotte were each other's rocks. If someone did to Zara what they did to Charlotte, I'm not sure I wouldn't have had a similar reaction. And as much as I'd like to, I can't condone her behavior, though I certainly understand where she's coming from.

"Will she see any leniency?" I ask.

Rice purses his lips. "Five murder charges, and she all but admitted to them. We're still going over all the evidence you gathered, but it looks like she was prepared for each one, either with a hazmat suit or something similar, which is why we didn't find any blood at the scenes. Dutton's men found a few unused ones at her hotel, I guess for her next victims. But my guess is she burned the used ones, or disposed of them where we'll never find them."

"It's a shame," I say.

"What's that?"

"All that cleverness. All that talent. She would have done well in a place like the Bureau. Maybe if she'd grown up in different circumstances…" I trail off.

"Yes, well." Rice holds out his hand and I take it, giving it a firm shake. "Thank you for all your help, Agent Slate. They were right when they said you were the person to call."

I chuckle. "Make sure you tell my boss that. I wish we could have gotten here sooner, maybe found her before her final victim. But I guess it's good we stopped her when we did."

He nods. "It's clear we still have a long way to go up here. Charlotte's murder should have been investigated more thoroughly. I've already had two interviews for an interim chief in Collins, and the governor is pooling more resources to shore up the force there. Even with all the open positions, we should be back up and running at full speed in a few weeks. It will take some time, but I'm determined to make this place somewhere the public can trust the police again."

I know how that goes, having just spent the past month and a half enduring constant questioning by Internal Affairs. Rice is a good man; I believe he really will turn things around up here. "Best of luck."

"Thank you. I'm just sorry for all the trouble we put you through."

"It was no trouble at all, considering how it all turned

out." I shoot him a wink, then leave him to his work. I need to get back to Zara at the hotel so we can finish packing. Sandel and Kane are already on their way back to D.C. but seeing as they get to fly, they don't have nearly the trip ahead of them as we do.

Back in the hallway as I'm making my way out of the offices, I catch sight of Eastly's attorney Wilcox standing near the door, his hands clasped behind him and a smug grin on his face.

"I'm surprised you're so cheerful seeing as you got absolutely destroyed in court yesterday," I tell him.

He moves into step beside me, and we both walk outside. "Ah, but that's the thing. For me it's about the thrill of the game, not whether I win or lose. Don't get me wrong, I love to win, but if I don't, I'm just happy to fight another day."

"Good for you," I tell him.

"You know, Agent Slate, you were quite the opponent. I haven't had so much fun in a long time. Perhaps you'd be willing to work together again sometime."

I turn to him. "Unless you didn't notice, we're not on the same side. Your client tried to get me fired and arrested."

"That's because he's a sad old man without any future prospects," Wilcox says. "But you...you have a bright future ahead of you. I can always tell the ones that will go far." He hands me a card from his inner jacket pocket. "Here. My contact information in case you ever find yourself in New York."

"Why would I need a lawyer?" I ask.

He gives me a smug smile. "You really never know. We're absolutely superfluous until we're not." For being a weasel, he's trying hard to gain my confidence, which only makes me suspect something else is up. I don't know what kind of game he's playing, but I want no part of it.

"Thanks," I say, slipping the card into my pocket, fully intending to tear it up as soon as I can. "I'm sure you're the first person I'll call." I leave him standing by the doors to the Adams County D.A.'s office.

"Take care," he calls after me as I head to my car.

Man, what a weirdo.

My drive back to the hotel is unremarkable, which is a welcome relief. All I want to do is finish packing then get back on the road with Zara, seeing as we have another *twelve hours* ahead of us. But she'll make the drive go quick; she always does. I'm lucky I didn't have to work this case alone; I'm not sure I would have handled it as well. Though I know she'll be itching to get back so she can return to her own cases.

When I pull up to the hotel, I'm surprised that she's not outside with her bags waiting. I only had a few additional things I needed to throw in mine; I figured she'd just toss it all in and be ready to go.

As I'm parking I get a text from her.

Where are you?

Just got here, why?

Get up here, now.

No emojis. That's a bad sign. I jump out of the SUV and dash into the hotel, forgoing the slow elevator and taking the stairs two at a time. When I get to the door I fumble with the keycard until it finally opens.

Inside Zara is sitting on her knees on the bed, her phone up, recording something. It's only then I realize the TV is on.

"What's going on?" I ask.

"Look," she says.

My heart is racing. What could be so important she made it sound like someone was having a heart attack up here? But as the TV comes into view my heart drops. My name is splayed across the bottom of the screen on the banner, along with my file photo from the FBI's website. I remember that day, they told us specifically not to smile, but I couldn't help but do it anyway.

"Once again, thanks to the efforts of Special Agent Emily Slate with

the FBI, along with her partner and D.A. Rice, our community is free of the corruption that sat at its very heart for nearly twenty years."

"How long has this been on?" I ask.

Zara shrugs, but keeps taping anyway. "I just flipped it over."

Man, I hate it when the news gets involved. "I was really hoping to stay off the radar."

"Hey, at least they said your name instead of 'partner'," she says.

I shoot her a quick glance, my expression soft. "You should really get most of the credit. You were the one who figured out how to trace the phone. And did it despite me saying not to."

She waves me off with one hand. "Nah, you keep that big ol' spotlight all for yourself."

I place my hands on my hips as the image of the anchor disappears and my picture enlarges to fill most of the screen. "Wallace isn't going to be happy about this."

"What are you supposed to do, put out a gag order? It's the local news, they can report on whatever they want." She stops recording as soon as a commercial comes on. "This one is going in the scrapbook."

I rub my temple, not wanting to deal with the headache that is sure to follow. And when I slip my hand into my pocket, I feel Wilcox's card again. I pull it out, tossing it in the trash.

"What was that?" Zara asks.

"Wilcox ambushed me. Gave me his card. I think he was hitting on me."

"Really? Ew."

"I know. I just don't get his angle. Doesn't matter now, we need to get on the road. Are you ready?"

"To ride with a local legend? Absolutely," she says, pulling her suitcase off the bed and sticking her tongue out at me at the same time. Zara is always in a good mood after we close a case.

"That's right, rub it in. You've got twelve hours. After that I don't want to hear about it ever again."

"Deal. But only if we stop for a frap." She waits patiently while I finish throwing my stuff together, then we head down to the car. As we're throwing our stuff in the back, I notice the view of Collins is as crisp and clear as I've seen it, a white blanket of snow covering everything. The air is clean, refreshing. It's a shame to head back without getting a little relaxation in.

But then I think back to the trashcan in my apartment. And what's still in it. As soon as I get home, I'm fishing it out and sending it down to Quantico. I'm tired of hiding from it. Sometimes we need to face the past if we're ever going to move forward.

It's time to be brave, stop pretending like it doesn't exist, and deal with the problem.

Whatever that letter is, whatever it means, I know I won't have to face it alone.

Epilogue

"ONCE AGAIN, thanks to the efforts of Special Agent Emily Slate with the FBI, along with her partner and D.A. Rice, our community is free of the corruption that sat at its very heart for twenty years."

I smile as I see her picture down in the corner of the TV. It's been too long since I've seen her face. Emily has blossomed into a beautiful young woman.

I can't believe I've missed so much. And yet, I feel like we've never been closer. The anchor disappears and Emily's face fills the screen, bringing a tear to my eye. She's gorgeous. Perfect. Just like I knew she would be. She's everything I could have ever wanted and everything I've ever needed. Why did I wait so long?

I get up from my worn leather seat and head for the kitchen. Tea is boiling. I can hear it on the stove. Emily Slate. Emily Slate...FBI agent. *Special Agent* Slate, that's how she introduces herself. That's what she says, like it's a badge of honor. And why not? She's earned it.

Oh, how I wish I didn't have to do this. But she needs to know. She can't stay in the dark forever. After seeing her on TV when she found all those girls from that *sick bastard*; I knew then I couldn't stay away forever. I tried...I really tried not to reach out. But I'm out of options. Emily is my last hope.

But what if she can't handle the truth?

"She'll handle it, all right. She'll have to," I say. She's strong. The FBI has made her strong. But she has no idea what's coming her way. I need to prepare her. I need to break her down a little bit. If I don't, she'll never be able to understand. She'll just judge me like all the rest.

No, I will make sure she's ready. And until then, we have to take things slow. She'll try to hurry it along, just like she always does. She'll want this over with. But that's the thing about the unknown, it lives on its own schedule.

I will decide when it's time for her. And until then, I need to chip away at her, little by little. Piece by piece, until I can build her back up again, stronger and more resilient than ever. Only *then* will she be ready to accept her own history.

I pull the tea kettle off the stove and set it on the table beside a pile of letters that have yet to be sent. Each of them addressed to her. Each of them with a specific purpose.

Emily, my sweet, sweet girl. I am so sorry to have to do this to you. But it's for your own good.

I'll see you soon.

The End?

To Be Continued...

Want to read more about Emily?

You never know what's hiding behind your walls.

Special Agent Emily Slate is a woman on a mission. Someone is sending her letters written in her dead mother's handwriting, and she's not about to stop until she finds out why.

But when she receives a mysterious phone call from town where she grew up, Emily doesn't believe it's a coincidence. After all, where better to start tracking down the person who wrote the letters than in her own hometown?

Except, when she arrives, she finds herself in the middle of a murder investigation. Initially a suspect, eventually she learns that the body of a missing seventeen-year-old girl was found in the walls of what used to be her childhood home. Not only that, but the victim was the sister of Emily's one-time best friend.

With an entire town on edge, Emily isn't willing to leave the investigation up to the local cops. And as the secrets surrounding the girl's death begin to unravel, Emily finds herself in the crosshairs of a dangerous killer—one who has operated unchecked for over twenty years.

Will she be able to find out who buried a body in the walls of her old home before anyone else goes missing? Or will the killer catch up with her first?

It all comes back to *The Girl in the Wall*.

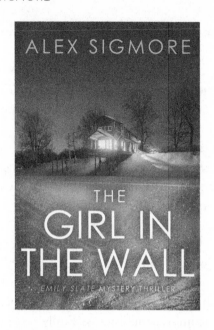

To get your copy of THE GIRL IN THE WALL, CLICK HERE or scan the code below!

FREE book offer!
Where did it all go wrong for Emily?

I HOPE YOU ENJOYED *A LIAR'S GRAVE*. IF YOU'D LIKE TO LEARN more about Emily's backstory and what happened in the days following her husband's unfortunate death, including what almost got her kicked out of the FBI, then you're in luck! *Her Last Shot* introduces Emily and tells the story of the case that almost ended her career. Interested? CLICK HERE to get your free copy now!

Not Available Anywhere Else!

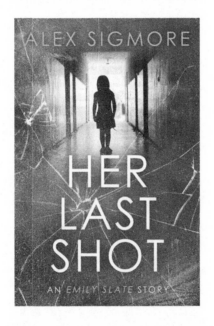

You'll also be the first to know when each book in the Emily Slate series is available!

Download for FREE HERE or scan the code below!

The Emily Slate FBI Mystery Series

A Note from Alex

Hi!

I want to extend my deepest gratitude to you for taking the time to read my latest book, A LIAR'S GRAVE. Your support means the world to me, and I am thrilled to hear that so many of you enjoyed have loved this series as much as I have.

As you know, this book marks the eighth entry in the series, and I am delighted to say that there will be more to come. Every book is an adventure and I am excited to continue unraveling the mystery surrounding Emily's mother with you in the upcoming books.

A LIAR'S GRAVE was a book that I poured my heart and soul into, and it was a joy to craft every twist and turn of the story. Your messages, reviews, and feedback on the rest of the series have been invaluable, and I am grateful for each and every one of you who has joined me on this journey.

Because I am still relatively new, all I ask that you please take the time to leave a review or recommend this series to a fellow book lover. This will ensure I'll be able to write many more books in the *Emily Slate Series* in the future.

Thank you for being a loyal reader,

Alex

Made in the USA
Las Vegas, NV
01 June 2024

90604586R00152